Crown Princess Ioanna

blessing a secret for twenty years. In any other nation, her powerful magic would be cause for celebration. But Xytae's patron is the war goddess Reygmadra, and the future empress is expected to be a brutal warrior.

Reserved and peaceful by nature, Ioanna knows the court sees her as a disappointment. She does her best to assuage their worries every day, working quietly beside her mother to keep the empire running while her father is away at war. But when news of the emperor's untimely death reaches the capital, Ioanna finds herself ousted by her younger sister Netheia, who has the war magic Ioanna lacks.

Princess Vitaliya of Vesolda has come to Xytae to avoid her father's upcoming wedding, which she sees as an affront to her mother's memory. Vitaliya has absolutely no interest in politics or power struggles and intends to spend her time attending parties and embarrassing her family. But when she saves Ioanna's life during Netheia's coup, the two are forced to flee the capital together.

Despite their circumstances, Vitaliya enjoys travelling with Ioanna and realizes that the future empress's shy and secretive nature is the result of her unhappy childhood. Ioanna is equally unaccustomed to being in the company of one as earnest and straightforward as Vitaliya, for she has spent her life surrounded by ambitious and cutthroat nobles.

Ioanna cannot allow her sister to continue their father's legacy, and plots to rally supporters to her side so she can interrupt Netheia's coronation. Vitaliya knows she ought to leave Xytae before the nation is ripped apart by civil war but finds she is unwilling to abandon Ioanna. But Ioanna's enemies are always watching...and they've realized that Vitaliya is a weakness to be exploited.

THE EMPRESS OF

XYTAE

Tales of Inthya. Book Four

Effie Calvin

A NineStar Press Publication

Published by NineStar Press
P.O. Box 91792,
Albuquerque, New Mexico, 87199 USA.
www.ninestarpress.com

The Empress of Xytae

Printed in the USA
First Edition
December, 2019

Print ISBN: 978-1-951057-99-2

Also available in eBook, ISBN: 978-1-951057-98-5

For Jasper, the new kitten in my life.

THIYRA

Rhodia

Etren ✦ Dossau

Enas

SIABAELD

Strentard

Cira

Verarin

IOSHORA

The Xylian Empire

Lytlaria

Visoddia

AQUIIM

Masim

Coplar

Silos Lslas

THE WINTER STRAIT

THE SUMMER STRAIT

TO
ANORA
KOITU

TO
EWEN
LANDS

Prologue

REYGMADRA

The Imperial Palace at Xyuluthe buzzed with anticipation. Empress Enessa had finally gone into labor, and the heir to the Xytan Empire would be born within a few hours. The archpriest of Adranus and the archpriestess of Pemele were both there to aid with the birth along with countless members of the imperial court who would bear witness to the historic event.

Reygmadra, Goddess of Warfare and Eighth of the Ten, waited just outside the empress's chambers, unseen by all who passed. She would not deny she was beginning to grow impatient. She was only here to bless the child, the future empress. Then she would be on her way.

If the child ever arrived.

Reygmadra had no tolerance for children, nor for the tedious conversations that always surrounded a birth—discussions of size, weight, and bodily functions. She had left the empress's room because she had grown tired of the pointless hysterical screaming, but this was undoubtably worse.

Unfortunately, she could not grant a blessing to a mortal until after it had taken its first breath. This was one of the rules she and her fellow gods had agreed upon when they'd first set out to create Inthya. Even Reygmadra could see the value in this one, for if babies could use magic in the womb, nobody would ever risk giving birth ever again.

Emperor Ionnes was occupied, as always, by his campaign in Masim. He would not return to meet his new daughter for several months. Some of the members of the court were muttering about this, but Reygmadra did not see the trouble. What help could Ionnes be right now? He would only be in the way if he tried to help. At least in Masim, he was serving his nation by leading the army.

She longed to be there, whispering ideas in his ear as he slept, soaking up the power she received when tens of thousands of warriors prayed to her in unison. Of course, the prayers would find her no matter where she was on the mortal realm of Inthya or in the celestial planes of Asterium. But there was nothing like experiencing it firsthand.

Babies seemed to bring out the stupidest, weakest aspects of mankind. One of the Xytans was now relaying a tale of someone else's labor, and Reygmadra decided to take a walk before she lost her temper and stabbed someone.

She moved through the palace like a specter, her face unseen and heavy footsteps unheard. She was dressed as she usually did when she manifested on Inthya, as a common soldier with short sword and breastplate. If someone did somehow see her, they would think nothing of her.

One of the rooms led out into a garden, and Reygmadra decided she had been indoors for too long. She stepped out into the sunlight, into the fresh air.

Reygmadra didn't think much of gardens—they were really just a waste of space—but this one was empty, so she would stay for a while. As she moved, she kept an ear to the palace, hoping she would soon hear distant cheers.

"Still waiting?"

A woman dressed as a Xytan noble stood there among the flowers. She had olive-toned skin and long, wavy ebony hair, and her face was impossibly, supernaturally beautiful. The dress she wore was simple but elegant, all wine-colored silk that perfectly emphasized wide hips and a narrow waist. Despite her disguise as a mortal woman, Reygmadra recognized Dayluue—Goddess of Love and Seventh of the Ten.

"It will be a while yet," said Reygmadra. "Why are you here?"

"I'm feeling neglected," Dayluue said. "You haven't come to see me in ages."

"I'm busy."

"You're always busy." Crimson lips pressed together in a pout as Dayluue adjusted the neckline of her dress aggressively. "Maybe I should call on someone else. I wonder what Nara is doing."

Possessive rage seized at Reygmadra, and Dayluue began to laugh. But the sound was cut short when Reygmadra grabbed her by the shoulders. A moment later, she had Dayluue pressed between the garden wall and her own body.

"I love it when you get jealous," Dayluue said breathlessly. "Kiss me?"

Reygmadra brought her lips to Dayluue's throat. Dayluue tilted her head back, hands clasping at Reygmadra's hair, and laughed again. "I have missed you," she said.

"I don't believe you," said Reygmadra because expecting strict monogamy from Dayluue was like expecting a bird to refrain from flight.

"I'll prove it, then." Dayluue's eyes sparkled.

"No. I'm busy."

"I never took you for the sort to get excited over a birth. Or are you finally realizing what I've been saying about the population—"

"No. I'm just giving her a blessing, and then I'm leaving."

"It might be a while," warned Dayluue. "Labor can last an entire day."

Reygmadra shuddered. "Awful."

"Well, they wouldn't have to do it so often if you didn't keep convincing them to kill one another."

Reygmadra rolled her eyes. "Did you come here just to argue?"

Dayluue pressed her lips to Reygmadra's. "Only if you really want to," she murmured into her mouth. The scent of her mortal body, flowers and sweat and pheromones, was intoxicating.

They were antithesis to each other, and yet, there was an undeniable symmetry to their domains. They were two primal forces, mindless impulse given sentience. And sometimes the fiery lust Dayluue elicited from her felt identical to the thrill of battle.

Perhaps that was why Dayluue always returned to her. Perhaps that was why Reygmadra did not object to Dayluue's wandering.

When they met like this in Asterium, it was a union of selves, of auras and magic, and two becoming one in the way none but their own kind could hope to understand. It was delightful to have Dayluue's energy surging through her, to feel her own spirit within Dayluue. Reygmadra always came away from these unions feeling softer, lighter. But not weaker. Never weaker.

On Inthya, with warm bodies made of blood and flesh, things were different. On Inthya, Dayluue was in control, and Reygmadra was helpless under her expert fingers.

"Kiss me again," said Dayluue. "But lower, this time."

WHEN REYGMADRA OPENED her eyes, the sun hung low in the sky, and Dayluue rested against her chest, fingers tapping out a pattern on bare skin. Reygmadra ran her hand through Dayluue's hair absently.

Somewhere, not too far away, a baby was crying.

The ridiculous paints Dayluue wore on her face should have been ruined, but, of course, they weren't. She looked as perfect as ever with not even a curl out of place. Her silk dress was tangled in a rosebush a few meters away.

A baby was crying...

Panic shot through her as realization hit. She shoved Dayluue off and leapt to her feet, donning her armor as hastily as possible and leaving half the straps undone.

"Wait!" began Dayluue, but Reygmadra was not listening. There was no time to waste. With nothing more than a thought, she transported herself to the private chambers of Empress Enessa.

The room was dim, and the empress was asleep, her breathing soft and even. In the chair just beside her, an attendant fanned her face leisurely. Two guards stood on either side of the bed, silent and watchful. They did not react to Reygmadra. Their eyes slid over her, past her, through her, blank and uncomprehending.

And by the window a nurse hummed softly, rocking a small bundle in her arms.

Reygmadra peered down at the baby. It was wrinkled and red and dreadful, but at least it was quieting down, soothed by the nurse's song.

"Let me see her," Reygmadra commanded the nurse. The woman looked at her with unseeing, unquestioning eyes and held her arms out, tilting the child so Reygmadra had an unobstructed view of her.

Reygmadra brought the blessing to her hands. It manifested, as always, as rust-colored light. Carefully, she touched two fingertips to the baby's heart, pressing the magic down.

But the magic was not taking. Reygmadra frowned and dismissed the blessing, only to call it again. This time, she jabbed the child in the chest so hard it began to whimper again. But the magic fell away as though the blessing had been repelled. And now that she paused, she could see the golden kernel of magic already embedded there.

Realization, cold and bitter, rose up in her throat like bile.

"Iolar!" she screamed, spinning away from the baby and the nurse. Nobody reacted; not the child, nor the guards, nor the empress. "Iolar! She was meant to be mine!"

"We had no agreement." The voice came from directly behind her. She turned to see her brother standing in the doorway. Perhaps he had been there the whole time, watching silently. "But I understand your anger. You may have the next one, if you so choose."

Reygmadra clenched her fists. "That is Ionnes's heir! No second-born will make up for what you have stolen from me!"

"What I have stolen from you?" repeated Iolar. "Are you certain you wish to continue this line of conversation?"

"Just wait! You'll regret this, I swear!"

"What will you do in retaliation? Push Xytae even further into darkness?" retorted Iolar. "Continue down this path, and these Men will turn on you before I even have a chance to act."

"We shall see," said Reygmadra. "You do not know the Xytan people as I do. They will not tolerate a soft, peace-loving empress."

"Then you have nothing to fear, do you? Eran tells me Ionnes will have two more children before he leaves Inthya. Select either to be your champion, and we shall see who emerges victorious."

Reygmadra did not dignify this with a response. She wanted to rend, to tear, to break, to destroy. She wanted to scream out her rage until the rest of the world felt what she felt. But there was nothing here she could fight. She shoved past her brother and stormed out into the hall where Dayluue waited.

There was sorrow in her face, but all Reygmadra could think was she would have much preferred to see pain.

"You're allied with him now?" spat Reygmadra.

"I am allied with mankind," said Dayluue. "I am allied with the millions of souls that trust us to protect them. Can't you see what you're doing isn't sustainable? You're going to destabilize the entire continent and—"

"Shut up!"

"Why won't you listen to me?" There were tears in Dayluue's eyes. "Why won't you even acknowledge what I'm saying? Are you that desperate for power?"

"Why should I believe a single thing you say when you've just established yourself to be a liar?"

"I wasn't lying," said Dayluue. "I've missed you. Please, I don't want to fight with you. Let's just talk. Please."

"No. No more of your games." Reygmadra took a step backward. "Nothing can replace what you have taken from me."

Chapter One

IOANNA

When Ioanna of Xytae emerged from her bedroom, she was not expecting to find a body sprawled across her doorway. Corpses were rare—though certainly not unheard of—in the Imperial Palace, and usually the servants were quick enough to tidy them away before they could inconvenience anyone.

Ioanna held her breath and prodded the body with her foot, trying to roll it over so she could see if it was anyone she knew. The corpse groaned, and Ioanna exhaled in relief. Not a corpse, then. Just a drunk.

"Hello. You're on the floor," said Ioanna pleasantly. "You might want to get up."

"I can't find my room," the prone figure mumbled. Then she covered her eyes with her hands. "Why is everything so white?"

"Because it's all made of marble. Can you stand if I help you?"

"Maybe. I don't know."

"What's your name?"

"You'll never believe me," the young woman said with a groan. She looked to be about Ioanna's own age, around twenty years old, but Ioanna did not recognize her as a member of the court. "Vitaliya. Of Vesolda. Gods, why is it so bright in here?"

Ioanna knelt and positioned Vitaliya's arm over her own shoulders, so she could help her to her feet. "Where are you staying?" she asked once they were upright.

"Uhum..." Vitaliya looked around blearily. Her brown hair was hopelessly tangled, and her face was red and blotchy. Despite that, Ioanna could tell she had a pretty face, round with a soft nose and delicate lips. "Somewhere..."

"It's probably not far. We put all the visiting royals down this way," explained Ioanna, taking a few steps to the right. Vitaliya remained limp and unresisting as Ioanna pulled her along. "Is any of your family here with you?"

"No." Vitaliya squinted ahead as they walked. "That one! That door! That's mine; I'm very nearly sure."

"Do you have your key?"

Vitaliya rummaged in her pockets, and eventually one of her hands emerged with a heavy bronze key. She managed to unlock the door, and they staggered into the room together. The curtains were still drawn, and Vitaliya sighed into the cooling darkness.

Once Ioanna's eyes adjusted, she realized dresses were strewn all over the place like Vitaliya had tried each of them on briefly, and then discarded them. She tried her best not to step on any as she helped Vitaliya toward the nearest chair. "Didn't you bring any friends or servants with you?"

"No, none at all," said Vitaliya cheerfully. "They'd rather be at the wedding than here, so I came alone. Who needs any of them?"

"What wedding?" asked Ioanna.

"My father's! He's marrying some horrible woman, so now I hate him forever."

"That's not true," Ioanna said quietly.

"No, it is! The wedding's in just a few months. And I'm not going." Vitaliya crossed her arms and sank deeper into the chair. Closing her eyes, she muttered, "I hope Pemele strikes him dead."

That last part was another lie, but Ioanna did not acknowledge it. Instead she said, "I don't think Pemele does that."

"She should consider it!" Vitaliya opened her eyes again. "My mother's only been dead six years! She's practically still warm! And for some reason, I'm the only one who can see how awful it is! And do you want to know the worst part?" Vitaliya didn't give Ioanna a chance to reply before barreling on. "The woman. Just guess who she is? You'll never guess. She's a *shepherdess*. A shepherdess! Marrying my father! Marrying a king! A shepherdess!"

"Oh, yes," recalled Ioanna. "I remember hearing about that. It was quite a scandal, wasn't it?"

"I thought all his advisors would drop dead from shock!" Vitaliya appeared to cheer up. "She's not going to be queen, at least. The nobles would revolt. He's giving the throne over to my brother right before the wedding. And then they're going to ride off to a castle by the seaside and probably die of happiness."

"Oh my," said Ioanna.

"Thank you, though," concluded Vitaliya. "For getting me back here, I mean. I was with Princess Netheia and her friends last night. Things might have gotten out of hand. I shouldn't be surprised I didn't quite make it back."

"You nearly did, though."

"Right! Points for trying." Vitaliya smiled. "I hate to throw you out, but I'm not going to be able to stay awake much longer. Did you tell me your name?"

"Ioanna."

"Augh!" Vitaliya slapped herself in the forehead. "No! Tell me you're joking!"

"I'm afraid not. Don't worry. I understand. We all have bad nights. And bad mornings."

"I'm sure you have so many important crown princess things to do, and I've just been sitting here complaining about my problems." Vitaliya looked stricken. "And you're so much nicer than Netheia said you'd be."

Clearly Vitaliya was still a little bit drunk. Ioanna felt herself smile. "I'm glad to hear it."

"I think she wants to kill you."

"Oh yes," said Ioanna. "She certainly does."

"Just don't drink anything she gives you." Vitaliya's bleary-eyed confusion had been replaced by concern. "Maybe it's not any of my business. But—"

"I won't," Ioanna promised because this was easier than explaining how poisoned foods always glowed sickly green-gold to her eyes. She stepped back, setting her feet down carefully to avoid the discarded dresses. "If you'd like someone to come clean your room, you only need to ask."

"Later," said Vitaliya, waving her hand dreamily. "When I'm alive again. If I remember. If not, maybe I can pick up my own dresses. Expand my horizons. Will I see you again?"

"I don't know. I don't go to very many parties."

"That's too bad." Vitaliya sighed. "It's nice to talk to someone who doesn't think punching is meant to be punctuation."

"I know what you mean." Twenty years spent living at a court where many were blessed by Reygmadra had made her very, very fast with a shield. "Don't take it personally."

Vitaliya smiled, nodded, and closed her eyes again. Strangely, Ioanna regretted leaving. She knew her reputation at court was one of solitude, even reclusiveness, but Ioanna didn't think that was her own fault. Everyone at Xyuluthe had an ulterior motive. Their false praise gave her a headache, and each hollow compliment felt like a slap to the face.

Iolar's Truthsayer blessing was wonderful for an empress, but terrible for a girl.

Ioanna's parents had been...disappointed, to say the least, when they first learned of her ability to conjure up warm golden light, Iolar's signature blessing. Everyone else in the Isinthi family carried Reygmadra's magic. It was nearly synonymous with their name. The Ten were supposed to be equals, but Reygmadra was venerated over any other deity in their nation. This, her father claimed, was because Xytae's destiny was to conquer the world.

Ioanna remembered her parents' pained smiles as the news of her blessing spread through the palace. And she remembered the resulting confusion. Why would any child of the emperor have Iolar's magic? As the God of Law and Fourth of the Ten, Iolar was known to grant blessings to regents of other nations but never in Xytae.

Then a little bit later, Ioanna had explained to her parents they shouldn't tell lies because it made her head hurt, and their disappointment turned to panic.

She must never tell *anyone* she could detect lies, they'd instructed her. If the imperial court found out she was a Truthsayer, she would be in grave danger. Bad enough she lacked Reygmadra's magic altogether. If they knew the full extent of it, nobody would ever trust her. Nor would they tolerate her as their empress.

Unlike her ability to conjure Iolar's light, Truthsayer magic was extraordinarily rare, perhaps the rarest in the world. Sometimes priests and paladins had a knack for sensing deception, but Ioanna's magic went deeper than that. Whenever someone lied in her presence, she could feel it in her mind, a pinch of *wrongness*. Small lies did not hurt so badly, unless they became too numerous. But the large ones sometimes felt like being struck with a hammer.

When Ioanna entered the throne room that morning, she found Empress Enessa already there on her throne. Today the empress wore a long violet dress and a matching necklace and earring set of gold and amethysts. On her head rested the heavy golden crown of the consort inlaid with rubies. It was impressive on its own, but nothing compared to the regent's own crown, the crown that would someday be Ioanna's.

Beside Enessa, Emperor Ionnes's throne remained empty, though draped with a banner with Reygmadra's emblem to signal he was away at war. On her other side was the little chair and side table where Ioanna always sat.

Ioanna's father spent more time in Masim than he did at home, and so Enessa handled domestic affairs. It had always been this way for as long as Ioanna could remember. The emperor and his generals seemed to be under the impression his plan to reestablish Xytae as a true empire was not only attainable, but on the verge of complete success. The fact they had no hope of ever taking back Ibaia, let alone Ieflaria or Vesolda, never occurred to them. Nor did the reality of the ongoing war with Masim. They spoke of it like a glorious endeavor, but Ioanna only saw an endless bloody conflict draining the empire's treasury.

"Ioanna," said Enessa, sounding surprised but not irate. "Is all well?"

"I was delayed," Ioanna murmured, unwilling to say anything that might damage Vitaliya's standing with the court. She did not know if they'd be impressed or scornful if they heard the princess had tried to keep up with Netheia and her friends.

"I was afraid I'd have to send the guards after you," said Enessa, her tone friendly and conversational. "I'd hate for you to miss something important."

Ioanna nodded, understanding what her mother expected of her. When people came to the throne to make complaints or requests, sometimes they would misrepresent situations in hopes of getting more resources out of the empress or improving their own standing at court. When Ioanna detected this, she would run her fingers through her hair. Most observers would not even notice, for they would be fixated on Her Imperial Majesty. And if they did, who would think anything of a young lady playing with her hair?

But to Enessa, it would mean something was amiss, a signal to ask more pointed questions or verify claims before granting a request. She'd gained a reputation as a shrewd and ruthless negotiator as a result.

Ioanna knew she ought to be grateful nobody besides her sisters and grandmother had caught on to the fact she was a Truthsayer—or if they had, they were wise enough to keep it to themselves. But some small, selfish part of her wished for a little bit of acknowledgment.

In any other nation, her blessing would be an incredible gift. It seemed a cruel mistake that she'd been born in Xytae. Already the nobles worried her blessing from Iolar meant Xytae would change once she took the throne. No longer would they value strength, freedom, courage. Instead there would be laws, *endless* laws, freedom sacrificed for the sake of maintaining order. The Temple of Reygmadra would weaken as she diverted resources away from the army. And anyone who refused to go along with it would find themselves pushed out.

Knowledge that she was a Truthsayer would only escalate those fears. And then everyone would band together to deal with the threat.

Every day, Ioanna stood beside her mother as she conducted the empire's business. She never questioned an order or an edict. She remained silent, inoffensive, unthreatening, praying the nobles would soon realize she meant them no harm, and the changes she privately dreamed of were for the good of all their citizens.

"Empress Enessa," said a new voice, pulling Ioanna from her thoughts. "How lovely you are today. Is there any news from Masim?"

Ioanna turned to the speaker, a minor noble from one of the western provinces, who alternated between promising more soldiers for the war effort and saying he needed them back to defend his lands. Nobody took him very seriously, least of all Ioanna. Like many of the others filling the room, he had no complaints or requests to make today. He had only come here to observe, gossip, and be admired. When Ioanna looked him in the face, he averted his eyes.

"I will make an announcement when I receive word that can be shared without compromising our soldiers," replied Enessa in a cool tone, and the man drifted off.

The first noble with a genuine request approached Enessa, and Ioanna forced herself to focus. But today, she felt restless and distracted, and she did not know why. Her eyes drifted to her mother's crown. Idly, Ioanna wondered if she would someday have a consort of her own. If she did, she supposed it would be a political alliance.

Whomever her spouse turned out to be, she only hoped they were not inclined to lie.

The morning dragged on with Ioanna only occasionally having to brush imaginary strands of hair out of her face. When the requests trickled to a stop, Ioanna turned her attention to her books. She kept a few of them at the table for those times when there was nothing to do but sit and wish she were well-liked enough for people to approach her. The Temple of Iolar had a wonderful library, and there she first discovered tales of ancient kings and noble warriors, who contributed to the unending fight against chaos. Some of the stories were obviously meant to be metaphorical, but others claimed to be historical accounts.

In later years, she'd turned her attention to the books that had been too complicated for her younger self, the ones that contained no illustrations and discussed questions of morality, or justice, or law. Some were tedious and dry, but others were bright and engaging. Some had been written as a direct response to other writings, which meant Ioanna had to double back and cross-reference, occasionally venturing into other temples to see if they had what she needed—for devotees of Iolar did not only quarrel amongst themselves, and debates could stretch across theological lines.

As a child, she'd only gone to the Temple of Iolar for a quiet place to hide. The priests had been wary of her, at first. She could not blame them after everything her father had done. But it hadn't taken them very long to realize she was nothing like her father.

Archpriest Lailus taught her the prayer to conjure golden shields, saying it was a sin to waste a blessing as beautiful as hers. Until then Ioanna had never thought of her blessing as beautiful. She'd never thought of it as anything except a disappointment. A little later, she learned how to put a blessing on a weapon so it would glow with holy light. It was a paladin's prayer, and neither Ioanna nor the priests cared much for weapons, but the pride in their faces warmed her, nevertheless.

When she grew a little older, Lailus taught her how to call down cleansing golden fire. *It is rare that one is powerful enough for it*, he'd cautioned. *Do not be disappointed if you can't do it.*

But by then they'd all realized there was very little her blessing could not do.

When the doors to the throne room opened again, Ioanna's eyes flicked up from the page. A winged woman, dressed in the familiar blue-and-white uniform of the couriers, entered the room. In her hands she held a thick sealed letter. She started for Enessa, but one of the guards blocked her path with his spear. Another took the letter from the courier's hand and brought it to Enessa.

The empress accepted the letter and broke the seal. Ioanna tried to lean closer to see what it said, but her mother held the page too near to her own face for Ioanna to read the words.

"Mother?" asked Ioanna, after a long pause. Enessa did not reply, and Ioanna stood. "Mother?"

"Go fetch your sisters," ordered Enessa, her voice simultaneously harsh and wavering.

"What has happened?"

"I said *go!*" Enessa cried. Ioanna turned and fled unthinkingly, propelled by the force of her mother's words. She did not stop until she was outside the throne room. Only then did she question the oddity of her being sent on this errand as opposed to one of the many palace guards.

Where would Netheia be? With her friends probably, hunting or sparring or still sleeping from last night's party. Iulia, only ten years old, was likely with her tutors and would appreciate the rescue. She would go to her youngest sister first.

When Ioanna arrived at the emperor's private library, Iulia's tutor was in the middle of explaining something, gesturing to spots on a map to emphasize his points. Despite this, Iulia's chin was rested in her hand, and her eyes were vacant. Ioanna cleared her throat, and they both turned to the doorway.

"I need to borrow Iulia," said Ioanna. "Our mother has summoned us."

Iulia did not need any further explanation. She shoved her book away and jumped to her feet eagerly. "What's going on?"

"I do not know," Ioanna said. "Come on, we need to find Netheia."

"Do you think it's about Father?"

"I imagine so. But she wouldn't tell me anything, except to fetch you."

"Do you think he's taken Ayvadisi?"

"No," said Ioanna.

Iulia huffed. "You don't have to tell the truth *all* the time, you know."

Ioanna smiled and poked Iulia in the ribs to make her flail and shriek. "Don't ask questions if you don't want answers."

They found Netheia lounging in the east garden with a few of her friends. Most were sprawled out on blankets or under embroidered awnings. Netheia herself was nearly asleep on a low chaise, dressed only in the short tunic and boots favored by many warriors.

From the look of her, one might expect Netheia to be the eldest of the sisters. They both had the same tightly curled hair and similar oval faces with dark-brown eyes. Netheia had sun-bronzed skin and a perfectly toned body from the endless hours she spent sparring. Ioanna, so thin and pale in comparison, always found herself self-conscious beside her.

"Netheia," said Ioanna, trying to speak gently so her sister would not be shocked awake. One of Netheia's eyes opened, and immediately a look of irritation came over her.

"What do you want?" she demanded.

Netheia had joined their father in Masim several times. Ioanna herself had never been asked to go, and she was grateful for that. She had only the most rudimentary skills with a weapon, learned in early childhood back before the priestesses gave up on her completely. More importantly, she could not bring herself to take an active role in the battle against the Masimi, who were only protecting their homes.

Ioanna did not spend much time around Netheia, for her sister made no secret of the fact she wanted nothing to do with Ioanna. If Netheia really wanted her gone, she would launch into an impromptu rendition of "I am the sun," a song of her own invention that never failed to give Ioanna a headache because it was nothing but a list of falsehoods. It began, "I am the sun, I am a bird, I'm the town baker, I am a herd (of cattle)," and continued in this manner until Ioanna fled or Netheia ran out of rhymes.

Sometimes Ioanna wondered at the fact Netheia had not revealed Ioanna's blessing to the entire court in an effort to drive her away forever. Perhaps Netheia's hatred did not run quite that deep. Or perhaps she was only biding her time. Ioanna could ask, but Netheia would probably refuse to answer or give a deliberately ridiculous reply out of pure contrariness.

"Mother wants to see us," said Ioanna. "All three of us."

"So she sent you?" Netheia sneered but made no move to rise from the couch. "I suppose you do make a better messenger than a princess."

Ioanna ignored the insult, for there was no point in acknowledging it. "Come on, she's waiting for us."

"You should come, Netheia," urged Iulia. "What if it's a message from Father?"

"Neither of you tell me what to do!" snarled Netheia.

"Very well." Ioanna shrugged. "I'll tell her you refused to come."

Netheia jumped up like a flash of lightning, but Ioanna was ready for her. A golden shield blossomed from her palm. A moment later, Netheia slammed against it, hissing with rage. She beat her fist into the barrier, but it held.

"You're being ridiculous," said Ioanna.

"Fight me, you coward!" screamed Netheia. "You never will! I'd beat you in a real fight! You're lucky you can hide behind your magic! I'd kill you! I'd kill you!"

Ioanna did not need her blessing to know her sister told the truth. It was why she did not lower the shield yet. Netheia would burn herself out eventually, for the blood rage could not last long before subsiding, especially if Ioanna did nothing to feed it.

"What are you *doing*?"

The fury in Netheia's face vanished, only to be replaced by shock. Ioanna turned, though she did not yet drop the shield, and saw Enessa entering the garden flanked by four guards.

"What in Asterium are you two doing?" Enessa's eyes were bright with rage. "Are you fighting? Now?"

"Mother—" Ioanna began, retracting her shield.

"I'll fight if I want to!" Netheia interrupted. "What's it to you? To anyone?"

In Ioanna's opinion, Enessa tolerated a great deal of disrespect from Netheia. But perhaps their mother had finally reached her limit, because she drew her arm back and slapped Netheia across the face.

The garden fell silent. None of Netheia's friends moved or spoke. Nor did Netheia herself, obviously struggling to understand what had just happened.

"Come with me, immediately," ordered Empress Enessa. "Your father is dead."

THEIR FATHER'S STUDY was understood to be one of the most secure rooms in the palace. Protective charms and enchantments had been laid on nearly every stone, so many that the hair on Ioanna's arms raised whenever she stepped inside.

"This can't be true," said Netheia, snatching the courier's letter from Enessa's hand. "Who sent this? Commander Caelina? I never liked her. I never trusted her."

"Netheia."

"I won't accept this!" screamed Netheia. She hurled the letter at Ioanna so rapidly and with such force it struck her in the face. Well accustomed to this sort of behavior and knowing that issuing a complaint would merely result in an order to be less sensitive, Ioanna only scrambled to grab the letter before it hit the floor. "You look at it! Tell her that it's a lie!"

Discerning written lies was significantly more difficult than spoken ones. As far as Ioanna could tell, it depended upon how long ago the writing had been done. Anything older than a few weeks would have no traces upon it. Almost as though the page retained the memory of its author for only a brief time. But this letter could not be too old, so perhaps she had a chance.

Ioanna set the letter down on her father's desk and closed her eyes so the words would not distract her. She put both hands over the page and felt for Commander Caelina's intentions. But no twinge of deceit pricked at her fingertips, no matter how she strained.

"It's true," she said. "Or else, Commander Caelina thinks it's true." For her magic could only detect deliberate deception. Errors in judgment or genuine misunderstandings were not included in that. Nor, despite the name of her blessing, could she sense *truth*. She could only state the absence of a lie. And there was a difference between the two.

Netheia snatched the letter back as quickly as she had thrown it. "I'm going to Masim, then! I'll either prove he's still alive or avenge his death!"

"You are going nowhere," said Enessa. "Your father died because of his own foolishness and pride. I won't allow you to do the same."

"What happened?" asked Ioanna.

"One of the Masimi commanders challenged him to single combat." Enessa's eyes grew cold. "He accepted."

"What?" Ioanna shook her head, incredulous. "Why would he agree to such a thing?"

"As I said. Foolishness and pride." Enessa glared at Netheia. "I suggest you *not* replicate his actions."

"But that means Ioanna is empress now," said Iulia quietly. "Doesn't it?"

Netheia squared her shoulders. "We'll see about that. Nobody wants an empress without Reygmadra's blessing."

"Enough," said Enessa. "The coronation will be at the end of the mourning period, in exactly one hundred days' time."

"Mother!" objected Netheia.

"I said *enough*! Or do I need to lock you in your room?"

"But she's going to ruin everything!" Netheia's face burned crimson again. "This isn't what he wanted! You know it! We all know it! He hated Ioanna! He wanted her to *die*! He was going to name me his heir! He promised me he would, after he returned from the south!"

Perhaps this ought to have shocked Ioanna, but it did not. She did not feel anything at all. Netheia might as well have informed her the sky was blue. She could think of nothing to say except, "He shouldn't have put it off, then."

Netheia screamed in rage, flying forward to collide with Ioanna's shield again.

"*Netheia*!" roared Enessa. But her words were lost as magic, rust-red in color, overtook Netheia's body. Ioanna could not stifle a gasp. It appeared as though her sister had been set alight.

"You want to be empress, but all you know how to do is hide!" screamed Netheia, punctuating each sentence with a blow to Ioanna's golden shield. "You're an embarrassment! You're a mistake! Reygmadra didn't bless you because she saw you're *weak*!"

Her fist shattered through Ioanna's shield. Ioanna gasped as the magic splintered like broken porcelain. She'd never seen this from her sister before, nor anyone else. Had Netheia been hiding magic from her?

Netheia lunged again, nothing stopping her as she collided with Ioanna. Her fist slammed into Ioanna's jaw, and then her eye.

Golden light exploded from Ioanna's hands, blasting Netheia back and slamming her into the far wall. It would not hurt her badly, for Iolar's light was meant to fight demons and chaos gods, not mortal women. And besides, Netheia barely felt pain when she was in a rage.

Ioanna's attack only slowed Netheia down for a moment before she was up and moving forward again. But this time, Enessa seized her by the back of the collar and hurled her in the direction of a chair. Netheia landed in it haphazardly, and the strange magical glow faded from her body.

"Kill each other on your own time!" yelled Enessa. "Or I'll tell the guards to lock *both* of you up! Neither of you is empress yet!"

Ioanna expected Netheia to retort with something biting, but her sister was now staring down at her own hands. After a moment, Ioanna realized they were red—*burned* red. From the celestial fire? But that should have been impossible. Ordinary people could be injured by Iolar's light if it was thrown with enough force, but the purifying burn was reserved for evil creatures.

Netheia was many things, but she was not evil.

"Are you all right?" asked Ioanna, moving forward to examine the burns. "How did—"

But Netheia leapt back to her feet and jammed her hands in her pocket, obscuring them from view. Then before anyone could stop her, she pushed the door open with only her shoulder and stormed out of the room.

Chapter Two

VITALIYA

Princess Vitaliya of Vesolda had been in Xytae for two weeks, but she was not sure how she felt about it yet. She was grateful it was not home, but at the same time, she could not see herself remaining here forever—regardless of the fact she'd made that exact claim to the Vesoldan court.

But the world was bigger than just Vesolda and Xytae. Perhaps she would go somewhere else once she tired of the capital. She appreciated Xytan parties, for they were just the sort of loud and mindless indulgence she'd been seeking. But the Xytan courtiers were a little too... Vitaliya was not sure how to describe them. Intense? Forceful?

Angry?

Xytae clung to the title of empire even though all its subordinate territories had broken away long ago, one by one declaring independence and driving the soldiers out. Yellowing ruins still dotted the Vesoldan countryside, but most had been cleared away or built over in a deliberate rejection of Xytan imperialism.

Despite this, Vitaliya felt no resentment toward Xytae or her people, only a mild curiosity. Vesolda's oppression had taken place centuries ago. It was ancient history. She could hardly care less about it.

The architecture of the Imperial Palace was truly stunning, all high ceilings and elegant pillars, plinths, and endless gardens. But maybe the empress needed to hire more servants because Vitaliya frequently saw dust gathered in corners or on steps, and garden pathways were strewn with dead leaves or fallen branches. Some of the exterior walls were beginning to discolor to a nasty greenish-black color as though nobody had scrubbed them in a very long time. Vases held long-dead flowers, and dishes were frequently cracked and chipped.

When Vitaliya emerged from her room, feeling much better than she had when Ioanna found her, it was nearly noon. As she walked down the halls, she passed groups of servants whispering to one another in low voices. But when she slowed down to eavesdrop, the conversations immediately halted. She pursed her lips together, offended by this exclusion.

Luckily, she soon found a familiar face—Decima. Decima was one of Princess Netheia's closest friends, as far as Vitaliya could tell. A failed acolyte of the Temple of Reygmadra, she'd been cast out for her inability to take orders. Decima claimed this was fine by her since she'd rather fight with her own hands anyway, not bless soldiers. But she'd yet to enlist in the army, for her friendship with Netheia protected her from having to fulfill her civic obligations.

"Decima," said Vitaliya. "What's going on? Did someone die?"

Vitaliya had meant it as a joke, mostly, but the other girl blanched.

"You haven't heard yet?" she asked. "Come with me. Emperor Ionnes is dead."

"What?" Vitaliya shook her head. "That can't be true!"

"I heard the empress say it with my own ears," insisted Decima. "All three of the princesses went off with her, and I haven't seen them since. The rumors say he was killed in a duel with one of the Masimi leaders."

"Why would he be dueling anyone?"

Decima shook her head. "I don't know!"

"Isn't that what his entire army is for?"

"I'm just telling you what they're saying." Decima huffed. "In any case, if he really is dead, that means we'll have a new empress. Enessa's only the consort. She can't rule on her own."

"So, Ioanna, then?"

"Maybe," said Decima. "Maybe not."

Vitaliya chewed the inside of her cheek. "I don't think she'd be so bad." Maybe that was silly—she'd only spoken with her for a few minutes. But the crown princess had seemed kind. At least, kind enough to not deserve what Netheia so obviously wanted to do to her.

"If that's how you feel, maybe you should stay out of it," said Decima. "The Xytan people don't want someone like Ioanna. Our empress should be a warrior."

"It was just a thought!" Vitaliya protested. "Is that really so important to you?"

"She's got Iolar's magic. Don't you know what his followers are like?"

"Well—"

"They try to force everyone to do things *their* way, no matter what. They think there's only one right way to live. And if you try to argue, they accuse you of being corrupted by evil!"

That was a rather extreme view of things, and certainly did not fit with Vitaliya's experiences at home, where the Temple of Iolar was just as influential as any other. But she did not argue. She'd learned fights at the imperial court were hardly ever settled with words, and she knew she had no chance of holding her own against Decima.

If it came down to it...if Ioanna and Netheia decided to fight for the throne, and it turned into a civil war, staying in Xytae probably wouldn't be a very good idea.

But what were her alternatives? Return home to Vesolda, and have everyone think she'd forgiven her father? No. Better to go to Ieflaria, or maybe Ibaia. Vitaliya considered this. She'd been to Ieflaria several times before, but she'd never seen Ibaia.

Ibaia was a strange sort of place where they had no kings, queens, regents, or even ranking nobility. They selected their rulers by majority, which seemed like a good way to guarantee one's rulers would be beautiful and nothing else. Still, it might be interesting to visit and pass judgment. The journey to Ibaia would be long, but she was not in any hurry.

She hoped things would end well for Ioanna, but there was nothing she could really do to help. Even if there was, she wouldn't ever want to claim to represent Vesolda in a conflict. She was angry at her father, not at their citizens. And especially not at any soldiers who might be sent to fight if Xytae decided to take offense to Vitaliya's interference.

No, it would be best to leave immediately.

"I've got to go," said Vitaliya. "I haven't eaten since last night, I need—"

But Decima wasn't listening. She pushed past Vitaliya, eyes locked on something up ahead. Vitaliya rose up on her toes to peer over Decima's shoulder. Princess Netheia was storming down the hallway. She looked furious—and like she'd been in a fight, with a long tear in the collar of her dress and her hair in disarray.

Vitaliya decided it was time to be somewhere else. She turned away and darted around the nearest corner. Luckily, Netheia had barely noticed her.

"I can't believe her!" Netheia cried loudly enough that Vitaliya could still hear her. "She's just going to—to stand back and let this happen!"

"Who?" asked Decima.

"My mother! Of course!"

Decima gave a sigh and lowered her voice. "What did she say?"

"She said Ioanna was going to be empress, and I needed to shut up and go die somewhere."

"What did she *actually* say?"

Netheia huffed. "She said the coronation's in a hundred days."

"Whose coronation?"

"Ioanna's, obviously..." Netheia's voice trailed off. "She didn't specify."

"And what else did she say?" Decima pressed.

"To kill each other on our own time." Netheia's thoughtful tone twisted into something sinister.

"We don't need one hundred days. We could have this done in an hour," whispered Decima eagerly. "Enessa's not supporting Ioanna; she's just being clever. She wants to be able to claim she supported the winner all along."

"I know I can get the guards on my side," Netheia whispered back. "It would be so easy..."

Vitaliya hurried away in the direction of her room, not daring to turn around and glance back over her shoulder. Her suspicions had been correct. She needed to leave Xytae immediately, before the swords and torches came out.

As she rummaged in her pockets for her key, she remembered Crown Princess Ioanna. It really was too bad she was probably going to die. But that was the way of things in Xytae, or so Vitaliya had always been told. The parties were marvelous, wasteful and extravagant, and they very nearly made up for the backstabbing and poisonings and sinister plots.

Vitaliya went into her room and began to collect her dresses from where she'd strewn them about over the course of the last few days.

I should warn her.

Vitaliya paused.

No. Stay out of it. Keep Vesolda out of it.

But warning Ioanna wasn't really interfering, was it? It was just stating a fact. And besides, who would ever know? Nobody would find out. Even if Netheia suspected someone had said something to Ioanna, there'd be no proving Vitaliya's guilt—and no real reason to suspect her. She'd only met Ioanna once, for a few minutes.

But Ioanna did not deserve to die.

Vitaliya allowed the dresses she'd gathered up to fall back to the ground. She would sneak out and warn Ioanna, just to assuage her conscience. Then she'd throw all her things into a carriage headed for Ibaia and forget all about it.

That was enough. That was more than enough.

Vitaliya opened her door cautiously and glanced down the hallway in both directions. People were around, but nobody paid any attention to her, and she doubted they would when the gossip was this good.

It wasn't far to Ioanna's room—nor was there any mistaking it for someone else's, given the size of the doors and the ornamentation around them. Vitaliya gave one of the doors a tentative knock. A small part of her hoped there would be no response.

"Who is it?" called a gentle voice from within.

"It's Vitaliya." Why hadn't she used her title? "I, I must speak with you."

There was a long pause, and Vitaliya feared Ioanna would order her away. And really, who could blame her? Ioanna was surely mourning the death of her father. The last thing she needed was some foreign, barely sober stranger in her private rooms.

But then the door opened, and Ioanna stood before her. Vitaliya was struck by her resemblance to Netheia and marveled at the fact she'd been so drunk she hadn't immediately identified her this morning. The princesses' faces were so similar, and their dark curls were practically identical. But while Netheia's body might have been carved from marble, Ioanna was made of glass.

"Vitaliya." Ioanna's dark eyes were warm, and she did not appear as though she had been crying. "I was not expecting to see you again, and so soon. Come in."

Ioanna turned, and Vitaliya followed her. The room was enormous, even by extravagant Xytan standards. She'd seen Netheia's room, and while it had been large enough to host a party, it was only about half the size of Ioanna's.

Netheia's room had been decorated with weapons, armor, and trophies, but Ioanna's was mostly clear of any sort of decorations, except a few bookshelves. Still, it didn't feel bare or impersonal because the architecture of the room was so impressive it hardly needed decoration at all. The floor was pale, gleaming tiles, and every surface had been intricately carved with designs of people, flowers, and patterns. Daylight streamed through every open window, giving the room a free, airy feeling.

"I'm sorry," said Vitaliya. "About your father, I mean."

To her surprise, Ioanna only shrugged. "It was inevitable," she said in a very soft voice. "And really, I hardly knew him. And he hardly knew me."

"I'm sorry," said Vitaliya again.

"No, no, I am. What are you meant to say to that?" Ioanna smiled ruefully. "But I thank you for thinking of me."

"That's not why I came, though," said Vitaliya. "That is, I *am* sorry. But there is something else I must tell you. Your sister, Netheia..."

The faint smile faded from Ioanna's lips.

"I think you need to leave the palace right now. You need to leave the city. She's coming to kill you, and she's getting guards and soldiers on her side." Vitaliya swallowed, wishing she'd been more eloquent. Netheia was Ioanna's sister, and who was she? Just some foreigner. She'd be lucky if Ioanna didn't have her arrested for slandering the princess.

But Ioanna nodded sadly. Then she sighed. "I should have expected this. Thank you for informing me."

"You believe me?"

"Of course I do."

"Well..." Vitaliya had not expected convincing her would be so easy. "Do you have somewhere safe to go?"

"Yes."

Vitaliya waited, but Ioanna said no more. But then, that was probably wise. Better that Vitaliya not know where the princess was going.

"I should go, then," said Vitaliya. "I need to pack my things."

"I am sorry this has been your first impression of Xytae," Ioanna murmured. "I hope, in the future, we will be more worthy of such a guest."

Vitaliya grinned and shook her head. "Don't let my title fool you. The only reason I haven't run off to become a playactor is because my grandmother forced me to swear on her deathbed I wouldn't."

Despite everything, Ioanna laughed. The sound was soft and short like she was afraid to be seen doing it. It disappeared as quickly as it had come.

Vitaliya thought of all the things she'd heard about the crown princess—not just from Netheia, but from *everyone*. How she was the first member of the Isinthi family in living memory to not have Reygmadra's war magic. Instead she was blessed by Iolar. Worse still, she was famous for hiding behind those celestial shields when it came to a fight—something the Xytan court could not respect.

Vitaliya had never said so, but she didn't think there was anything shameful about not wanting to be hit. That was just common sense, wasn't it?

Ioanna did not duel. She did not even spar. She did not attend parties. She could not throw a javelin or swing a hammer. She had never gone to Masim with the soldiers. She barely spoke to anyone, except her own mother. She stayed in her room and read dreadful boring books about theology and history. She attended Sunrise services. She thought she was *better* than the rest of the court.

Vitaliya wasn't certain she believed that last one. In Vesolda, Ioanna would be considered shy, at worst, and her silence would likely be viewed as an indicator of wisdom.

Xytae was such a strange place.

Vitaliya turned away from Ioanna and began to walk back toward the door. But just as she reached for it, it swung open from the outside.

"Oh, hello," said Netheia. In one hand, she held an unsheathed short sword. She released the handle to spin it as though it was a toy, then caught it before it fell. "Look, Decima. You were right. I'll never doubt you again."

"Yes, you will," drawled Decima. Vitaliya pulled her eyes away from the gleaming blade and looked up at the other young woman. She held some kind of polearm, leaning on it casually like a walking stick. And behind her, Vitaliya could see more people, some familiar, some not.

"I was just offering my condolences—" Vitaliya began.

"Shut up." Netheia ran her tongue over her teeth. "Don't think I won't kill you too. Don't think I'm afraid of a war with Vesolda. Personally, I'd love a reason to take it back—"

"Is this necessary?" interrupted Ioanna.

"You shut up too!" Netheia jabbed her sword in Ioanna's direction in the same way a tutor might use a pointer to emphasize a lesson. Ioanna did not flinch. "I don't want to kill you if I don't have to. No, that's not what I mean. I mean, Mother would rather me not kill you. And I don't want to hear about it for the next thirty years. So, I'm trying it this way first."

Vitaliya moved further back, further into the enormous room. Her eyes fell, once again, on the open windows. If she could get to one... If she could get *through* one...

It certainly wouldn't be the first time Vitaliya had escaped out a window.

"You don't deserve this." Netheia advanced on Ioanna at a leisurely pace. The elder princess did not move. Nothing affected her. "Even you know it. The empire is *meant* for me. You can go join the temple or something. Like you've always wanted. I won't bother you, and you won't bother me."

Ioanna still didn't reply.

"I'm being very generous," Netheia added. "More generous than you deserve."

"And what about her?" Ioanna tilted her head in Vitaliya's direction.

"I haven't decided yet." A smile crept across Netheia's lips. "I wonder how much King Marcius will pay in ransom. Or maybe I'll execute her. Start a war. Take Vesolda back by force. The world is so full of possibilities, isn't it?"

Ioanna moved, so lightning fast not even Netheia could respond in time to stop her. She was moving toward the window, having apparently had the same idea as Vitaliya. One arm caught Vitaliya around the waist, pulling her along. When they reached the windowsill, Ioanna did not hesitate. She flung herself, and Vitaliya, over the edge.

Vitaliya screamed. Climbing out a window was one thing; hurling oneself out of it was quite another. And they were high up enough that the landing was not going to be pleasant, unless—

Ioanna stretched her arm out toward the approaching ground. Golden light sprang from her hand, and Vitaliya flinched, expecting it to burn when they inevitably collided with it.

But it did not burn. It was warm, certainly, but nothing resembling the descriptions of righteous celestial fire that featured so prominently in stories. And it was soft, too, like a cushion made of light.

A moment later, the princesses struck the ground. It wasn't a gentle landing, but Ioanna's shield took the worst of the shock out of it. Vitaliya turned her face up to the window they'd fallen from. Decima stared down at them, looking about as surprised as Vitaliya felt.

"Are you all right?" asked Ioanna.

"I think so—"

"Come on." Ioanna grabbed Vitaliya by the arm, nearly dragging her to her feet. Vitaliya had no idea what Netheia was complaining about; Ioanna seemed like a model Xytan woman to her. "Before the guards come after us."

"But where—" Vitaliya looked over her shoulder at the palace. "I left all my things—"

"That's not important right now."

Maybe it wasn't, but Vitaliya wasn't sure how far they'd get with only the clothes on their backs and whatever coins happened to be in their pockets. Ioanna continued to pull her along, veering into an area where life-size statues and untrimmed fruit trees shielded them from view.

The Imperial Palace was massive, at least twice the size of her father's castle at Bergavenna. They hurried deeper and deeper into the gardens, to areas Vitaliya had never seen before. The quality of the gardeners' work deteriorated the further away they moved from the palace, and Vitaliya found herself stumbling over loose stones and fallen branches while overgrown brambles caught on her sleeves and tore at the fabric.

But Ioanna was still moving, her face pinched and determined. "There's exits hidden all over the grounds," she muttered to Vitaliya. "I'll find us one."

Noise rose behind them—Netheia's soldiers were searching for them. They reached the high wall surrounding the palace grounds. The exterior side was kept clean and bright, and Vitaliya had been impressed by it when she'd first entered the city. But inside the wall was discolored and overgrown with an array of different plants, so thick in places that it seemed the wall itself had been shaped from greenery rather than stones.

Somehow, Ioanna found a door in the mess. Vitaliya didn't spot it at first, not even when Ioanna put her hands on it, for it was so covered in plants. Ioanna struggled to reach the ancient handle without gouging her hand on the sharp thorns wrapped around it.

"Here, let me," said Vitaliya, calling her own magic to her hands. Green light, Eyvindr's blessing, flickered at her fingertips.

The brambles were old and stubborn and did not want to move for Vitaliya. No gardener had ever tended them, and so it took some coaxing before they parted, leaving the door exposed. Unfortunately, Vitaliya could now see it was kept sealed by heavy chains and a large lock.

But Ioanna took the lock in her hands and pulled. It was more rust than metal, and after only a moment, it snapped. At the same time, a few of the chain links broke too.

"Lucky you haven't had any assassins," observed Vitaliya.

"Assassins come in through the front door," Ioanna replied.

Outside the wall, thankfully, there was not a bustling street. Instead, they found a quiet alley. Given the amount of refuse piled up, it was almost hard to believe they stood in the shadow of the palace wall. Vitaliya stumbled over a few empty sacks, which had been stacked haphazardly here and there. A few rotted boxes were beginning to collapse on themselves, and quick movement caught her eye for just a moment—mice, or probably rats. Ioanna closed the door behind them, breathing deeply.

"If we're quick, we might be able to get out of Xyuluthe before Netheia realizes we're not in the palace anymore." Ioanna began to undo the complicated braids her hair had been woven into, running her fingers through them so her curls fell free. "Put your jewelry in your pockets. We don't want to appear too wealthy. And stay near to me—I might need your help."

"I don't know the city very well." Vitaliya hadn't spent any significant amount of time outside the palace since her arrival. But Ioanna shook her head.

"If I get a headache...if there's too many people, or if it's too loud...just grab my arm and get me somewhere quiet. Don't let me sit down."

Vitaliya was not sure what to make of this, but she nodded. She had no intention of staying in the city for a moment longer than she had to.

Chapter Three

IOANNA

Xyuluthe was an enormous city, but Ioanna had spent very little time exploring it. Even if she'd been inclined to—which she was not—she was not permitted to go beyond the Great Temples, which were all clustered near the palace.

She'd studied maps of the city, usually in the context of which areas were easiest to defend, and which directions an invading army might want to approach from. She'd been told from an early age there were many secret ways out, but she did not need to know them because someone would guide her there if the time ever came.

Ioanna had detected some of these secret paths without aid over the years. Hidden things tended to draw her attention, though in a softer way than lies and deception did. Most of the paths within the palace went downward into the sewers, and presumably let out near the river. Ioanna had never ventured all the way to the end of one, fearing she'd become lost and not be able to find her way back.

And of course, there were the forgotten doors all over the palace grounds like the one she and Vitaliya had slipped through. A more adventurous princess might have used these to elude her guards and run all over the city.

But the city was so loud, and so full of people lying to one another. Ioanna saw no reason to subject herself to that.

If they kept to the quiet places, the narrow streets and darker alleys, they would miss the worst of the crowds. Open markets were to be avoided at all costs, for she knew the tiny lies told by the vendors regarding the quality and freshness of their wares would pile on her until she was nearly blind with pain.

Robbers might lurk in the shadowy places, but Ioanna knew her blessing would be enough to frighten them off if they tried a direct approach. Still, Iolar's magic was rare in Xyuluthe. Once the word got out that Netheia was searching for her, using her blessing would be as good as writing her own name across her forehead.

The road in front of them was quiet, but Ioanna could hear voices from the next street over. She wondered if news of her father's death had spread beyond the palace yet. Maybe whispers, maybe rumors, but nothing substantiated. Not until her mother made a public address.

"How are we going to get out of here?" asked Vitaliya in a low voice.

"The east gate. It's nearest to here, I think."

"And after that, where will we go?"

"Oredia."

Vitaliya looked confused. "Where is that?"

"North of here. Three days' travel by carriage."

"But you have allies there?" Vitaliya persisted.

"I suppose you could call her that," said Ioanna. "Oredia is the home of my grandmother, Irianthe Isinthi. The former empress. She won't let Netheia kill me, and I'm sure she'll be able to get you passage back to Vesolda too."

"Oh. Yes." But Vitaliya bit her lower lip. "I was actually thinking I'd go to Ibaia, though."

"Ibaia? Whatever for?"

"Now I need a reason?" Vitaliya sighed. "Though I suppose since I've lost all my things, I might as well go home. Ugh. Maybe I'll stay in Oredia for a few weeks instead."

"I imagine your family will be worried once they receive news of what happened."

"Let them worry! Anyway, you can't mean to walk all the way to Oredia. We'll never get there before Netheia finds us."

"If we ride, we might be able to make it in two days," said Ioanna. "But I don't know if we can afford to purchase horses with only our jewelry."

"Buy a peasant's dress, and sell the one you're wearing," advised Vitaliya. "And I'll do the same. They might not give us a fair price since we're in a hurry, but at least we'll be less conspicuous. And it will get us some coins."

Ioanna looked down at her dress. She certainly owned nicer ones, but Vitaliya had a point. Anyone who saw her would know she'd come from the palace. "I'd hoped to avoid the merchants."

"What for?"

Ioanna could not possibly explain. She'd kept her blessing a secret from the world for such a long time; the very idea of telling Vitaliya filled her with panic. She knew Vesoldans lacked the fervent devotion to Reygmadra that had marred Ioanna's childhood, but she still could not guess how Vitaliya would react. Even if she was not disgusted, she might be frightened and turn her in to Netheia. Or worse, seek to use Ioanna as a pawn in Vesoldan politics.

"I'd just hoped we might leave the city quickly," Ioanna said weakly. As far as lies went, this one was benign. Nevertheless, uttering the words still made her forehead ache briefly.

"Leaving quickly won't matter if they catch us before sunset," asserted Vitaliya. "Trust me, I know all about running away from things. If we leave without supplies or disguises or anything, we'll be sorry later."

"We don't have time to commission dresses."

"We don't have to. You can buy them ready-made from shops, you know! That's what the ordinary people do!" Vitaliya began to look around. "We might have to find a livelier area, though. I think this is residential."

Ioanna allowed Vitaliya to link their elbows together and pull her along. Vitaliya was already smiling like she considered this more of a silly misadventure than a potential life-and-death matter. Maybe, to her, it was.

As they made their way to the more crowded areas, Ioanna braced herself for pain, the sort that always overcame her whenever she walked into a party or even a too-crowded room. But either the common people of Xyuluthe were feeling particularly pious today, or they were simply less inclined to lie to one another than the nobles were. After a moment, her shoulders relaxed.

Ioanna considered herself fortunate she didn't leave the palace frequently enough for most citizens to recognize her face. Everyone knew Netheia, for she was always riding about with her friends, sparring publicly, and participating in athletic events. Ioanna was not nearly so sociable. When people did pause to look at them, their eyes lingered on Vitaliya—whether because of her Vesoldan clothing or pretty face, Ioanna did not know.

After a bit of searching, Vitaliya pulled Ioanna into a dressmaker's shop. As Ioanna stared around at the interior, marveling at how much had been crammed into such a tiny space, Vitaliya shouted happy greetings to the shopkeeper and her assistants, so familiar that for a moment Ioanna wondered if Vitaliya had come here before. But no, she'd said she didn't know the city.

Ioanna had always envied people like Vitaliya, who could greet strangers like they were old friends and be met with equal enthusiasm. There was a sort of magic in it—though her mother always said anyone could do it, if they put the effort in.

Ioanna couldn't detect a lie in that statement, but that didn't necessarily mean it was true. It might only mean Enessa believed it wholeheartedly.

"We're here to sell our dresses, and buy new ones," Vitaliya announced to the entire shop. One of her hands wrapped around Ioanna's waist, and she pulled her close. Ioanna made a sound of surprise, but Vitaliya didn't appear to notice. "My love and I are running away. Her father has ordered her to be married in a week to a man she hates. To a man we *both* hate. We need disguises."

Ioanna closed her eyes. The lie was silly and didn't pain her as badly as the ones she heard so frequently at home.

"We're going to run away to the south and become—" Vitaliya paused, though Ioanna wasn't sure if this was for dramatic effect, or simply because she hadn't yet thought of an occupation. "—fishermen. Fisher*women*. We'll build a little hut from driftwood and trade with the mer for sunken treasure."

Ioanna did not know if the seamstresses truly believed Vitaliya's tale, or if they were simply indulging the wealthy noblewomen that had entered their humble shop. Ioanna supposed it did not really matter. The assistants began to select dresses from the racks, and Ioanna could see they were very nearly finished, with only the hems in the sleeves and skirts left unsewn, so they might be fitted to whoever purchased them.

At the same time, the head seamstress took the heavy fabric of Ioanna's skirt in her hands, feeling its weight and quality. Her face grew dark with concern. "I cannot buy this from you. There is not enough money in this shop."

It was not a lie. Ioanna, who had been fully prepared for the shopkeepers to attempt to cheat them, found herself so taken aback she could not think of a reply.

"That's all right. I expected that," interrupted Vitaliya brightly. "Just give us what you can."

Ioanna knew she was thin by Xytan standards. She had neither muscle like Netheia, nor curves like Vitaliya. Servants were always leaving dishes beside her while she read, or worked, as though they were afraid she might starve to death unless they took an active role in things. Whenever she had to visit the palace dressmaker, they tutted and fretted and poked and mumbled.

But these women did not comment on Ioanna's shape, or lack thereof. They brought out dresses of varying lengths, including the ankle-length ones worn by richer women or those who worked indoors, and the knee-length garments soldiers and workers wore. Ioanna instinctively reached for the more familiar design, but Vitaliya said, "You might want the shorter kind if we're going to be riding."

Ioanna didn't particularly want to show her knees to the entire world, but Vitaliya seemed to know what she was talking about, so she picked a shorter garment, simple and without any ornamentation, save that it had been dyed sage green. Even the customary belt at her waist was nearer to a piece of rope than a girdle. Paired with her sandals, she thought she looked like a messenger, one of those young people who ran all over the city delivering packages or letters. They were frequently small and skinny too.

Vitaliya's dress was white, accentuating her deep-olive skin. Her shoes, silk Vesoldan slippers, did not at all match and would be a poor choice for traveling, so one of the assistants went scurrying out to find a pair of boots. Vitaliya also asked for traveling cloaks and rucksacks to carry their things.

The cloaks were made of heavy wool, and while it was probably too warm out to wear them right now, Ioanna knew she'd be grateful for them at night once the sun went down. As they waited for Vitaliya's boots, Ioanna tried not to appear too tense. But she could not keep her eyes off the door, expecting soldiers to burst in at any moment, swords gleaming, to drag her back to Netheia.

The seamstresses were cheerful, though. Maybe they were already thinking of how rich they'd be once they sold Ioanna's dress, but it seemed to her they were genuinely untroubled. Clearly, no rumors of her father's death or Ioanna's subsequent flight from the palace had managed to reach them yet.

Besides, the shop was a curious sort of place. It was nothing like the beautiful rooms of the palace dressmaker, orderly and pristine. Bolts of fabric were stacked nearly high enough to brush the ceiling, and Ioanna kept well away from these towers for fear they might come crashing down on her head. Countless threads were underfoot, and when the light caught them the right way, dropped pins gleamed.

Finally, the boots were delivered, and Ioanna and Vitaliya emerged into the daylight once more. Ioanna glanced around for soldiers but saw only a single member of the city watch, leaning against a wall and staring off into the middle distance. He'd received no orders from the palace—or if he had, he wasn't expecting to spot a runaway princess during his shift.

Nevertheless, Ioanna was relieved when Vitaliya pulled her in the opposite direction, talking about how they had to get horses next.

Ioanna knew how to ride, though she didn't spend much time at it. Netheia owned several horses, all very expensive and very aggressive. When Ioanna rode, the hostlers always found her a gentle, calmer mount—the sort Netheia said were no good for anything except pulling a plow. Ioanna knew Netheia exaggerated, but nevertheless it kept her from attempting to join any activities where she might be required to ride.

All of the gold coins they'd accumulated were not quite enough to purchase them two mounts, so Vitaliya traded one of her gold bracelets away while Ioanna chewed anxiously at her lower lip. Guards might spot them at any moment. She would not relax, not until they were out of sight of Xyuluthe's walls.

When they finally exited the city via the north gate, Ioanna feared her heart might be on the verge of failure. She clutched at the reins as tightly as she could, and this was the only thing that stopped her hands from trembling.

They rode onward until Xyuluthe's walls grew too distant for Ioanna to see. Still, she frequently looked back to see if anyone was riding toward them. They passed other travelers, some on foot and some in wagons. She wondered how far they were from the nearest town, and if they might make it there by nightfall.

But whenever they passed someone she might ask, Ioanna's tongue froze in her mouth, and an icy terror came over her. She'd spent so little time outside the palace, outside the court. Surely if she tried to interact with her citizens, she'd only humiliate herself, and then they would examine her more closely, and perhaps her description would fit with someone the city guards were asking after.

She glanced over at Vitaliya. Maybe she should ask the other girl to do the talking. It came naturally to her. But she could not bring herself to say anything to Vitaliya either. She did not know *what* to say.

After a few hours of painful silence, just as the sky was beginning to darken, Vitaliya pulled her horse to an abrupt halt. Ioanna did the same, afraid something was wrong. But Vitaliya slid down from her mount's back and rushed over to the roadside. "Yes!" she cried. "Finally."

"What's wrong?" asked Ioanna, glancing back and forth to make sure no soldiers were approaching.

"Nothing's wrong! Everything's perfect!" Vitaliya threw her arms around one of the many trees bordering the roadside. "Oh, you're beautiful!"

"What are you doing?" asked Ioanna.

"I'm starving. It's an orange tree."

"But it's not..." Ioanna looked up at the branches. "There won't be any fruit for months. It's too early."

"Says you!" cried Vitaliya happily, calling bright-green magic to her hands. She pressed it into the trunk of the tree, and it flowed upwards, curving into the lowest branch, the only one within arm's reach. Within minutes, fresh leaves emerged from the cold branch and unfurled like the wings of countless butterflies. And nestled amongst them Ioanna could see small, dark-green pearls that gradually lightened in color as they swelled to the size of a fist.

"I've never seen that done so fast," marveled Ioanna, watching as the fruit changed from green to orange. People with Eyvindr's magic could wake fruit trees out of season if their blessing was strong enough. But in Ioanna's experience, it still took days for the fruit to ripen.

"Give them fifteen minutes to get darker," Vitaliya advised. "They'll taste better."

"I'm a little envious," said Ioanna. "It's a very useful blessing."

"I help the farmers, sometimes. Not so much recently, but in the past. We have some large farms near Bergavenna."

Ioanna looked at Vitaliya with wide eyes. "Your parents allowed that? Or you did it in secret?"

"Actually, it was their idea. They brought in a priest to teach me after they realized I could make the roses bloom. He told them my blessing was strong, and so they wanted to put it to good use. I thought I'd hate it, being in the sun and the dust...but it's nice. And I might as well contribute to something, right? In any case, I wasn't allowed to do the *real* work. The tilling, the planting, and the carrying heavy things. Magic's nothing compared to that." Vitaliya flopped down onto the grass smiling, and apparently not concerned about getting dirt and leaves in her hair.

"Those farmers must have been honored."

"I didn't do anything an ordinary priest wouldn't have," denied Vitaliya. "And slower and clumsier at first. But they were kind. I thought it was just because of who my parents were, but it didn't *feel* like that. It felt genuine."

"Has the Temple of Eyvindr tried to recruit you?" Eyvindr, God of the Harvest and Third of the Ten, was an extremely powerful god, and his temples were influential. She would be surprised if the Vesoldan temple hadn't taken an interest in Vitaliya.

"Oh yes, of course! But I won't join. I'd have to give up my title and go live in the temple. And there's no promise I'd stay in Bergavenna—what if they sent me to some dreadful farming town in the middle of nowhere, and I died of boredom?"

"I don't think they'd do that to you," said Ioanna. "Even if you gave up your rank, everyone would know who your family was. They'd never treat you like an ordinary priestess."

"Maybe, but I don't want to risk it. Besides I just don't think I'd *enjoy* being a priestess. That kind of life has so many rules. I would look very nice in green, though, wouldn't I?"

Ioanna felt herself smile, briefly. Their situation was certainly not ideal, and perhaps she ought to be annoyed to be saddled with such a silly traveling companion. But Vitaliya was kind and soft in a way that was rare at the imperial court. Yes, she told the occasional lie, but they were harmless with no malice or machinations behind them.

They tied their horses and sat under the tree to eat. The oranges were good, sweet, ripe, and they had no trace of magic in their flavor, nothing to suggest they hadn't grown naturally over the course of several months.

Ioanna wondered what Netheia was doing now. She wondered what her mother was doing now. Were they searching the city for her, or did they think it wasn't worth the trouble? Was her mother worried or just relieved? Was she happy?

Mother would rather me not kill you, Netheia had said.

In a twisted way, the words warmed Ioanna. Her mother did not hate her as much as she could. She did not hate her enough to want her dead. Only...driven away. Or perhaps, knowing Enessa, she wanted Ioanna to cheerfully surrender the crown, and then remain at court so they could continue to use her blessing to their advantage.

Maybe that was the reason why Enessa wanted her alive. Not because of any maternal affection, but because Ioanna's blessing was rare and powerful and they'd be fools to let it go to waste even if the name of it did terrify the court. Her heart sank at the realization.

And what of the way Netheia's hands burned under Iolar's light? As though she was a chaos cultist! But Netheia had Reygmadra's blessing, and nobody could carry the magic of more than one god. Everyone knew that.

Had she imagined it?

In that case, had she imagined Netheia's blessing overtaking her body, and Netheia's fist shattering through her shield—two things that ought to be impossible?

"My hands are sticky," complained Vitaliya, pulling Ioanna away from her worries. "Let's find some water. The horses will need it too."

Ioanna glanced toward the sky. The sun was low, and soon it would be too dark to travel. "I was hoping we'd make it to a town before nightfall, but I suppose we'll have to camp." It would be unpleasant, though, since they had no bedrolls or tents.

"Oh! Don't worry!" said Vitaliya happily. "I know what to do! But first, water. There's got to be some nearby if there's so many fruit trees growing wild." She jumped to her feet, sending torn pieces of orange rind everywhere, and began to move deeper into the trees. Ioanna stayed with the horses but balanced on the tips of her toes in order to keep Vitaliya within her line of sight.

"I knew it!" cried Vitaliya distantly. "There's a little stream back here."

Ioanna looked at the trees. It would probably be safer to sleep among them rather than directly beside the road. If any soldiers came looking for them, they'd be more difficult to find, especially in the darkness. Maybe they would even ride right past without a second glance. And if not, they'd make enough noise moving through the woods Vitaliya and Ioanna would hear them coming and be ready for them.

Ioanna wasn't sure if she could kill someone even if they were trying to kill her. She hoped she wouldn't ever have to find out. With any luck, a demonstration of her blessing might be enough to make them decide they weren't being paid enough to risk dragging her back to Xyuluthe.

Ioanna took the horses by the reins and led them carefully through the trees. She found Vitaliya kneeling before the little stream, splashing water on her face. Ioanna tied the horses, giving them enough rope so they could reach the water as well, and went to submerge her hands.

"I think this is nicer than the capital," said Vitaliya cheerfully, drying her hands on her skirt. Oddly enough, it was not a lie. "Everyone in Xyuluthe is so angry all the time. I'm much more relaxed now."

Ioanna wasn't sure what to say in response to this. She watched as Vitaliya stood and brushed mud and bits of broken bark from where they'd stuck to her knees. Then she went and removed the saddles from the horses, setting them down on the ground.

"Well," began Ioanna. "You said you knew something about making camp?"

"Oh yes!" Vitaliya looked around. Then she pushed her way into a patch of long grass. "Just wait."

Ioanna watched as more green magic flowed from Vitaliya's hands and into the surrounding wildlife. The plants began to grow longer and thicker, rising up until they were nearly Vitaliya's own height.

Vitaliya moved her arms, as if directing the plants, and the long grasses began to weave themselves into a basket shape, large enough for a person to rest comfortably inside. Ioanna stood out of the way and observed quietly. When Vitaliya turned back to Ioanna, she smiled.

"I used to make these when I was younger. I'd go outside, read, and fall asleep," explained Vitaliya. "They're really very soft!"

Ioanna tried not to think of spiders crawling across her face as she slept, or snakes slithering into her pockets. Vitaliya knelt down and climbed inside the nest.

"See?" she called, shifting around to peer out at Ioanna. "It's nice. And it smells wonderful."

"I see."

Vitaliya stretched out and closed her eyes. Then after a moment, they snapped open again. "I'm not tired yet," she said. "You know what would be funny? If there's a town only a few more minutes down the road."

"I think it's better to stop now, instead of risking—"

"Oh no, you're right! I just think it would be funny." Vitaliya closed her eyes again. "Maybe I am tired after all.

You can come in if you want. There's enough room for both of us."

Ioanna wondered if it would be rude to ask Vitaliya to weave a second nest. She did not believe the other princess would attempt anything untoward, but she'd never slept beside anyone before. She wasn't accustomed to it.

But she didn't want Vitaliya to think she was ungrateful, odd, or any other number of negative things. And Vitaliya already used her magic several times today for rather impressive feats. She might very well be drained.

Ioanna decided she would tolerate sharing and hope Vitaliya did not kick or punch in her sleep. She found a sharp stone and began to carve runes in the dirt as the priests of Iolar had taught her.

"What are you doing?" called Vitaliya.

"Drawing a protective circle. If any guards or soldiers come for us, it will wake me."

"Oh, yes! I've heard of those. The paladins use them!" Vitaliya smiled, and a bit of Ioanna's anxiety lifted at the realization Vitaliya truly didn't object to the use of Iolar's magic. "Does it work against ordinary people? I always assumed it only caught chaos gods and things like that."

"No, it will catch anything except animals. It can't sense animals. Not even a hungry wolf. I think it's because—" She stopped, realizing Vitaliya neither wanted nor deserved a lecture on the nature of protective circles.

But Vitaliya's eyes were bright and curious. "Because why?" Her tone did not at all sound mocking or sarcastic. It sounded genuine.

"Well, we don't know for certain. But I don't think animals are capable of evil, really. Most of the temples agree. And the circle is Iolar's magic, so it—"

"*Most* of the temples?" interrupted Vitaliya. "Who's going around arguing animals are evil?"

"Well, it's not like that—" Ioanna realized she was doing a very poor job of explaining. "It's not something anyone seriously debates. It's more for thinking about. Most people agree animals aren't capable of evil, but then the question becomes if they're capable of good."

"They are!"

Ioanna waited for Vitaliya to explain her reasoning, but the other princess merely shifted into a more comfortable position in the nest. She clearly felt she'd delivered a good argument that required no further details. Ioanna found this oddly endearing.

Ioanna murmured the prayer to activate the protective circle. The runes glowed with familiar gold magic, then faded to a dull, inconspicuous shade of brown that would not be visible from the road.

"I always thought it seemed difficult having Iolar's magic," observed Vitaliya. "All that memorizing! I could never do it."

"I don't know. It always came naturally to me." But Ioanna understood what she meant. Iolar's magic functioned most efficiently when channeled through recitations and runes, rather than willpower or emotion like most of the other gods' blessings. The prayers were easy enough to remember, but drawing runes required concentration and a careful hand.

Inside the woven grass nest was more comfortable than Ioanna anticipated, and it did smell nice. Vitaliya was a heavy weight beside her, and Ioanna tried to keep herself from rolling into the other girl.

"I am sorry about all this," began Ioanna.

"What? Oh no, it's not your fault! You didn't ask your sister to chase us off. Besides, I've been in worse spots than this."

"You have? When?"

"Well..." Vitaliya's voice trailed off as she considered. "All right, maybe I haven't."

A tiny laugh escaped from Ioanna. Vitaliya had been so convinced she was telling the truth that, in the moment, Ioanna had been unable to detect any lie.

Only rarely did Ioanna encounter people who were exactly what they professed to be. There were so many lies at court, so much deception. But Vitaliya's lies could not be called cunning manipulation. They were more akin to childish hyperbole, the sort Iulia occasionally indulged in when she was feeling particularly emotional.

Ioanna knew she and Vitaliya were the same age, but Vitaliya seemed so much younger. Ioanna supposed it was the lack of responsibilities. Vitaliya may have been a princess, but clearly nobody expected her to be any sort of heir. Maybe that was for the best, though. Ioanna could not see the girl ruling a nation. Not that she would ever say such an impolite thing out loud.

"What do you think you'll do once you get to Oredia?" asked Vitaliya.

"I suppose that will depend on what my grandmother says," Ioanna admitted. "I'm certain she'll provide us with a safe place to stay, but I don't know if she'll tolerate my trying to take back the throne."

Vitaliya said something, but Ioanna barely heard it. She was already lost in her own thoughts. If only she'd been faster! The Order of the Sun *would* come to her aid; she was certain of it. But now it would be days before she could even send them a letter, and weeks before she could expect a reply.

The paladins of the Order of the Sun had been exiled when she was only five years old for the crime of refusing to join the emperor's army. Perhaps her father had thought they would yield if faced with banishment, but they had not. They'd simply withdrawn to the surrounding nations. Archpriestess Seia of the Temple of Reygmadra told anyone who would listen that some had even gone to Masim to fight *against* Ionnes, proving once again Iolar's followers couldn't be trusted.

When Ioanna tried to recall individual paladins, their faces were always blurred like ink splashed with water. But she vividly remembered the armor they wore, their gleaming silver chainmail and white tabards, and how they never, ever gave her a headache when they spoke.

Some days, when the Xytan court seemed particularly cruel, Ioanna fantasized about running away to join them. She never would—Iolar meant her to be an empress—but the thought was tempting. She could live in Vesolda, or Ieflaria, and it wouldn't matter she was awkward and clumsy with a sword because Truthsayers were far too rare and precious to send into battle.

Ioanna closed her eyes and listened for the sound of hoofbeats, shouting, or swords being drawn. None came.

It occurred to her that perhaps she ought to pray. If any situation warranted prayers, surely it was this. But though Ioanna attended Sunrise services regularly, she would admit she had fallen out of the habit of addressing personal, spontaneous prayers to Iolar since he never responded to them. Reciting old prayers from memory, or reading them from books, was easier because then she didn't get her hopes up waiting for an answer.

Ioanna knew she was not entitled to a reply, nor an explanation of why her patron god had given her such a dangerous blessing in such an inhospitable country. But she would have appreciated it. Even if he could not tell her how to convince the imperial court she meant them no harm, it would have been comforting to know he watched over her, or at least he had not forgotten her name.

Chapter Four

VITALIYA

Vitaliya awoke the next morning as the sun rose, still cradled in the grass nest she'd spun for herself and Ioanna. In the night, a few wildflowers had bloomed around her, a side effect of the magic she'd poured into the spot.

Vitaliya looked around, expecting to see Ioanna still asleep. But the space beside her was empty. She tried to get up, but her legs had become tangled in the long strands of woven grass, and she fell to the soft ground.

Ioanna stood by the horses, staring out in the direction of the road. Her fingers were slightly curled like she was preparing to summon her magic. But she did not. She merely stood and watched.

"Hello," said Vitaliya. "Do you want more oranges?"

Ioanna turned around, her face unreadable.

"I can get us some," continued Vitaliya, determined to be helpful. She wasn't really in the mood for oranges. She wanted something warm and substantial, but they had no options. "Maybe I'll pack some? In case we can't find more food later."

Ioanna nodded, and Vitaliya went to the tree she'd poured her magic into last night. The branch was still laden with fruit, and she grabbed as many as she thought would fit in their bags.

"Have there been any soldiers?" asked Vitaliya.

"Not that I've seen. Perhaps they passed us in the night. Or maybe..."

"Maybe Netheia gave up!" suggested Vitaliya, determined to interject a bit of cheer into the conversation.

"Mm," said Ioanna.

"I can't wait to meet your grandmother. I've heard of her, but nobody really seems to know much about her. She's a very mysterious figure in Vesolda."

"In Xytae too," said Ioanna, turning away from the road at last. "I don't think there's anyone in the world quite like her."

"I'd like to know why she gave up her crown. It must have been a difficult decision."

"Not at all." Ioanna struggled to place her mount's saddle on its back, and Vitaliya came around to help her with it. "She's never made any secret of the fact she hated her title, and she's quite pleased with herself for managing to shake free of it."

There were few people on the road at such an early hour, and the sun was not too strong yet. They rode along in silence for a time, and Vitaliya watched as the woods beside the road changed to neglected farms with broken fences.

"These fields look terrible," she observed, canting her head in their direction.

"Well, it's not time for planting yet," began Ioanna, but Vitaliya shook her head.

"This is more than just a season's worth of growth. These fields haven't been cleared or tended for years."

"Oh," said Ioanna. "Well, I don't know. Perhaps the soil is tainted?"

"I don't think so. The weeds are growing just fine." Vitaliya would not pretend to be any sort of authority on farming practices, but her time spent using her blessing for the benefit of Vesolda had managed to teach her a few things. "I'll ask when we go into town. That's very strange."

Besides, everything Vitaliya knew about Xytae suggested they were shipping a significant amount of their harvest out to the war effort. She'd even heard rumors they were decreasing their sales to Thiyra, the mountainous continent to the west not suited for farming.

Soon enough, Vitaliya caught sight of a little village with thatched roofs and more fields. As they rode toward it, Vitaliya glanced over at Ioanna. Her face appeared as solemn as ever, but her shoulders were tense as she examined the road ahead of them. Doubtless she was expecting soldiers to come intercept them. Vitaliya couldn't bring herself to worry about that very much, though. They were outside of the city now, so surely Netheia would have given up? Vitaliya certainly would have if she'd been in Netheia's place.

But then, Vitaliya would never be in Netheia's place. She had no intention of ever standing between her older brother and the Vesoldan throne. Being the Queen of Vesolda might be fun for a few days. But once the coronation and parties were all over, everyone would expect her to settle down and listen to their problems and never leave Bergavenna or do anything fun ever again. They might even try to talk her into getting married.

Vitaliya looked at Ioanna again and wondered if she ought to suggest Ioanna forget about being empress and try to enjoy her life. Perhaps it would be a little insensitive given everything that had happened yesterday. Maybe it would be better if Ioanna worked it out for herself.

As they arrived in town, Vitaliya could not help but compare it to the farming communities she'd visited to help with the harvest. True, those had all been within a few hours of Bergavenna, but they weren't terribly far from Xyuluthe now. Yet this town looked rather sad. The homes were all in need of repairs, and a few of them were so poorly maintained Vitaliya hoped they were standing empty. No flowers, nor statues, nor any other kind of decoration added any sort of charm or personality to the community.

Desperate to see something other than a dusty main road and wilted, withered trees, she looked around for a building that might be a temple. Back in Vesolda, a place like this would probably have a Temple of Eyvindr. Or if it wasn't large enough to justify such a thing, they might have an undedicated temple, plain and simple, kept tidy by the children of the town and open for any traveling priest or priestess to use. The priestesses of Pemele, who performed marriages, and the priests of Adranus, who performed healing and cared for the sick or performed funeral rites for the dead, were the ones most frequently traveling from place to place.

"Does anyone live here?" murmured Ioanna.

That was an eerie thought. What if the entire town had been deserted? What if they went inside the nearest building and found corpses ravaged by a plague or mauled by a monster?

"Maybe we should go," suggested Vitaliya. "Forget this place. Forget the fields. Let's just leave."

"No," said Ioanna. "What if they need our help?"

"Then they could have walked to Xyuluthe and asked." Vitaliya hadn't meant for it to come out as cruelly as it did, but she still thought she'd made a good point.

They were only a day's ride from the capital, even if it didn't feel like it. Standing there in the middle of a quiet village, surrounded by nothing but sad, overgrown fields, it was difficult to believe they could be back at the Imperial Palace before sundown if they decided to give up and turn themselves in.

It seemed as though they'd stepped into another world.

"Maybe this is Iestil," murmured Vitaliya, naming the plane of Adranus, God of Death and Tenth of the Ten. "Maybe we're dead. Maybe we died in our sleep."

"It can't be. I'm going to Solarium," said Ioanna very seriously. "Besides, Iestil isn't empty either. It's filled with hundreds of thousands of people."

"Dead people."

"It's just a village," Ioanna insisted. "Come on, let's knock on some doors."

Vitaliya wished she had a knife. All the Xytan nobles carried weapons, some openly at their belts and some tucked away. During her brief time in the palace, Vitaliya had taken note of rings that concealed needle-sharp blades, or long, decorative pendants that came to a sudden point, and even metal hairpins that had been sharpened into knives.

If she carried such things in Vesolda, everyone would think she'd gone mad. But in Xytae it was normal, even expected. She wondered if Ioanna had any hidden weapons. From what she'd heard and seen, Vitaliya doubted it. And Ioanna had Iolar's defensive magic, so perhaps she didn't need such things.

Vitaliya thought of her own magic, trying to imagine a way it might be turned into something she could use to defend herself. The only thing she could think of was calling up thorny vines, but that would be reliant on what plants were around at the time, and anyone with a sword would be able to cut through those in an instant.

Besides, Eyvindr would probably be displeased if he saw her using his blessing to hurt people, even if only in self-defense. Not that Vitaliya believed she'd be able to grow anything fast enough to intercept a soldier.

Ioanna got down from her horse and moved in the direction of the nearest house. Vitaliya slowly did the same, remaining far enough behind her that she could turn and flee if there was something dreadful within.

But Ioanna knocked, and knocked, and there was no reply.

Vitaliya wasn't sure if she wanted to suggest trying to force the door open. On the one hand, answers might be inside the house. On the other hand, so could any number of awful things…a trapped monster, a waiting wildcat, a rotting corpse.

But Ioanna was already moving in the direction of the next dwelling, unafraid. "There must be people living here," she insisted, despite all evidence to the contrary. "Even if it's only a few."

Vitaliya turned her eyes back to the neglected fields. "Let's just go. Please? I'm scared. This place is eerie. I feel like something's about to jump out at us."

"It's just a village," Ioanna insisted again. But perhaps she was beginning to feel unsettled too because she nodded. "All right. We'll just check the temple, and then we'll go."

The temple, as Vitaliya had expected, was undedicated. It was very small, about the same size as the surrounding houses, and built from plain gray stone. The lack of decoration gave it a cold, austere feeling. But as they rounded the side to approach the front door, Vitaliya's eyes fell upon a small, open-topped wagon and a donkey.

"Someone's here! Someone's alive!" She went to the donkey and patted its neck affectionately. "Or if they're dead, I guess we have a cart now."

"Stop saying people are dead," said Ioanna.

"People *are* dead. People have been dying for thousands of years."

"Maybe, but you don't have to keep bringing it up."

The sight of the wagon made Vitaliya feel better, but she still stood back and allowed Ioanna to open the door to the temple. She stepped inside, and Vitaliya followed cautiously, keeping one foot in the doorway so the door could not slam shut and trap the two of them inside forever.

The inside of the temple was made from the same plain stones as the exterior. A few small windows let in a little bit of daylight, but none of the candles had been lit. The floor had not been washed in a long time, and dried mud stuck to the flagstones. Enormous balls of dust gathered in each corner, and cobwebs grew over every surface. A few rows of hard wooden benches filled the largest part of the room, and near the front was a plain altar.

But the temple's strangest feature was certainly the red-brown chickens that wandered through the rows, pecking at spots on the ground and clucking softly as though they had every right to be there.

And standing just before the altar, folding a blanket into careful quarters, was a middle-aged man in brown robes. At the sound of the door opening, he jumped and gave a cry of shock.

"Oh!" he yelped. Then he took in the sight of Ioanna and Vitaliya. "Ladies—you nearly scared the life out of me! I thought I was the only one here."

He was a priest. The color of his robes meant he was from the Temple of Cyne. Cyne was the God of Animals, and Eleventh of the Ten in Ioshora. Mostly priests of Cyne were called upon to serve as healers to animals that were sick or injured. They could usually be found in farming communities.

"We're sorry," said Ioanna. "We were only passing through and hoped to purchase supplies here. But it seems this village is abandoned."

"It is," confirmed the priest. "All the residents have gone to war, died, or moved away. I only stopped here for the night to take shelter in the old temple. You're not far from Xyuluthe, though. You can purchase whatever you need there."

"That's where we've just come from, unfortunately," said Ioanna. "We're headed north."

"You've been to Xyuluthe?" The priest looked curious. He tucked his blanket under his arm, pulled a large leather rucksack onto his back, and began to walk toward them. "Here, let's talk outside. I forgot how badly this place needs to be cleaned. I might have been better off in the cart after all." He made a sound with his tongue, and the chickens hurried after him, their long claws clicking on the stone floors.

"Has this village been abandoned for long?" asked Ioanna as they emerged into the daylight.

"A few years, I think," said the priest. "It didn't happen overnight. I've lost a few small communities to the war, and I expect I'll lose more in the coming years. You'll probably pass more if you're going to be traveling. Be careful—bandits have been known to use them for camps sometimes."

"I was never told of any abandoned villages," said Ioanna, frowning deeply. "I'd think that would be important news."

The priest shrugged. "I'm sure it was a decade ago. But they're quite common now. We've grown accustomed to them."

Ioanna did not appear to be at all consoled by this, and Vitaliya didn't blame her.

"I heard a rumor last night," added the priest. "They say Emperor Ionnes is dead."

Ioanna nodded. "That is what they're saying in the city as well."

"Two priestesses came through last night a few hours after I arrived here. From the Temple of Reygmadra. They were looking for two young ladies. Princesses." He gave them both a meaningful look.

Vitaliya really didn't want to have to fight a priest, especially one of Cyne's. She looked to Ioanna for help. But Ioanna's face was stony and impassive and gave no indication of whether she thought the same thing.

"What else did they say?" asked Ioanna.

"Emperor Ionnes is dead, and Princess Netheia had been named his heir." The priest paused again. "I asked how she could have been named after he was already dead, and they threatened to stab me. Very unpleasant women."

"It's not true," said Ioanna. "She's not been named heir. She just...believes she ought to be."

"That's about what I expected," said the priest. "My name is Otho, by the way. I've got some spare robes if you want to be my acolytes."

Ioanna frowned. "You want to help us?"

"If it means a chance at no more of this?" Otho made a broad gesture with his arm, indicating the entire abandoned village. "Yes. Certainly. If you don't mind riding with the chickens. You *are* the princesses they're looking for, aren't you?"

Vitaliya liked to believe the best of religious figures, and priests of Cyne were not known for their ambitious natures. But what if Otho's intentions were bad? What if he turned them in to Netheia for a reward, and set aside his wagon and chickens for a life of leisure?

But for some reason, Ioanna wasn't suspicious. "Yes," she said. "I am Ioanna of Xytae. And this is Vitaliya of Vesolda. We'd be very grateful for your aid. We're very poorly equipped and don't know this area."

"Where had you hoped to go?" asked Otho.

"To my grandmother's estate in Oredia."

Otho nodded. "The area I am assigned to does not cover that far north, but I know the way. I do not think anyone will miss me for a few days. It is not the lambing season yet." He pulled some brown robes identical to his own from the back of the wagon. "Put these on. If the priestesses come this way again, I'll tell them I'm training you."

The robe was loose enough that Vitaliya could wear her clothes underneath. It was a little too long and too large, but she supposed that was better than it being too tight. She drew the rope belt around her waist and knotted it, then looked over at Ioanna.

Vitaliya stifled a laugh. Ioanna was all but drowning in the oversized robe and resembled a child dressing in her mother's gown. She'd never pass for an acolyte.

"Do you have scissors?" Vitaliya asked Otho. "We need to trim some fabric off, or she'll break her neck when she takes a step."

Otho finished placing his things and his chickens in the back of the wagon. Then he removed a heavy set of shears from one of the many bags obviously meant for sheep. "Hold still," he warned Ioanna. "I don't want to cut any fingers off."

After the robe had been trimmed down to an acceptable length, Ioanna looked a little more dignified. And once she was back on horseback, it was harder to tell that beneath the robe was mostly air.

"Are the chickens your only companions?" asked Vitaliya once she was back up on her mount.

"Along with Daisy," confirmed Otho, resting one hand on his donkey's neck. "I had a dog, but he went to Ferra last winter, and I can't bring myself to replace him yet. I expect one will adopt me soon enough, though. I've found I don't frequently get a say in the matter."

Vitaliya knew she wouldn't be able to tolerate the lifestyle of a traveling priest, but she thought it sounded nice in its own rustic way. Especially if animals were involved. Still, she'd spent enough time among farmers to know it was not all delivering litters of puppies and brushing horses. Cyne's work could sometimes turn ugly or tragic. It was the nature of...well, of nature.

As the wagon began to move, Vitaliya realized they wouldn't be able to get to Oredia as soon now. But maybe slower was safer in this case. Especially if priestesses of Reygmadra were searching for them both. Besides, she wasn't exactly in a hurry. She couldn't go home until after the wedding, or else everyone might think she'd forgiven her father.

She wondered how long it would take for news of what had happened in Xyuluthe to reach Bergavenna. Would everyone assume she'd been killed during Netheia's coup? Vitaliya curled her toes in delight. They'd be so sorry! She imagined them at her funeral (for, of course, they'd have to hold a massive state funeral for her), murmuring their regrets to one another. *If only we'd listened to her. If only we hadn't told her she was being a melodramatic child. If only we had mourned Queen Isabetta a little bit longer.*

"What are you smiling about?" Otho asked Vitaliya.

"Vengeance!" Vitaliya cried happily. Otho gave a snort of laughter.

"Vengeance?" repeated Ioanna. "On Netheia?"

"What? No. I'm hardly even mad at her anymore." Besides, getting vengeance on Netheia would probably be more trouble than it was worth. "I meant on my family. I'm sure they'll be worrying about me soon once they learn what happened."

"What does that have to do with vengeance?" asked Otho in confusion.

"Oh, never mind," said Vitaliya because she couldn't think of a way to explain the situation that didn't make her sound deranged. "It's not important."

"You said you've lost communities to the war," said Ioanna, and Vitaliya was grateful for the change in subject. "Do you mean they were all drafted?"

"Not all. Just enough the smaller ones could no longer sustain themselves. Villages don't do well when there's only tiny children and their grandparents. With no one to work the fields or the forges, they just wither. The children are orphaned or sent to live with distant family, and the grandparents die of old age or leave for larger cities."

"I'm sorry," said Ioanna. "I didn't know—or else, I didn't know it was this bad. If it's any consolation, it's always been my ambition to end the war with Masim. I've never seen the point in it."

"That sentiment might gain you some support," advised Otho. "The war might be popular in the capital, but I've seen nothing but suffering come from it. And for what? Are we all meant to migrate to Masim once the war is done? I've no intention of doing that. Xytae is my home and always will be."

"I don't know," admitted Ioanna. "My father did always say Masim was a better place to live than Xytae."

"Did nobody tell him he could have just bought an estate?" asked Vitaliya. "No need to mess around with soldiers and wars. He could have had a very nice mansion and a pet lion and a giant statue of Zeneen in the front hall."

"I do not know," said Ioanna. "I have never understood him. And he never understood me. I expect he did intend to make Netheia his heir. I suppose I can count myself fortunate he never had the chance."

Vitaliya was not sure what to say. Her instinctive response of *why would anyone want to be an empress anyway?* felt no less insensitive than it had earlier.

"Well," she said, "do you think your grandmother will support you?"

"No," admitted Ioanna. "I just think she won't let Netheia kill me."

"It's a start, I suppose. And maybe we can change her mind. Even if she doesn't care about rightful succession, maybe she'll care about not letting the country go to ruin."

"I don't know if she'll see it that way. I've never met a noble who thought the war with Masim wasn't a glorious enterprise."

"Well, they would say that if they didn't want to be in trouble with your father, wouldn't they?"

"Perhaps," granted Ioanna, but Vitaliya could tell she didn't really believe this.

They rode on in silence for a time, moving at a sedate pace so they would not leave Otho, Daisy, and the chickens behind in the dust. As the day wore on, a few travelers passed them, some moving away from Xyuluthe but most traveling toward it. Everyone they encountered asked if they'd heard rumors of Emperor Ionnes's death and wanted to share rumors. Whenever this happened, Ioanna stared down at her mount's mane and let Otho and Vitaliya do the talking. Vitaliya imagined she must be nervous, afraid one of the passersby would manage to identify her. Or perhaps she simply hated to be reminded of her father's death.

Or maybe, like Netheia had claimed, she wasn't very friendly.

But Ioanna had been friendly to Vitaliya from the moment they'd first met. She was certainly shy—and who wouldn't be, growing up at such a miserable court—but obviously she just needed someone to show her a bit of kindness, and she'd open up. Vitaliya could do that.

The first town they encountered was quite small, by Vitaliya's standards, but the fields were well-tended and clear, ready for the planting season, and she could see children running in the street as they approached. This would not be another eerie abandoned village.

"This is one of my towns," said Otho with some pride. "We can get supplies here."

"We need names!" Vitaliya realized. "They're going to ask you about us—you'll have to come up with fake names. Especially for Ioanna."

"You're right," said Ioanna. "In that case—"

"I want to be Kreszentia," interrupted Vitaliya, afraid Ioanna might have had the same idea and not wanting to lose out.

"That's an Ieflarian name," pointed out Ioanna. "And you're obviously not Ieflarian. They'll know you're lying."

"My mother was Ieflarian," proclaimed Vitaliya. "I take after my father! Who was Vesoldan! But died! In a tragic...falconry accident."

Ioanna groaned and pressed her hand to her forehead.

"Fine!" huffed Vitaliya. "I'll be Floriana. *You* can be Kreszentia."

"Nobody is being Kreszentia."

"Why are you being so difficult?" sighed Vitaliya. "Fine. You're Lucia. Otho, can you remember that? Floriana and Lucia."

"I'd like to hear more about the falconry accident," commented Otho. "I've never known anyone to die in that way. And I've seen quite a lot."

"Oh, it was horrible!" cried Vitaliya, cheering up now since someone was playing along. "That's why I won't treat birds. I'm traumatized from the experience. If I see one, I'll go into a panic. Cows and horses, certainly. Goats? I adore goats. But birds? I simply can't stand them. I don't even like couriers. The sight of them fills me with existential dread."

"You are traveling with chickens," Ioanna pointed out, casting a glance in the direction of the wagon where the two were settled, apparently accustomed to the bumping and rattling.

"Chickens don't count as birds. They can barely fly."

"Perhaps we ought to let Otho do the talking," advised Ioanna. "He knows these people best, after all. We don't want to arouse anyone's suspicions."

As they moved into town, people called greetings to Otho, pausing in their work to wave or, once they realized he was accompanied by two strangers, come over for a closer look. Vitaliya had the sense there wasn't very much to do in town, and so someone coming by for a visit was more exciting than it had any right to be.

"Floriana and Lucia," explained Otho, once enough people had gathered that he wouldn't have to repeat himself. "The temple in Xyuluthe has asked me to take on acolytes to gain practical experience. They'll be assisting me for a while."

"You were in Xyuluthe?" asked one of the women. "Did you hear news of the emperor? There are rumors he was killed in battle."

"That is what I am hearing as well," agreed Otho. "It seems to be the truth. But the empress has made no formal announcement yet—or if she did, I missed it."

Nobody in the crowd appeared particularly shocked or saddened by the news. Vitaliya wondered who they believed would be their next ruler. Would they prefer Netheia, or Ioanna? Or did they see them as interchangeable?

"We had priestesses of Reygmadra visit last night," commented another man. "We thought they'd come to convince more of us to join the army. But they were asking about the crown princess. Seems she's gone missing. Claimed the empress had sent them to find her."

"We saw them too," said Otho. "Rather aggressive. We were glad to see them go. They didn't give you any trouble, did they?"

"Searched every house," said the man. "Had some of us wondering if they were priestesses at all, and not robbers who found some spare robes. But they didn't take anything and left in a hurry. Doesn't make any sense the crown princess would be gone, unless she doesn't care to be empress after all. Like her grandmother."

"Who knows?" said Otho. "In any case, we've come to see what supplies you can spare. Ah, yes—" he added as a child thrust a kitten at him. "Is this one of Snowdrop's? You see, she didn't need our help after all, did she? Cats are clever like that. Would you like me to take a look at her anyway?"

Otho would probably be a while, Vitaliya realized. Even if it wasn't time for the lambing, the people of this town probably kept plenty of other animals they cared deeply for. She wondered if it would be the same for her if she'd joined the Temple of Eyvindr. If her farmers would be just as happy to see her when she came to town. Probably not. She wouldn't make a very good priestess. It was better for everyone that she not have a job as important as taking care of the kingdom's crops. Anything could go wrong.

She felt a little guilty Otho would have to use part of his stipend to purchase supplies for her and Ioanna, but she knew they could give him more of their jewelry to cover the cost. He would come out better for having helped them in the end.

The villagers went back to their business, and Otho went to see to their animals. Vitaliya and Ioanna, still in the role of his acolytes, followed after to see if he would need any help.

"I'm sure you've never seen a town like this before, have you?" Vitaliya murmured.

Ioanna shook her head.

"Don't worry," said Vitaliya. "I was intimidated too. When my parents first sent me to the farms, I mean. But I think people are just about the same no matter where they're from or how they live."

Vitaliya could not tell if Ioanna was consoled or offended by this observation because her expression of calm indifference never changed. Vitaliya hoped she did not take offense to the implication she was frightened of the townspeople. She only wanted Ioanna to feel more comfortable.

Their first visit was to Snowdrop, a white housecat who refused to come down from the roof where she slept and only flicked her tail a little when Otho called her name. The little boy who owned her said she sometimes went up there to get away from her kittens.

After that, they conducted an examination of the sheep, who were all in good health, and a visit to a very old dog named Amble, who rose up on shaky legs to greet them as they approached. Otho said there was nothing more that could be done for him as his owner already fed him a special blend of herbs to ease the pain in his joints. He explained how to make it and said the concoction worked on Men as well as animals.

Vitaliya found this very interesting, having never studied healing or alchemy even though her blessing would probably be conductive to the latter. She'd never really considered it even as a pastime. It might be fun to keep a little room filled with interesting plants, liquids, powders, and glass bottles. But maybe it was like farming: a bad idea for one as irresponsible and reckless as herself.

Fortunately, there were no terrible injuries to tend or other tragic events that required Otho's aid. Vitaliya hoped most of his visits were as pleasant and easy as this one had been.

They left the town shortly after noon, the wagon loaded with enough supplies to last them into tomorrow, or perhaps the day after if Vitaliya found more fruit trees in the meantime.

"Will we reach another town before nightfall?" asked Ioanna.

"Unfortunately, I don't believe we will," said Otho. "But don't worry, we'll just set up a camp. I do it quite frequently when I'm caught between settlements."

"I wonder if we'll see those priestesses," said Vitaliya.

"I doubt it. They're probably far ahead of us now," Otho stated confidently. "Besides, don't worry—they're looking for noblewomen, not acolytes."

Vitaliya nodded and hoped he was correct. If he came to harm because he'd chosen to help them, she would never forgive herself.

Chapter Five

IOANNA

Vitaliya's grass beds were unquestionably the strangest place Ioanna had slept in her entire life, but she supposed she preferred them to the wagon, all hard wood slats and chicken feathers. In any case, the grass nests weren't terribly uncomfortable, just odd. Her only real complaint was she could never shake her worry that insects were crawling across her body and burrowing into her hair.

"Do we have eggs?" she heard Vitaliya ask. "Chickens! Do you have eggs? Yes! Eggs! Eggs for us!"

Ioanna opened her eyes and pulled herself free of the odd nest. Vitaliya sat in the wagon while Otho tended to the small fire they had built. Ioanna rubbed at her eyes and glanced toward the road, but once again, there were no signs of the priestesses.

"Ioanna! Look! Eggs!" cried Vitaliya eagerly, holding one up in the air like a prize. "We can have eggs!"

"Do you know how to cook?" asked Ioanna.

"No! But I'll work it out!" A cast iron pan clanged against the back of the wagon. "You just take food, add fire, and then it just sort of comes together—"

"Let me help you with that," said Otho, hurrying over. "Don't want to burn yourself."

"Burning is learning." But Vitaliya let him take the pan away and went back to cradling her eggs.

Two eggs among three people was not a very generous meal, but Otho had a loaf of bread, which was only stale on one side. Vitaliya had spotted another orange tree yesterday, and the wagon now held a generous pile of fruit. Tiring quickly of oranges, though, Ioanna decided she would keep alert for vineyards today. She could not identify fruit trees out of season, but anyone could spot the special trellises farmers built to grow grapes.

After a quick and not terribly satisfying breakfast, they set out again, headed north. Otho said they would probably reach another settlement before noon, a larger one where they could purchase hot meals at the inn. Ioanna suspected he didn't frequently indulge in such things but perhaps was trying to accommodate the two princesses traveling with him.

Ioanna appreciated the effort but wished she had the confidence to tell him it was not necessary. Only her fear he'd find her rude or ungrateful stopped her.

After a few, uneventful hours, they came upon an obstruction in the road. At first, Ioanna took them for more travelers, coming from the other direction. But it didn't take her long to realize they weren't moving, and there were quite a lot of them, though all on foot.

"Ah, yes," said Otho. "Let me handle this."

"Who are they?" asked Vitaliya. "Soldiers?"

"Bandits," said Ioanna.

"Don't worry. Once they realize we're with a temple, they'll probably let us go without any trouble," Otho reassured them.

"Probably?" whimpered Vitaliya.

"I don't know. I've never seen any this near to the capital. Most have the sense to keep out of sight." Otho shook his head minutely. "Let me do the talking. I can handle them."

Bandits were a fact of life, but the high percentage of the population with blessings from the gods meant they were not as common as they might have been otherwise. It was a risky line of work, and not just because the Xytan military would kill any they found and not bother with trials. There was no telling when an ordinary traveler had enough magic to fight off an entire gang with ease.

"Hold," called one, stepping forward. Ioanna supposed he was probably the leader. "This is a toll road. If you want to go any further, you've got to pay."

He was not, Ioanna realized, the burly, middle-aged fighter she'd been expecting. In fact, his face appeared soft and fair like a child trying on his father's helmet. He was about the age he would probably be drafted into the army, if anyone could find him. Ioanna looked away from him and studied the other bandits gathered behind him. Some held bows, and others had short daggers, and all had hard, angry expressions on their faces. But nevertheless, there was no hiding the fact they were all *young*.

"But you're hardly bandits at all!" Ioanna exclaimed before she could stop herself. "You're children!"

"You—*you're* children!" sputtered the leader. "Shut up! Or I'll slice you open!" But Ioanna had spent a great deal of her life hearing threats far more detailed and credible than this, and so it had little impact.

"Now, wait," began Otho. "Let's not lose our tempers."

"You shouldn't have to resort to banditry at your age," Ioanna said earnestly. "I'm certain we can help you."

"Shut up!" said their leader again. "Give us—just give us whatever you've got!"

"You can have some oranges and these lousy boots, but you're not getting the chickens," said Vitaliya. "You don't deserve them."

The bandit leader swung his sword in a wide, unpracticed arc. Ioanna was ready as it came around toward her. The sword was clearly cheaply made, and somewhat rusted as well, for the blade broke cleanly from its hilt as it collided with her shield.

"What—?" he began, and the bafflement on his face made him look younger still. "How'd you—you can't—"

"Now you don't have a sword," observed Ioanna. "You should probably let us go."

"But you can't do that!" cried the young man. "That's not Cyne's blessing!"

"Well, that's what happens when you accost strangers on the road. You're bound to get surprised. Now, why are you doing this? You're too young to be living this way."

"Maybe we want to! Not everyone is content staying in a boring town, working a boring farm, and having boring children. Out here, we're nobody's slaves. We do as we please and don't answer to any priests or nobles."

The young man delivered the words confidently, but they were all lies. These children had turned to banditry because they had no other choice.

"Where are your parents?" Ioanna asked.

"Who cares? We don't need those either!" That, strangely enough, was not a lie. Ioanna supposed these children had been alone for so long they legitimately believed they didn't need guidance from their elders.

"I expect they were all drafted," said Otho. "And with no one to provide for them..."

"Why are we drafting parents with children to care for?" Ioanna demanded of nobody in particular. "That's ridiculous!"

"Well, you go on and tell the emperor that, then," sneered the young man. "Sure he'll be properly impressed and send everyone back home."

"Haven't you heard?" asked Ioanna. "He's dead."

The young man was so taken aback that he didn't reply. But one of the children behind him lowered their bow and said, "He is?"

Ioanna looked at the child, dressed in a short but billowy robe, sewn in the style of those frequently worn by neutroi in Xytae. Clothing was not always a reliable indicator of gender, but in this situation, she could only make her best guess until she had a chance to clarify.

"Yes," said Ioanna. "We received the news only yesterday."

"She's lying!" cried the young man. "She's just tryin' to distract us! Don't listen to her!"

"Cassian, we're not gonna rob her," said the child patiently. "She's got magic. Good magic. We don't have a chance. I wanna hear if he's really dead."

"He was killed in battle," explained Ioanna. "In a duel. One of the Masimi challenged him, and he accepted. Or at least, that's what I heard."

"Who cares?" demanded Cassian. "So a rich man died! What does it matter? The next one'll be just as bad as him! Nothing's gonna change! They're all the same in the capital! We might as well be dead if we're not fighting in their wars or paying their taxes."

"I'm sorry," said Ioanna, stricken. "I had no idea things were this bad."

"Then you don't have eyes, do you?"

"Don't be rude, Cassian," said the child. "She's just a priestess. It's not her fault the nobles—"

"She *talks* like the nobles."

"Well, nobles are allowed to become priestesses if they want."

Cassian eyed Ioanna warily. "Is that true? You're a noble?"

"My family," said Ioanna. "But I don't agree with them on many things." She waited for the pain to hit her, but it did not. It was all technically the truth. "I wish I could do more to help you."

"We're all right," said the child, which was also a lie but a soft one. "It's the priestesses of Reygmadra we have to watch out for. If they see you, they'll bring you in to help the soldiers—taking care of horses, carrying things, or doing the washing."

"What is the Temple of Pemele doing to help you?" asked Ioanna. Orphans ought to fall under their jurisdiction, not the Temple of Reygmadra's.

"The priestesses are nice, but they warn you if you go to their temples for help. They warn you that if you stay, you might get taken, and they can't do anything about it. Some children decide it's worth it. We didn't think so."

"I'm sorry," murmured Ioanna again, and it felt so pathetic and inadequate against everything she'd just been told. "I didn't know."

"The priestesses of Pemele are nice," the child said encouragingly. "Right, Cassian? And most of the other temples too, except Reygmadra's. They don't report us, and we try not to bother them."

"Except now," said Vitaliya. Then perhaps sensing she was being unkind, she added, "I meant it about the oranges, though. We've got lots. Or, no, wait! I can wake up the fruit trees for you! Are there any nearby?"

The child looked puzzled but nodded.

"Lead me to them, and I'll make them grow some fruit. It won't last more than a few days, but it will help you."

"But that's not Cyne's blessing either," said Cassian helplessly.

"There's no rule saying you have to have Cyne's blessing to join the temple," Otho pointed out. "That's just the assumption most people make. But we don't bar anyone from joining."

"I've got Eyvindr's blessing, but you can't hug a plant," said Vitaliya. "Or maybe you can if it's big enough. But it's not the same." She leaned forward and embraced her mount around the neck. "See? So much nicer."

The children still seemed a bit uncertain, but Vitaliya said, "Never mind that. Show me where the trees are! You need to eat something."

The children led them further down the road, though they refused to travel on it. Instead, they kept to the trees, ducking in and out of shadows and peeking warily ahead before continuing onward. Ioanna supposed she understood this and wondered what would be worse—being caught by soldiers or being caught by the priestesses of Reygmadra.

How had she failed to realize things were so terrible outside the capital? She spent every day at her mother's side, and though she was concerned about the war draining their resources, she'd never had the slightest inkling things had come to *this*. Someone...someone ought to have said something.

Did her mother know things were this bad? Did her father? She might believe her father hadn't known, for he was so seldom at home. But her mother had no such excuse. Unless the nobles had been deliberately keeping it from her, for fear that implying the war was having adverse effects on their people would provoke her ire.

Or perhaps she knew but did not care.

"Oh, very nice!" cried Vitaliya happily, pulling Ioanna out of her thoughts. Ioanna realized she was peering into the trees. She watched as Vitaliya got down from her mount and walked into the woods.

"What is it?" asked Ioanna.

"Fig trees. See those big leaves? That's how you can tell. There's a whole grove of them deeper in."

Now that Vitaliya mentioned it, the leaves were a little odd, but Ioanna would have never noticed it on her own.

"Be careful," said Ioanna. "Don't, don't drain yourself."

"I'll be all right." But then she paused, considering. "I'll have to go more slowly than I usually do and put less magic into each plant. They'll take longer to give fruit, but they'll have more in the end."

"I'll go with her," Ioanna said to Otho. "Just...in case." It was not that she mistrusted the children, for attacking them now would be the most foolish decision the group could make. But Vitaliya just seemed like the sort of person who needed looking after. There was no telling what she might do if impulse struck her.

Ioanna tied her horse and the one Vitaliya abandoned to the wagon, leaving Otho there on the road. Hopefully, if any travelers passed by, Otho would be able to think up an explanation for why they'd stopped.

She tried to step carefully, avoiding large stones that might cut her sandals and branches that might trip her, but she was unaccustomed to moving through such dense greenery. By the time she caught up to Vitaliya, she was already pressing her hands onto the trunk of the nearest tree.

But this time she did not remain at the tree for long before she removed her hand, still glowing green, and pressed it to the next tree, and then the next, and the next. Within minutes, Ioanna could see the start of new growth in the branches. Little green bulbs would soon darken to purple.

The children all began to shout eagerly, and Vitaliya laughed. She took a step backward but stumbled, and Ioanna rushed forward to catch her. Vitaliya laughed again like she was drunk.

"I think I'm out of magic now!" she cried. "I hope we don't have to fight a...a something. Something that hates plants. What hates plants?"

"Come on. You can rest in the wagon," said Ioanna.

"With the chickens!" But Vitaliya sounded excited rather than disgusted. "They're so nice."

"I suppose," said Ioanna, who had no real opinion on this.

The children followed them back to the road but seemed reluctant to step out of the trees.

"She's fine. Just drained," Ioanna reported to Otho. Vitaliya pulled free of her and climbed awkwardly into the wagon.

"Wait. Let me put down a blanket first—" began Ioanna, but Vitaliya had already collapsed onto the dirty wooden slats. Her eyes were already closed, but one of her arms curled around a chicken.

"Is she all right?" called one of the children.

"She'll be fine. She just needs to rest," explained Ioanna. Did none of them have magic of their own? She supposed they must not, or they'd have gone to the temples instead of living out here. She pulled one of the blankets out and draped it over Vitaliya. Then she took as many of the oranges as she could carry and brought them back over to the group.

"Now, be careful in the next few days," Ioanna advised. "The priestesses of Reygmadra might come back this way." She wished she could do more for them, but her Truthsayer magic was worthless in this situation. *Could* she bring them to Oredia? No. A gaggle of children would raise countless questions and might cause people to look more closely at Ioanna and Vitaliya.

Ioanna told herself she had to be rational. If she was captured now, she would never be able to help these children as empress—or anyone like them. For she knew for certain these children weren't the only ones who had been forced to turn to banditry to survive. If they'd made it for this long, they could probably survive a few more weeks.

She hoped they could.

With great reluctance they moved on, leaving the would-be bandits behind, but the matter weighed on Ioanna's mind. Did her mother know about this? Did any of the nobles? First the abandoned villages, and now this. *Someone* had to know what was happening outside the capital.

The Temple of Reygmadra always spoke as though freedom was the most important thing in the world, and the only way to ensure it was with military might. But what about the freedom of those children? They'd been forced into banditry when their parents had been drafted, and they'd likely be drafted too if they were caught. Was that freedom?

She could visualize Archpriestess Seia's sneer and her response. *More proof that Iolar's followers hate freedom.* No, that was unfair of Ioanna. Seia could make better arguments. She would probably say the children could earn their freedom through military service, and it wasn't the Temple's fault they'd chosen to hide away.

Vitaliya remained sound asleep in the wagon, so still she might have been dead. Ioanna had no idea how anyone could sleep with the road so badly maintained, but Vitaliya did not stir.

Ioanna had never run out of magic before—at least, not by accident. There was never much reason to use her blessing for prolonged periods of time, and detecting lies did not seem to drain her the way actively conjuring shields did. The priests had forced her to drain herself once, though, just so she could see what it felt like. When she was about nine years old, she'd held a shield for *hours* while Archpriest Lailus read to her from a book to keep her entertained.

The exercise had not been done out of sadism nor scientific curiosity. The priests insisted she must know, for her own safety, what it felt like to become drained of magic. It had taken a very, *very* long time, but gradually the world had grown quiet, and Ioanna realized Archpriest Lailus's voice sounded like it was coming from somewhere far away even though he sat directly in front of her. When she tried to step forward, she'd stumbled, and the world had tilted. *This* was what being drained was like, Lailus explained to her. And if she ever felt this way again, she must stop whatever she was doing and rest. If she carried on for too much longer, her life would be in danger.

It was rare for someone to die of overusing magic, but it did happen occasionally. Every temple had an anecdote about some foolish young person who had only wanted to prove they were more powerful or talented than their mentors. They would feel the drowsiness come on but convince themselves they could hold out for just a little longer. Soon the drowsiness would turn to searing pain, and by then it would be too late.

Ioanna looked at Vitaliya again. It was hard to tell, given the movement of the wagon, but she was still breathing. No doubt she had been just as carefully trained as Ioanna herself—if not more so—and underwent the same exercise as a girl, pulling up crops at accelerated speeds or making flowers bloom until she grew too tired to continue, followed by a stern warning to never forget the feeling.

Ioanna knew that if Vitaliya was not crying out in pain, she would be fine after she rested.

Still, it was very quiet without her around. Ioanna had nothing to distract her from her own thoughts and how dreadfully useless she felt. The Xytan people were faring badly, and there was nothing she could do to help them. Not in the way Vitaliya could.

The only thing Ioanna's magic was good for was frightening people.

Chapter Six

VITALIYA

"What's the matter with this one?"

The words, harsh and *far* too loud, pulled Vitaliya out of her sleep. For a moment, she wondered where she was and why her back hurt so badly, and then she remembered. She'd fallen asleep in the wagon.

"She drained herself" came Otho's voice from a little further off. "Earlier today. Dealing with an injured horse. We're letting her rest until..."

"I'm alive!" Vitaliya opened her eyes and sat upright, nearly smashing her forehead against the woman leaning over her. It was only the other woman's quick reflexes that saved them from collision. "Oh! No! I'm so sorry!"

The woman, Vitaliya realized, was a priestess of Reygmadra, dressed in a short red robe over padded leather armor. Vitaliya decided to try to smile. The woman did not smile back. Instead, she turned away from the wagon and said, "Remember what I've told you."

"I will," promised Otho. "Good evening."

For it *was* evening with the sun sinking low in the sky. Had she slept the entire day? She'd never drained herself so completely before, not even when she'd gone to the farms. There had always been priests and guards there to keep an eye on her to make sure she didn't overexert herself.

She felt fine now, but running out of magic was never fun. At least she'd managed to help those children.

Vitaliya looked back at the priestess, but the woman walked away, either satisfied or just too irritated to ask any further questions. She watched as the woman moved further down the road where a second priestess on horseback and another saddled horse were waiting. Within moments, they were gone.

"That was unexpected," murmured Otho. "I didn't think we'd see more of them."

"Those weren't the ones you met earlier?" asked Ioanna in an equally soft voice.

"No, and I'm glad for that. They'd have known I didn't have two acolytes yesterday."

"What happened?" mumbled Vitaliya. "I missed everything. I missed the whole day."

"Don't worry. I don't think they suspected anything," said Ioanna. "They came up on us so quickly that I didn't have time to wake you. Are you rested now, or do you want to go back to sleep?"

"I don't know." Vitaliya paused. "I suppose I'm rested. Or rested enough to weave us some beds."

"You don't have to do that. We're going to reach a town within the hour," said Otho. "We'll stop there for the night. If we're lucky, we might reach Oredia by tomorrow night. If not, then certainly the day after."

Vitaliya got up and jumped down over the side of the wagon. Her horse had been tied to it, and she went to set it free. "Warm food?" she said. "I would die for warm food."

"I'm sure they'll give us some, if we ask," said Otho.

"I don't want to ask. I want to pay for it," said Vitaliya. "I feel bad just taking things, especially since times are so difficult." If only she hadn't left her coin purse behind when they'd fled! She had enough gold to revolutionize the entire region or perhaps bring it to ruin through inflation.

"Don't worry. These people are accustomed to sharing with traveling priests. We pay them back through our service. I do not keep track of how many animals I tend to, and they do not keep track of how many loaves of bread they give away. All will right itself in the end."

"If you're certain." Vitaliya glanced at Ioanna. She could tell the other princess was equally mistrustful of this philosophy. It certainly *sounded* nice, but Vitaliya had grown up in a world of paper, charts, and taxes, no matter that she'd done her best to keep away from all three. A kingdom could not run itself on goodwill. There would always be someone waiting to take advantage.

Her back was sore and stiff after spending so many hours asleep in the wagon. So she decided to walk rather than ride, leading her horse for when her legs grew tired. For now, though, she enjoyed stretching her limbs, and the wagon moved slowly enough that she could keep up easily.

The town wasn't too much larger than the last one had been. The residents greeted Otho in the way Vitaliya was growing accustomed to. Otho introduced the princesses as Floriana and Lucia again, prompting Vitaliya to wonder what might happen if she simply remained with Otho and went on being Floriana for the rest of her life.

Well, that probably wouldn't be allowed because the Temple of Cyne would learn about her sooner or later, and then someone would look at the books and realize there wasn't an acolyte named Floriana in Xytae—or if there was, she hadn't been assigned to Otho. And then the entire ruse would fall apart, and Otho would probably get in trouble because of her.

She could still join the temple on her own time, but joining officially seemed so permanent and intimidating. It was more fun to pretend because then she had the option to run away once things became too difficult.

Vitaliya looked over at Ioanna, who appeared as uncomfortable as ever under so much scrutiny. Vitaliya wasn't sure how to tell her it would only get worse once she became empress. But then, maybe Ioanna already knew and wouldn't appreciate the reminder.

The town had an undedicated temple, and Vitaliya was wary at first, remembering the awful, dirty place they'd seen when they first encountered one another. But when Otho opened the doors, Vitaliya saw this temple was clean and well maintained. There was also enough ornamentation within that she could tell it had once been a Temple of Eyvindr.

"You have a good eye," said Otho when Vitaliya commented on this. "The Temple of Eyvindr used to have a permanent presence here. Unfortunately, as many of them have been called to work the Imperial Fields, citizens have been forced to rely on traveling priests."

"The Imperial Fields?" asked Vitaliya. "What's that?"

"Land owned by the crown, located in the south nearer to the war effort," explained Otho. "Everything grown on those farms goes directly to the soldiers. I've never seen them with my own eyes, but I've heard they're quite impressive in size, and at their peak grew at triple the rate of ordinary farms, until..."

"Until what?" asked Vitaliya.

"I'm not sure; I'm not a farmer. But there have been rumors, in past years, the soil is beginning to weaken, and their output is not so impressive anymore."

Vitaliya knew weakening of soil was a natural thing and could be combated by growing different crops in the same fields, or by calling in priests to rejuvenate the soil with magic. "Why don't the priests restore the soil?"

"They can't," said Otho. "Or, at least, not as effectively as they once could. Perhaps there is a limit to how much magic the earth can take in such a short time. Or maybe there is some other reason."

"Like Eyvindr is displeased with them?"

"I would not presume to speak for Eyvindr."

"I might," said Vitaliya. "If he sees them going to the south, not helping ordinary people but contributing to the war, that would upset anyone, wouldn't it?"

"But what choice do they have?" asked Otho. "If they stand against the emperor, they'll certainly be imprisoned or worse."

"This country is awful," muttered Vitaliya. Then, not wanting to offend, she added, "I mean, the fact temples have to take direct orders and ignore ordinary people..."

"It is difficult," said Otho. "I count myself fortunate the Temple of Cyne has been largely overlooked by the war effort. And I have hope perhaps things will change in the future. And we will be able to go back to living as the gods intended."

Vitaliya looked over at Ioanna, but she had her back to them and was carefully unfolding the blankets and making up the beds. Vitaliya knew she'd heard the conversation, for they were nearly within arm's reach of each other, but Ioanna went on as though nothing had happened.

Vitaliya wasn't very tired yet, mostly thanks to the long rest she'd had in the wagon, and so she went back outside. The sun was setting, but it was still warm, and Vitaliya was seized by the impulse to find a tree to climb.

Maybe that would be a bad idea, though. She was supposed to be an acolyte, and therefore should probably attempt to conduct herself with some degree of dignity.

The door to the temple opened behind her, and Ioanna stepped out. She looked as solemn as ever, which meant Vitaliya was once again compelled to make her smile.

"This has been nice," said Vitaliya. "I mean, nicer than I'd have expected, considering the circumstances."

Ioanna did not reply, and Vitaliya feared she'd been insensitive.

"I wouldn't have thought I'd ever ride in a wagon pulled by a donkey," Vitaliya hurried to add. "And wear a robe. And visit a town so tiny. And give fruit to bandits. Things like that."

"It might still end badly," said Ioanna quietly.

"Maybe! But it's not bad *now*. And I think that's important too." Vitaliya gave an encouraging smile. "I think Cyne or someone sent Otho to us. We'd be lost without him, wouldn't we?"

"Yes," agreed Ioanna. "Those priestesses would have certainly had us today if not for him."

"He's quite familiar but not in an impertinent way. Don't you think? I like it. It makes me feel ordinary."

"Yes," said Ioanna. "I think so."

Vitaliya smiled and looked up at the sky to see if she could pick out any stars. But it was still too early. "I think it will all turn out all right somehow. And maybe that's silly. But it's what I think."

"I can't see how."

"Well, neither can I. But we don't know what we're doing yet. Once we get to your grandmother's house, we can stop worrying about hiding from guards and priestesses and come up with a proper plan."

"It seems impossible."

"What? No, she's only a few days travel away. We'll make it for sure."

"No. I mean...coming up with a feasible plan. Defeating Netheia. Everyone is already on her side. Sometimes I wonder if it might just be better to give them what they want and disappear."

"Well, that would be the easier thing," granted Vitaliya. "And if I was you, that's probably what I'd do. But you're smarter than me, and more responsible than me. So, I expect you'll do better than that. Besides, everyone needs you to come fix everything—to bring back the priests, the parents, and stop trying to draft children into the army and stop the whole ridiculous war!"

"I know that's what needs to be done," said Ioanna. "But I can't see the *path* to it. Everything I can think of only ends in my death."

"What's your best plan?" asked Vitaliya. "Or, what's your least worst plan?"

"I suppose I'll have to go to Ieflaria," murmured Ioanna. "That's where most of the Order of the Sun went after my father cast them out. I hope their knight-commander can call enough of them back to constitute a fighting force."

"The Order of the Sun? You think they'd help you?" Ioanna had Iolar's blessing, but would such a simple thing be enough for them to lend their support? They tended to stay out of political disputes, preferring to handle threats that were celestial in nature.

"Yes," said Ioanna, but she did not elaborate. "I was planning to write to them before Netheia confronted us. If we'd had more time, I might have sent a courier. But perhaps it would be better to go to them myself, so they can see I have nothing to hide."

"Ieflaria's nice," Vitaliya encouraged. "I've been there a few times—when the princesses got engaged, and married, and when the queen had her baby. It's a little colder than I like, especially since the capital is so far north, but everyone's very friendly. They've got a dragon."

"Yes," said Ioanna. "I heard."

"He's blue, and tame, and he talks! He was raised by the princesses from an egg, so they're like his mothers. Isn't that adorable? I'd much rather have a dragon for a child than an ordinary baby."

"He would be very expensive to feed."

"You're probably right," mused Vitaliya. "Still. I wonder if he would fight for them if there was ever a war? Or maybe not if the princesses are his mothers. They wouldn't want their son to go into danger."

"The Ieflarians are not inclined to war."

"It was just a thought. A silly one." Vitaliya gave her an encouraging smile. "You should think of silly things more often. All this worrying will make you sick. But let's find something to eat. Real food, I mean. If I have to eat another orange, I'll turn into one."

Ioanna's laugh was short, but Vitaliya was thrilled to hear it anyway.

THEY LEFT TOWN the next morning after Otho did his round of animal inspections. The residents seemed disappointed he was going so soon, but he said there was a pressing matter to attend to in another community, and he would return as soon as he was able.

"We're coming to the edge of my territory," Otho advised. "The next settlement we see will want to know what I'm doing there since I'm not their usual priest. We should tell them we've been called to a special assignment to the north, and we're only passing through."

"Do you know when we'll reach them?" asked Ioanna.

"I have a map somewhere back there," said Otho. "Given the area, it probably isn't more than a day out, so hopefully we'll reach it by sunset."

Vitaliya found the map under a bag of shearing tools and brought it out for examination. "It says here there's a town not far ahead," she reported, tracing the line that represented the road with a finger. "Or at least, I don't think it's far ahead."

"It's probably accurate," said Otho. "If it hasn't been abandoned in the meantime. But I shouldn't say that—if it's large enough to have been listed on a map, it's probably doing well."

"There's places that aren't on the map?" asked Vitaliya.

"Certainly," said Otho. "Small villages and the like. Camps. Side roads and streams too small to bother taking down on a cheap map like this."

Vitaliya looked down at the yellowed page and tried to imagine what *wasn't* pictured there. Logic said it probably wasn't anything interesting, but that wasn't as much fun as thinking they might unexpectedly stumble upon a hidden shrine or mysterious forgotten hanging gardens.

They arrived at the next town a few hours after noon and, as Otho had predicted, the inhabitants were openly confused by the arrival of a priest who was not their own. After reassuring them he had *not* come to replace their regular priest, and they were only passing through, everyone relaxed.

This town, Vitaliya realized, was home to far more young adults than she would have expected given how the priestesses were so aggressive in making certain nobody was able to escape military service. They were still only a few days from the capital, so it was not as though they'd escaped notice simply by virtue of living in a remote location.

Vitaliya turned to Ioanna to ask her if she'd noticed this as well. But before she could speak, she realized Ioanna had a very strange look on her face like she was about to be sick.

"Lucia," worried Vitaliya, tugging on her arm. "What's the matter?"

"Don't call me that!" snapped Ioanna. Vitaliya stared at her in shock, and then Ioanna shook her head. "I'm sorry. That was rude. I just—I can't...this place...something's wrong."

"Wrong how?" asked Vitaliya.

"Wrong," murmured Ioanna, running her hands up and down her arms as though to warm them—but Vitaliya could see her digging her fingernails into her own skin. "Something's here that shouldn't be."

"Should we leave?"

"Yes." But Ioanna began to walk away from Otho's wagon and further into town. "But if I know it is here, it probably knows I'm here too..."

"You're not making very much sense," said Vitaliya, hurrying after her. But Ioanna did not reply.

Vitaliya followed her though the town, passing houses, wells, and confused people, who all stared after them. Vitaliya tried to smile at them, to put them at ease. But she wasn't sure how successful she was since Ioanna marched so purposefully—and occasionally paused to close her eyes.

"Do you hear that?" asked Vitaliya. "That music?"

"Yes," murmured Ioanna.

The sound was faint, but still sweet and lilting. It vanished when the wind shifted, but Ioanna seemed to know where it came from. She veered off the road and across an open field, not seeming to mind the presence of whatever lived in the long grass.

"Ioanna," began Vitaliya, stumbling a little as her boot caught on something. "Ioanna, we've gone too far—Otho is going to worry—"

But Ioanna hardly seemed to hear her. As they came to the edge of the field, which was bordered by trees, Vitaliya realized the music sounded far more distinct now. It was coming from some kind of flute.

"This way," Ioanna said, pushing on through the trees.

"I don't feel like this is a good idea," Vitaliya murmured. But she could hardly let Ioanna wander off on her own, especially in such a strange, disoriented state. What if she fell off a cliff or stumbled into a wild boar? Someone would have to run away screaming for help. "Ioanna, I can move the briars out of the way if you slow down!"

But Ioanna did not seem to notice or care, and it was all Vitaliya could do to keep up with her. She wondered if maybe Ioanna was under a spell. If the music they were hearing had taken over her mind, and something awful waited for them at the end of the path.

But if that was the case, why did it only affect Ioanna and not Vitaliya?

Vitaliya paused to pick up a stick from the ground. It wasn't long, but it was thick enough that it might serve as a club if she needed to protect herself. She gave it a few experimental swings and tried to imagine herself bashing a monster or a person. It was a little difficult to think about. She had a bad feeling she might freeze up when the time came.

Ioanna was still moving, and so Vitaliya hurried to catch up with her once more. They came to a fence, half-rotted and falling over, and Ioanna followed it until the sound of the music grew so loud that Vitaliya squinted ahead to see who—or what—the source was.

They came upon a man, only a little older than themselves. He sat on the fence, looking rather relaxed given the decrepit state of the wood, and the fact it might collapse into a pile of splinters at any moment. In his hands he held a simple wooden flute, the source of the music.

There was nothing terribly unusual about the man, save for the fact he apparently spent his day sitting on a fence. He looked like any other resident of the area, dressed in a midlength tunic worn over long trousers and a shirt, but the clothes were covered in patches and seams from countless repairs. His dark hair was curly, and a little too long to be considered fashionable. As they approached him, he lowered his flute and raised one hand up to his eyes, as though shielding them from a strong light.

"By Asterium," he observed. "You hurt to look at. I thought I sensed something absurdly powerful, but I'd hoped you were only passing by."

"What?" said Vitaliya.

"Not *you*. Her. The princess." The man nodded at Ioanna, then lowered his hand from his eyes, though he continued to squint.

"How did you know—" Vitaliya began, alarmed. But Ioanna interrupted her.

"He's not a man," Ioanna said flatly. "He's what I've been sensing. Which one are you?"

"I'm not doing any harm," the man objected. "In fact, if I wasn't here, these people would have starved to death years ago."

"Ioanna, what's going on?" asked Vitaliya. "Who is he?"

"A chaos god. A little one." Ioanna's eyes narrowed. "But I'm not sure which."

Vitaliya looked at the man in disbelief. He was so painfully ordinary! He had a hole in his sleeve, right at the elbow as though the fabric had been worn out through overuse. And the flute he carried was cracked in places. How could he be a god?

"She doesn't believe you," said the man, amused. "Doesn't she know?"

"Know what?" asked Vitaliya, looking from Ioanna to the strange man and back again. "What don't I know? What's going *on?*"

The man lifted his flute to his mouth again and began to play once more.

"I am perfectly capable of destroying you," warned Ioanna, raising her voice a bit to be heard above the music. The man rolled his eyes, apparently indifferent to the threat.

"If he's a chaos god, then you probably should," murmured Vitaliya. Still, she couldn't bring herself to believe it. Chaos gods were monsters! They took on terrifying shapes and forced people to do awful things! They didn't sit on fences and play flutes.

"Go on, then," said the man, lowering the instrument once more. "Either incinerate me or run along. I've got things to not be doing."

"Have you seen the priestesses of Reygmadra?" asked Ioanna.

"Who hasn't? They're like cockroaches. Worse. At least I'm allowed to step on cockroaches."

"Are you going to tell them we're here?" Ioanna pressed.

"And get involved in this mess? Certainly not. I'm keeping out of it." He went to raise the flute to his lips again, but Ioanna snatched it away from him. He looked offended but did not try to grab it back. "I'll have you know I make special effort to not remind the Ten of my existence."

"I can't let you stay here and continue hurting these people," said Ioanna.

"I'm not hurting anyone. I told you they'd all be dead if not for me. Did I lie? I'm offering you a very generous deal, considering the circumstances. You didn't see me, and I didn't see you. That's very kind of me. If I went to Reygmadra, I'm sure I'd be rewarded."

"I'm confused," said Vitaliya. "You're a chaos god, but you help people?"

"I help *my* people," he corrected. "They worship me, and things go nicely for them. Birth records go missing, so people are never summoned to fight. Things grow where they were never planted. Empty bags turn out to have one more cup of flour in them."

"Yes, but what sort of things do you make them do in return?" pressed Ioanna. Vitaliya nodded in agreement.

She knew chaos gods often demanded blood sacrifices, or for their followers to go out and kill any who might oppose them, or even destruction for no good reason.

"How distasteful." The man looked offended again. "Who do you think I am?"

"I don't know because you won't *tell* me."

"That's fair," he said in a surprisingly agreeable tone. "Acydon. God of Apathy. Now don't you feel silly coming all the way out here to see someone so unimportant?"

Vitaliya looked at Ioanna. "Are we sure he's telling the truth?" For why wouldn't a chaos god lie? "He might be something much worse."

"She *really* doesn't know!" marveled Acydon. "Why in the world does she think you're out here to begin with?"

Vitaliya frowned, uncomfortable at being discussed as though she weren't present—and at the implication something was going on behind her back. "Ioanna, what is he talking about?"

But instead of replying, Ioanna hurled Acydon's flute back at him, aiming it directly at his head. He caught the instrument effortlessly before it could collide with his face.

"Come on," said Ioanna. "We've got to go."

"What?" cried Vitaliya. "But—he's a chaos god! You're going to let him just carry on? Making these people worship him?"

"He's right. This town would be gone without him," Ioanna said flatly. "I don't like it, but that's the state of things here. I'm not going to condemn these people to starvation just because I don't approve of the god they've chosen to worship."

"It's not just here," said Acydon. Vitaliya was not certain if his tone was meant to be mocking or helpful. "All over the empire, my siblings have stepped in to help those whom none of the Ten can be bothered to provide for. A generous empress might remember that, after all the fighting's done."

"You think you deserve your worship legalized just for keeping a handful of people alive?" Ioanna asked incredulously.

"You don't? It's more than your nobles are doing. You're far less sanctimonious than I would have expected, so I'm sure you can see my side of things."

"You are caring for them simply to increase your own power, not out of kindness."

"That is why *all* gods care for mortals, I am terribly sorry to inform you," said Acydon. "That includes the Ten."

"You may believe that, but I don't," said Ioanna.

Acydon shrugged. Clearly, he didn't care what Ioanna believed. "You should be moving on. It's not just priestesses she has after you." He raised his flute to his mouth once more and began to play a lazy, meandering tune. Ioanna stared at him, her fists clenching, and Vitaliya nearly expected to see golden light gathering at her hands. The way it *ought* to be.

For chaos gods could not be allowed to run around free! Everyone knew that! In Vesolda, they had paladins from the Order of the Sun to keep them under control, and even ordinary priests of Iolar knew how to bind and banish them.

And how could they be sure Acydon was who he claimed to be? Ioanna was intelligent, so why was she taking his word so easily? He might be *anyone*. There was no compulsion for him to divulge his true name or domain. And they had no proof he was responsible for this town's survival. For all they knew, he could be planning to destroy it the moment they left!

But Ioanna turned around and began to walk back the way they'd come. She really was just going to leave! Unless this was a trick to lull Acydon into a false sense of safety before she struck? But Ioanna was straightforward like a paladin. If she was going to attack, she wouldn't waste time trying to be secretive or clever. She'd just do it.

Vitaliya paused to look at Acydon again. There really was nothing to prove he wasn't an ordinary man, and if not for the fact he'd identified Ioanna so easily, she still would not believe it. Their interaction had been strange and surreal, but not nearly as terrifying as stories had led her to expect.

"Was that a good idea?" Vitaliya asked Ioanna as soon as they were out of earshot. "Letting him go, I mean."

"What choice did I have?"

"Well—" Vitaliya floundered, not wanting to outright accuse Ioanna of being foolish, but also not wanting to leave the town in the hands of an evil god. "—maybe we should verify his story? Before we go?"

"He was telling the truth," said Ioanna flatly.

"But we don't have proof."

Ioanna did not reply as she continued to push her way through the trees.

"Should we tell Otho about this?" Vitaliya worried.

"No," said Ioanna. "He doesn't need to know."

"What about me? Do I need to know?"

"What?" Ioanna finally stopped walking and turned to look Vitaliya in the face. "What do you—"

"He kept saying I didn't know something. That I didn't know why we're out here."

"Don't worry."

"How am I meant to not worry about that!? If we're not going to Oredia, if there's something else—some other plan you don't trust me with—" Vitaliya's voice broke.

"No!" cried Ioanna in alarm. "No, nothing like that. I promise! We're going to Oredia, we're going to see my grandmother, and you can do whatever you like once we arrive. Everything else is just...my own problems. You shouldn't have to worry about them. That's all."

"Of course, I'm worried! Especially after all—all that!" She gestured broadly at the woods behind them.

"It's difficult to explain. If nothing else, it will take a long time. And we should leave immediately. The sooner we get to Oredia, the better."

Perhaps Vitaliya shouldn't have been surprised, but she was. Did Ioanna really think Vitaliya might betray her? Even after they'd fled Xyuluthe together? After Netheia had threatened to kill Vitaliya and invade Vesolda? The realization hurt. If she hadn't proved herself by now, what more could Vitaliya do?

Maybe it had been her imagination all along, but she'd really thought maybe Ioanna was beginning to trust her.

Obviously she'd been mistaken.

Chapter Seven

IOANNA

Oredia was a peaceful community, a medium-sized town surrounded by farmlands located in the shadow of Irianthe's estate. Though certainly not the glamorous setting most members of the court would expect a former empress to gravitate to, Ioanna understood why her grandmother had selected it to be her primary home.

Some people thought Grandmother Irianthe foolish for giving up her crown so quickly. But Ioanna knew her grandmother was exactly where she wanted to be and doing exactly what she wanted to be doing. How many people could say the same?

Oredia was home to a Temple of Inthi, and Grandmother Irianthe was known to support the artisans and inventors there. A Temple of Ethi, neutroi God of Knowledge, had also been built within walking distance of her home specifically at her request, so Ioanna never went without reading materials when she visited.

Grandmother Irianthe almost never came to Xyuluthe anymore, though she expected visits from her granddaughters at least twice a year. She hated court life and spoke candidly about the myriad ways her life had improved since passing the crown on to her son.

Grandmother Irianthe had no spouse, no consort, and no lovers. Ioanna understood it was certainly possible for someone to have no desire for such things though not very common. But she'd still managed to have a child. Ioanna's father had no father of his own legally, and so Ioanna had no paternal grandfather. Nobody had ever come forward claiming to be Ionnes's father, and on the family tree a single line was drawn from Irianthe to Ionnes as though she had been his sole progenitor. Perhaps this was odd, but Ioanna felt no compulsion to pry further into the matter.

"I hope she's home," commented Vitaliya as they made their way up the road to Grandmother Irianthe's estate. They'd arrived just as the sun was setting, and Ioanna had been afraid they might not arrive before dark. "I mean, I hope she hasn't gone to Xyuluthe. And maybe we passed her without realizing."

Ioanna wondered if the news of her father's death had reached her grandmother yet. Had her mother sent a courier? In that case, did her grandmother also know Ioanna had been forced to flee the capital?

She supposed she'd find out soon enough.

They reached the gate surrounding Grandmother Irianthe's estate. As always, it was guarded, and Ioanna knew she did not come to Oredia often enough to expect the men stationed there to recognize her, especially dressed as she was and accompanied by a common priest.

"I'm here to see my grandmother," she announced in the most level voice she could manage. Before either of the guards could retort with something incredulous, she added, "She isn't expecting me. Please tell her Ioanna of Xytae is here, and Emperor Ionnes is dead."

That cut off any arguments the guards might have offered. One of them left in the direction of the manor house immediately while the other remained behind.

Ioanna thought the guard might return with the groundskeeper, or another servant who would be familiar enough with Ioanna to identify an outright fraud. But when he returned, he was still alone.

"The empress mother wishes to see you immediately," he said. "She insists you come now without delay."

Otho volunteered to go and find lodging in town, but Ioanna insisted he remain for his own safety. It was unlikely he was in any real danger, but he had gone to a great deal of trouble to see them to Oredia, and she would never forgive herself if something happened to him. If nothing else, he deserved a hot meal and a reward for his efforts.

Otho's humble wagon and donkey were absurdly out of place as they ascended the gradual incline of the road toward Grandmother Irianthe's home. Unlike the Imperial Palace, her grandmother's estate was pristine, and even the stones lining the path appeared to have been scrubbed. They passed tall healthy green hedges so neatly trimmed they might have been freshly cut that very morning as well as carefully arranged gardens that had not yet started to bloom.

Hostlers approached as they came to the front of the estate, taking the wagon from Otho and guiding it out of sight. Ioanna looked up at the front of her grandmother's villa. It was an enormous home, as those in the countryside tended to be, with a large walled courtyard in the front that one had to pass through in order to reach the residential area.

They were less than midway through the courtyard when Ioanna caught sight of a figure moving toward them purposefully.

Grandmother Irianthe wore a simple white dress decorated with a wide gold collar and matching belt. Her face was exceptionally youthful, given her age, with only a few lines creasing through her skin, though her hair was finally beginning to turn silver. She had no attendants with her, and she did not smile or offer any kind of greeting as she approached.

"Ioanna," said Grandmother Irianthe, sounding more tired than surprised. "So, it is true."

"Father is dead," Ioanna began. "We—"

But before she could say anything more, Grandmother Irianthe reached forward and took Ioanna by the arm. "Come with me. There are things I must tell you."

"But—" Ioanna began, turning back toward Vitaliya and Otho.

"They can manage without you for an hour or two, can't they?" asked Grandmother Irianthe. Then without waiting for a reply, she said, "We must talk. Now."

"But—"

"Not here."

Ioanna gave apologetic looks to Vitaliya and Otho, and they both shrugged helplessly in reply. Her grandmother pulled her away, and Ioanna allowed herself to be dragged further into the garden and toward the house. Once inside, Grandmother Irianthe steered her unceremoniously through the beautiful entrance hall and off to a side room, one Ioanna and her sisters had not been allowed to set foot in when they were children. Grandmother Irianthe pulled the door shut behind them.

"Sit down," she commanded, and Ioanna did, sinking cautiously into an upholstered bench. "Tell me what happened. From the beginning."

Ioanna had thought Grandmother Irianthe had wanted to tell *her* something, but she would not argue. "We received the news from a courier a few days ago. The letter said Father was killed in a duel with one of the Masimi commanders, and I couldn't sense any lies on it. I think it is probably true."

"Almost certainly," agreed Grandmother Irianthe, nodding somberly. Ioanna wondered if she'd received a courier days ago. "What happened after that?"

"Netheia told me Father always intended for her to be his heir. She was not lying about that, but I don't know if it's true or merely her perception of things. In any case, he never announced it while he was alive. But she still managed to gather enough supporters that I had to flee the capital."

"And what about your mother? Who is she supporting?"

"I don't know. She didn't seem impressed when Netheia announced she was the rightful heir. But just before I left, Netheia said something that suggested she knew about the coup and did nothing to stop it." Ioanna sighed. "I suppose it hardly matters what Mother thinks. Even if she did support me, nearly everyone else is on Netheia's side."

Grandmother Irianthe did not react to this. Instead she sat down on a similar bench across from Ioanna. "Who have you been traveling with?"

"The girl is Princess Vitaliya of Vesolda. She was in the palace, visiting for an excursion, when we received word of Father's death. She tried to warn me of Netheia's plan and was forced to flee with me. The man is a priest of Cyne who has disguised us as his acolytes, to keep the priestesses of Reygmadra from bringing us back to

Xyuluthe. They've been searching for us ever since we fled."

"Yes, I am aware," said Grandmother Irianthe. "I have twice ordered them escorted off my land. I suspect there may be some in Oredia still in disguise. But never mind them. They cannot overrule *my* orders."

"She'll send soldiers next," murmured Ioanna, staring down at the intricate mosaic tiles on the floor. "The moment Mother allows it, I just know she will."

"You mustn't hate your sister, Ioanna," Grandmother Irianthe said. "She's only a little piece in a much larger game, being pushed about by a hand with very sharp fingernails."

Ioanna looked up. "What do you mean?"

Grandmother Irianthe glanced back toward the door again, verifying she had remembered to close it behind her. Then she said in a considerably quieter voice, "In my experience, the worst thing about being empress was not the loud parties, the dreadful, tedious people, the poisonings, or the stabbings. It was the *shouting*." Grandmother Irianthe touched two fingers to her forehead. "Imagine, if you will, a woman following you about all day long, yelling terrible advice in your ear. *Kill him. Kill her. Invade Ibaia. Invade Ieflaria. Invade Masim. Raise taxes. Raise an army. Fight. Kill. Fight*."

Ioanna shook her head incredulously. "Reygmadra spoke to you?"

"At first," said Grandmother Irianthe. "Before she realized I wouldn't give her what she wanted, and then the speaking turned into screaming. At night when I dreamed, it was always of the battlefield. Of victories, of winning effortlessly, and people gathering around and praising me. I knew she meant for me to feel glorious and triumphant, but I couldn't forget the sight of the mutilated soldiers. The visions were so vivid I made my guards take turns watching over me as I slept and ordered them to wake me if I became distressed."

"You think they were visions?" asked Ioanna.

"I know they were," Grandmother Irianthe said. "And I hardly needed to call upon a priestess to interpret them. I don't deny I didn't care to be empress in any case, but they made the decision to abdicate easier than it might have been otherwise."

Did Netheia have those visions too? She'd never mentioned them—but then, of course, why would she speak of such things to Ioanna? Ioanna wondered if Netheia would find them disturbing or think them as thrilling and glorious as Reygmadra intended them to be.

Was Reygmadra already leaning over Netheia's shoulder, invisible, murmuring that she ought to kill Ioanna? Convincing her it was for the best because it was the only way to ensure stability, and Enessa would forgive her sooner or later?

"After you abdicated, the shouting and dreams, they stopped?" asked Ioanna.

"Better yet. The day I left Xyuluthe was the day I lost my blessing."

Ioanna's mouth fell open, and she gaped like a hooked fish.

"I've never told anyone before this moment," said Grandmother Irianthe. "Though I do frequently wonder if anyone has guessed. I suppose it hardly matters now at my age. Nobody is calling upon me to duel."

"She truly was angry with you then," marveled Ioanna.

"Like a little girl throwing a tantrum because she's lost a favorite toy." Grandmother Irianthe smiled fondly, her eyes pale and distant. "At the time, though, it was a rather devastating thing. You can probably imagine."

Ioanna nodded. For a blessing to be rescinded was rare and deeply shameful. Stories that described such an event usually featured an act of great evil as the catalyst. The loss of a blessing was a sign to the audience that the subject had moved beyond the possibility for redemption.

"She got what she wanted in the end, of course. Your father was perfect for her. I doubt she ever had to shout in his ear or send him visions. Netheia will be just the same if she takes the throne."

"I don't see the sense in it," said Ioanna. "Why should Xytae be at war with Masim, or anywhere else for that matter? None of those lands have done anything to trouble us, and there's hardly any advantage to us taking them. The priestesses speak of valor and glory, but I mean *practical* things—our people cannot eat glory. Besides, the Masimi are honorable people even if their interpretation of the Ten is a little different from ours. It is not as though they venerate chaos gods or send monsters against us, so I do not believe there is any glory in their defeat."

"What makes you so certain there must be sense in it?" asked Grandmother Irianthe. "She is the goddess of war, so she seeks war."

"War for war's sake?" Ioanna questioned.

"Can you blame her? It's only her nature."

"And when we've warred ourselves into extinction, and all her worshippers are dead on a battlefield? What does she intend to do then?"

"I do not know. Perhaps you ought to ask her if you believe you can reason her out of her own domain."

Maybe I could, thought Ioanna. But then she thought of Netheia. Of how even the most well-reasoned arguments consistently failed to touch her heart or her mind. Of how she would resort to rage and violence whenever she knew she could not win through logic. Perhaps Reygmadra was like that too. Perhaps Reygmadra was a thousand times worse.

"Animals cannot help their natures," said Ioanna. "But a goddess? It seems so wrong someone so powerful is no different than a mindless beast. Besides, doesn't our ability to reason come from the gods? How could they bestow something that they themselves do not possess?"

Grandmother Irianthe did not appear to find this as compelling as Ioanna did. "Do not trouble yourselves with the nature of the gods," she advised. "Your work is here."

"You do not wish for me to become empress. I know that is true."

"It was once," agreed Grandmother Irianthe. "I will not deny it—when you were young, your blessing was a great shock to us all. And I did not believe one with Iolar's light would be able to lead Xytae in the way her people were accustomed. But that was many years ago. Now I see what has become of our nation, and I realize you could hardly be worse than the rest of us."

"Do you believe I ought to be empress, then?"

"I don't believe *anyone* deserves such a terrible fate," said Grandmother Irianthe. "Let alone a girl so soft as you. I'd hate to see you turned harsh and bitter. Nor do I wish to facilitate a war between you and your sister. But it is clear to me that Netheia will only continue along the path your father laid down, and it will lead to our ruin."

Ioanna had come to her grandmother expecting little more than a luxurious exile, to only remain on the estate until she was thrown out for dragging political machinations into the former empress's home. But now Grandmother Irianthe wanted to be her ally. She had never bothered to even hope for such a thing.

"But even if I am crowned empress, what good can I do if everyone at court hates me?" asked Ioanna. "If they all band together to work against me…"

"Well, the easiest solution is to execute the loudest of them and give their titles to your friends," Grandmother Irianthe said. Ioanna cringed. "But I think you'll soon see their religious convictions are not so firm as they claim. Oh, I am certain they make quite a show of their devotion to Reygmadra now, but their true allegiance is to their own comfort—their families, their lands, and their gold. Let them go on as they always have, and they'll find it's not worth the trouble to stand against you."

Ioanna was not sure if she believed that.

"Now," said Grandmother Irianthe. "There are some people who are waiting to speak with you."

"With me?" Ioanna blinked. "Who—?"

"They arrived a few days ago." Grandmother Irianthe got to her feet and moved toward the door. "Wait there. I'll send for them. I'll admit I wasn't as hospitable to them as I might have been. I did not wish to believe they were telling the truth."

Baffled, Ioanna remained in her seat and listened as her grandmother called to a servant out in the hallway. Who could possibly have come to see her? Her only guess was some friends or allies of Netheia's—or maybe some priestesses of Reygmadra in disguise? She expected they'd come to warn her that the moment she took a step outside of Oredia, she'd be arrested. Or maybe they'd not bother with words. She flexed her fingers and prepared to summon a shield.

The door opened, and Grandmother Irianthe returned. Behind her stood a man who appeared to be about fifty. His clothing was simple but very fine in quality as though he was a nobleman who did not have to dress to receive visitors today. His hair was cut short in the style a soldier's might be, but he did not give Ioanna the impression he was searching for a reason to fight unlike the way her sister and her friends always did.

Ioanna looked up at him curiously, and he stared down at her. There was wonder in his eyes. Perhaps Grandmother Irianthe had not told him she would be waiting for him?

"Ioanna," said Grandmother Irianthe. "This is Knight-Commander Livius of the Order of the Sun. He arrived several days ago."

In that moment, Ioanna was seven years old again, crouched over a page in the darkness and writing an awkward letter to a man she could not remember. Back then, the world had felt big and terrifying and impossible to navigate, but she'd always hoped she'd grow to match it.

Ioanna leapt to her feet, not caring for the furniture or the myriad breakable ornaments Grandmother Irianthe had decorated the room with.

"Knight-Commander Livius," she gasped. She began to reach forward, to clasp his hands, but then stopped herself because surely that was too familiar a gesture. "What—how—it's, it's wonderful to see you. But how...?"

For Knight-Commander Livius had been exiled from Xytae along with the rest of the Order of the Sun. Ioanna had always supposed she would have to send for him sooner or later. She had certainly not expected him to come searching for *her*.

"I am glad to see you as well," said Knight-Commander Livius. "I was going to be terribly embarrassed if you never turned up. Your grandmother has been extremely patient with us, considering I had no proof of my claim."

"But if you arrived here days ago..." The journey from Ieflaria would have taken weeks. "How did you learn of my father's death before we did?"

"A dream," said Livius. "Or a vision, I suppose. The most intense, vivid one I have ever experienced. When I awoke, I knew I must go to Oredia immediately to meet you. I admit, I spent a great deal of time doubting myself and considered traveling to the capital instead. But now I am glad I did not."

"I am as well," said Ioanna. If Livius had been discovered in Xyuluthe, not even Ioanna could protect him from the consequences. The Order was not remembered kindly by most of the Xytan court. Still, she could not help but feel a bit neglected—why had he received a vision from Iolar while Ioanna had not? "Have you come alone? Or did you bring more paladins?"

"I have not come with an army," admitted Livius. "I thought it best to move discreetly until I could determine what the situation here is. I've brought two paladins with me, both disguised as common guards, simply for protection on the roads. When the time comes, the rest will join me here."

"I do not want a civil war," said Ioanna. "I don't want to see us turned against one another. I appreciate your aid, but there must be a way that doesn't involve us becoming exactly like our enemies."

"Iolar means for you to be empress," said Livius firmly. "And therefore, it is my responsibility to ensure that happens. I respect your blessing, and your title, but I know you have little experience commanding soldiers. If we are to work together, I ask you to trust my judgment in these matters. Believe me when I say I will never order my soldiers—or your subjects—into an impossible battle. But in times such as this, there is no high path to be taken. The only choice is to fight or be trampled."

Ioanna was not sure if she believed that. Even now, she felt certain there was some magical combination of words that, if she uttered them, would cause Netheia to finally see reason. She only had to discover what they were.

"What had you hoped to do?" she asked. "I do not have any sort of plan. In fact, I thought I might be forced to allow Netheia's coronation to proceed."

"I don't propose we go directly to Xyuluthe," said Livius. "I have been informed we still have three months before the coronation. I suggest we spend that time rallying more supporters for you."

"You mean the rest of the Order?" asked Ioanna.

"No," he said. "Though certainly more will come now that I've confirmed the situation here."

"Ioanna, Xytae is in turmoil," said Grandmother Irianthe. "We've painted a pretty glaze over it, but it is beginning to crack. Gather the people to your side by speaking of your plans for peace. It should not be difficult, given the condition of things."

"I cannot ask farmers to stand against imperial soldiers!" cried Ioanna. "I'd be a murderer!"

"And what do you call standing back and allowing your sister to continue your father's work?" asked

Grandmother Irianthe. "One way or another, they will die—whether it's on the end of a Masimi blade, or in their own villages when there's no food left in the storehouses."

"It cannot come to that," said Ioanna, but even as she spoke, she remembered all she had seen between leaving Xyuluthe and the present. "Xytae is not *that* near to ruin."

"These things can happen very quickly, Crown Princess," said Livius. "Especially now that the empire is so weak. How much of your harvest is being sent to the soldiers? What do you suppose will happen if there's a blight next summer?"

"I don't know—"

"Besides, I think we can get some of the minor nobility to your side," said Grandmother Irianthe. "The ones not wealthy enough to live at Xyuluthe year-round. I've no doubt they have felt the effects of the war far more keenly than anyone in the capital."

"I, I'm tired," murmured Ioanna. "Please...can we discuss this later? Tomorrow? I can't think—I need to—"

Grandmother Irianthe opened her mouth, and Ioanna knew she was going to object, but Livius spoke first.

"Of course," he said. "You've had a difficult journey, and I've given you quite a lot to think about."

Ioanna was escorted to the room she had always stayed in on the rare occasion she visited her grandmother. It was among the largest of the guest rooms, second only to the one reserved for her parents. In an odd way, Ioanna was grateful she had not been moved up to that room. She was not ready for it. Perhaps Grandmother Irianthe had known this.

She had no things to unpack, but the wardrobe standing in the corner was full of anything she might need. Some of the clothes were too small, left over from childhood, but plenty would be acceptable to wear in the coming days.

"Hellooooo," sang Vitaliya brightly, opening the door without knocking and making Ioanna jump. "This place is nice. Nicer than the palace, I think. Certainly cleaner—no offense meant. Are you doing all right?"

Ioanna did not reply, too taken aback to formulate an immediate response. By the time she managed a rather weak "You might have knocked—" Vitaliya was already chattering.

"They tried to send Otho into town, but I held my breath until they agreed he could stay. I don't think he appreciated it. He kept saying he was happy to leave! But he deserves to sleep in a proper bed, don't you think? Even if it's only for one night. These servants had better not be rude to him, or I'll be *so* difficult! You can't imagine how difficult I can be!"

"Are you going home?" asked Ioanna, closing the wardrobe and turning away from it.

"What?" Vitaliya sounded confused. "Am I—what?"

"Or to Ibaia? You said you wanted to. There's no reason for you to remain here. It may even be dangerous."

"What?" Vitaliya shook her head. "What are you talking about? No. I don't want to go anywhere. I want to stay here."

"Why?" *This isn't a game*, Ioanna wanted to say. *This is not some petty diversion. If I handle this poorly, it might ignite a civil war. Men will die. I could die. You could die. Do you understand? Do you understand how serious this all is? Do you even understand that serious things exist?*

"Well..." Vitaliya bit her lower lip. "I think I can do more good here than anywhere else. People are hungry, and I can make the plants grow. Maybe it's small, but it helps. And besides, even if it didn't..." Her voice trailed off.

"What?"

"You seem like you need someone to be your friend."

It was not a lie, and so Ioanna was at a loss. Had anyone, in her entire life, spoken those words to her and *meant* them? Surely Vitaliya had an ulterior motive. Everyone did. Even the priests, though genuinely kind, hoped someday Ioanna would put a halt to the constant, excessive veneration of Reygmadra and restore Iolar's worship.

"What else?" pressed Ioanna, stepping closer. "What do you want for yourself? For Vesolda?"

"Um..." Vitaliya shook her head again, more vigorously this time. "I'd like my things back. I mean, the dresses we had to leave behind in the palace. It's not terrible if I don't get them, but some of them I liked. And there's some jewelry too, if it hasn't been stolen already."

"What else?"

"I don't know!" Vitaliya sounded a little concerned. "Am I forgetting something? I feel like there's something you want me to say, but I don't know what it is."

Ioanna turned away and went to go sit down on the foot of the bed. "I don't think I've ever met anyone like you."

Vitaliya brightened up again. "In a good way? Or a bad way?"

"Good, I think," admitted Ioanna. "You're straightforward, and when you lie, it's only about silly things to make us laugh. You really don't *want* anything, do you?"

"I want lots of things," denied Vitaliya. "I want my own chickens."

"Not things like that. Things that nobles fight over. Power and titles and important things."

"I already have a title," said Vitaliya. "If I wanted a better one, I'd have to be a queen, and then I'd have to do queen things. Having power just means having a chance to mess everything up." She reached out to close the door behind her, then moved nearer to where Ioanna sat.

"What would you do if you had to be queen?"

"You mean, if everyone else died?" Vitaliya came and sat down beside Ioanna on the bed. The mattress sagged, and Ioanna set one hand down to brace herself. "I don't know. Maybe I'd do like your grandmother did. Run away. Except at least she was responsible enough to make an heir first. I suppose I'd have to do that too. I'd make one of the chickens my heir. *Then* I'd run away."

"You don't want to do anything for the world?" questioned Ioanna. "If you were a queen, you could change many things. Influence history. There's so many—"

But Vitaliya was already shaking her head. "I'd only hurt people," she said. "I wouldn't mean to, but it would all go wrong. And you can't say sorry to dead bodies."

"You wouldn't kill people."

"Not on purpose. But that wouldn't make them any less dead. You know me! You know what I'm like. I don't think about things long enough or hard enough. If I was a queen, I'd order something I thought was a good idea, but it would be awful, and everyone would hate me for a thousand years."

"I don't think you would," said Ioanna. "If nothing else, you'd have advisors telling you if your ideas were bad."

"I don't want to take that risk. I'm selfish, I suppose. I don't want history to remember me as the lady who ruined Vesolda."

"I don't think that's selfish if it's coming from a place of not wanting to hurt people."

"Well, I hope we never have to find out. I hope my brother has sixteen children, and then each of those sixteen has sixteen more." Vitaliya paused. "I do like helping the farms and making the plants grow. I don't trust myself to do it on my own and for big areas like Otho does, but do you remember how happy those children were when I grew the figs for them? That made me feel so important. Not in a showing off kind of way but like I had done something really useful."

"You did," said Ioanna. "It might have been the difference between survival and death for them."

"Oh!" Vitaliya shuddered. "Don't say that."

"Why not?"

"It's too responsible. Too much responsibility for me."

"But it's a good thing, isn't it?"

"I know. I know it isn't rational. But that doesn't stop it. I can't control my thoughts."

"Who taught you to think in such a way?"

"I don't think anyone *meant* to. But my brother and I were tutored together, and it was all so serious and important all the time. It's no wonder I decided to just not be important."

"I don't think you're unimportant."

"That's too bad. I try very hard at it!" Vitaliya smiled again. She smelled of jasmine, Ioanna realized, because a little sprig of it had been woven through her hair. Had she grown it herself in the garden? "If I'm annoying you, though, I can leave. Not just the room, I mean. The whole country."

"You're not annoying me." It was strange, considering, well...everything about Vitaliya, but it was the truth. "Maybe I've been needing someone like you. At court it's so easy to forget that sometimes people are just happy."

"I'm sorry you had to live that way. I'm sorry so many people in Xytae are living that way. But if anyone can change it, I think you can."

"I don't know," whispered Ioanna. "I should be grateful for my grandmother's support. I should be grateful for the Order of the Sun. But for some reason, all I can think of is how everything would be so much easier if I just gave up on being empress and let Netheia have her way. Maybe I'm just a coward."

"Not wanting to die doesn't mean you're a coward!"

"Or selfish. So many people will suffer if Netheia is empress. I shouldn't even be considering..."

"Thinking about possibilities isn't selfish," asserted Vitaliya. "You're feeling guilty for things you haven't even done yet. And probably won't ever do, knowing you."

Ioanna felt one side of her mouth curl into a smile.

"Well," said Vitaliya. "Maybe I should go—"

If Ioanna had ever acted on thoughtless instinct before in her life, she could not remember it. It was as though her body had been taken over by something else as she lurched forward and brought her hands to Vitaliya's face and pressed their lips together in a kiss. She only had a moment to consider Vitaliya's soft lips, and her warmth, and the sweet scent of fresh flowers about her before she regained her senses, and she pulled away, horrified with herself.

"I—I'm sorry—" stammered Ioanna, mortified. "I'm...I don't know why I—"

But Vitaliya was laughing. And it was not a scornful or derisive laugh either. It was happy.

"If you'd wanted me to stay, you could have said so!" She caught Ioanna's hands and grasped them loosely in the space between their faces. "Don't—don't be embarrassed. Please. You've been alone for so long. I'm glad you want me near."

"I should have asked—"

"I like surprises." Vitaliya leaned forward and pressed her forehead to Ioanna's. "Really. I promise."

It was not a lie. Of course, it wasn't. Vitaliya never lied when it mattered. Ioanna didn't know what to say. She had never thought she'd be in this position with anyone, let alone a foreign princess. Vitaliya seemed to realize it too because she said, "You've never courted anyone, have you?"

"No, I, I never accepted anyone who wanted to." Because they had all been scheming, seeking the sort of power only the emperor's daughter could grant, and Ioanna had never been lonely enough to overlook it. "In the palace—you know—they're all so..."

"Yes," agreed Vitaliya. "I don't think I'd want any of them either."

"They were all liars," Ioanna said, and the words came out in such a rush that she was afraid Vitaliya wouldn't be able to understand her. "They, they would bring me gifts and they would say all these things, the things you're supposed to say when you're courting someone. But it was always lies, and it was terrible, like being slapped again and again—"

"I am sorry," said Vitaliya. "I think I know what you mean. I've endured a few of those myself—people wanting to be friends or lovers, and then the moment I get to trusting them, they start telling me about some matter my father ought to change his mind on, or they've got some debts that need repaying."

"Oh!" Ioanna had never experienced that before. Her blessing prevented things from ever reaching such a point. "I'm sorry. That must be awful." Far worse than knowing about it in advance and being able to prevent it. Now she felt guilty for ever pitying herself. Did she think she was the only one in the world who had to endure scheming, manipulative people? Of course, she wasn't. It happened to everyone with a title, wealth, or anything worth having.

"Don't worry!" Vitaliya smiled again. "It's nothing, really. Rain off my back, as they say. Besides, even if it's not real, it can be fun."

I would not know, Ioanna did not say because she was twenty years old and surely Vitaliya would find that odd. "I wish I didn't care."

"I don't blame you. It's tiresome."

"I think there must be something wrong with me. That the only way people can say kind things to me is when they're trying to manipulate me."

"Well, maybe not all of them were," urged Vitaliya. "You don't know—"

"Yes, I do." Should she tell Vitaliya? Would Vitaliya even believe her? Or would she think Ioanna was delusional and call her a liar, and Ioanna would be forced to prove it by making Vitaliya tell stories of her childhood and identifying the false ones like some sort of fortune-teller at a festival?

It was not how Ioanna wanted to spend the evening.

Or what if, even worse, Vitaliya saw the potential of Ioanna's blessing and turned ambitious and deceitful and...

No. That was not Vitaliya.

"Well—" Vitaliya squeezed her hands, and then released them. "—I can say kind things to you too. And I swear I won't lie."

"You don't need to—"

"Yes, but I want to. You were the first person at the Imperial Palace that I thought seemed like a good person. I'd been there for weeks, and you were the first. What do you think of that?"

"You only spent time with my sister and her friends."

"It still counts. It counts. I like that you've never once hit me. Your sister always—I think I've said that before, haven't I?"

"When we first met," Ioanna recalled.

"That's right! Oh, that feels like years ago, doesn't it?" Vitaliya smiled.

"How much of it do you remember? You were quite ill."

"I remember you found me...where was I?"

"In front of my door."

"What!" Vitaliya burst into laughter and fell back upon the bed. Her long hair splayed out across the soft blankets. "Was I really? I don't think I ever realized!"

"I'm afraid so."

"Oh, I'm such an embarrassment." But Vitaliya did not sound at all ashamed. She was still smiling, and Ioanna felt herself smile too, so widely that it made her face hurt. "Oh! And I told you not to trust your sister. And I was right!"

"Yes, you were."

"I was hoping I'd see you again after you left."

"I think I was too," Ioanna admitted. She felt awkward, towering over Vitaliya, and so she lay down beside her. There was more than enough room for both of them. "I'm sorry it turned out like this."

"It wasn't your fault! And besides, this isn't so bad." Vitaliya leaned in toward her to touch their foreheads together, just as she had before. "You can kiss me again if you want to."

Ioanna hoped she was not as clumsy and unpracticed as she felt. But Vitaliya's lips were soft and yielding, and she pulled Ioanna closer, so close that their bodies were pressed against each other. Ioanna wondered if Vitaliya could hear her heart racing.

"I'm so glad we're done with wearing robes. I like you in the shorter dress," Vitaliya murmured in a voice that sent a pleasant chill through Ioanna's body. "We don't have those in Vesolda."

"I hardly ever wear them. My legs are so thin—"

"I know. I *wish* mine were that thin!" sighed Vitaliya. She rested one hand on Ioanna's hip, then slowly drew it downward across her thighs and came to rest on her knee.

"I like how you look. I wish I had more of a shape." Ioanna stared at Vitaliya's hand, wishing she would move it up back up again. Should she ask?

She settled on resting her own hand over Vitaliya's, which was a little difficult given her position. Ioanna had to bend her knee to bring it within arm's reach, but that had the added benefit of drawing Vitaliya's hand into hers.

"What are you thinking about?" asked Vitaliya.

"You, mostly," said Ioanna, guiding Vitaliya's hand higher. This time, when they came to the fabric of Ioanna's skirt, Vitaliya slipped her hand underneath.

"Do you want—" Vitaliya began.

"Yes," interrupted Ioanna.

Chapter Eight

VITALIYA

Vitaliya woke to a few thin shafts of morning sunlight filtering through the shutters, and the weight of Ioanna's body pressed against her own. One of Ioanna's arms splayed across Vitaliya's chest, and her face rested against Vitaliya's shoulder.

After a few minutes of deliberation, Vitaliya decided she did not need to hide in a wardrobe or sneak out the window. She probably shouldn't be here, but logic dictated Ioanna could do whatever she wanted. Who would reprimand the future empress? *Maybe* her grandmother. But Vitaliya could not bring herself to worry about an old lady, even if she'd once been one of the most powerful women in the world.

Ioanna always appeared so solemn and thoughtful, but in sleep she seemed happier. She did not quite smile, but she was relaxed, and her breathing was soft and deep. Vitaliya played absently with Ioanna's dark curls, winding them around her fingers.

Soon enough, the pattern of Ioanna's breathing changed, and she opened her eyes. Vitaliya smiled at her.

"Hello," she whispered.

"I'm a Truthsayer," said Ioanna.

Vitaliya blinked at her lazily. "You're supposed to say, 'good morning' or something like that."

Ioanna stared at her for a long moment. Finally, she said, "Good morning, then."

"And there's no Truthsayers in Ioshora."

"Yes, there are. They have one in Ibaia. An old man. And there's me."

"Oh." Vitaliya rubbed at one of her eyes, not awake enough to be impressed by this yet. "It's a secret, then?"

"Yes."

"That's too bad. I'm terrible at secrets." She rotated her wrist to rub at her other eye. "You should not have told me."

"I can't believe I did." Ioanna's face was difficult to read. "I don't know *why* I did. I wasn't planning on it. It just happened. Are you upset?"

"About what?"

Ioanna shrugged, a bit awkwardly since she was still resting on her side. "You don't feel like it's an invasion of your privacy that I can tell when you're lying?"

"It's not like you asked to be blessed with—oh, wait!" Vitaliya brightened up as an idea approached her. "*That's* why the Order of the Sun likes you so much, isn't it?"

"Yes."

"That makes sense." Vitaliya closed her eyes again and pressed her face into the feather pillow. The sheets on this bed were so wonderfully soft and smooth against her bare skin. "Is that all?"

"I think so."

"No other secrets to tell me?"

"None that I can think of at the moment," said Ioanna. Still, from the way she bit her lower lip and refused to meet her eyes, Vitaliya could tell she wanted to say something more.

"What's the matter?" she prompted.

Ioanna moved her fingers, brushing them across Vitaliya's skin. "You stayed."

"Was I supposed to leave?"

"No!" Ioanna cried, surprising Vitaliya with her vehemence. Then, perhaps realizing most of the residents of the villa were probably still asleep, she lowered her voice. "I just, I thought you might."

"Why?"

"I don't know. Just a...a feeling I had."

"Do you want to talk about it?" In Vitaliya's opinion, nobody in Xytae spent enough time talking about their feelings. "It might help."

"I don't want...I don't want you to feel like you need to, to—" Ioanna struggled for the words. "—to coddle me. To treat me like you care for me, or we're courting, if that's not how you really feel. I know you think I'm some delicate thing that needs love and protecting, but I don't want that out of pity, or because you feel guilty—"

"I don't feel guilty," Vitaliya said calmly. "Maybe I do pity you a little bit, but I'd feel sorry for *anyone* in your place, and it's not why I came to you or why I stayed afterwards. I don't do that sort of thing."

"What do you want, then?"

"I told you last night. Chickens. And my dresses back."

"What do you want *from me*?"

Vitaliya shrugged. "What are you offering?" When Ioanna only blinked at her in confusion, she laughed. "Why don't you tell me what *you* want?"

Clearly Ioanna had not been expecting Vitaliya to turn the question on her. As she struggled to come up with a reply, Vitaliya said, "If you want me to come back tonight, and the night after, I will. If you want me to stay in my own room, I will."

"So, this was meaningless?"

"No. I don't think so. Temporary things can still be meaningful. Meaningful things can be temporary. It doesn't cheapen them."

"I don't want to be...to be temporary," said Ioanna. "And maybe that's a ridiculous, impossible thing to want. But—"

"I don't think so. Plenty of people prefer long courtships."

"Yes, but our situation is different. Now isn't a very good time for—and besides, I'm meant to be empress."

"You worry too much," said Vitaliya. "Why don't you just let it happen? And see where it leads?"

"Maybe," whispered Ioanna. Then she gave a little sigh. "I should get up."

"Empresses get up when they feel like it," said Vitaliya.

"I'm not an empress. And besides, we have a lot of work to do."

"I find the act of working to be morally indefensible." Vitaliya paused. "Do you think I could get some new dresses made? I've only got the one." And it seemed she'd lost track of it. She shifted to peer over the edge of the bed and spotted a bundle of mostly white fabric crumpled on the floor. When she reached out to pick it up with her little finger, she noticed how dirty it had become in the last few days and grimaced. She really did not want to put it back on.

"Some of Netheia's should be in the next room. You'll probably fit better in hers than mine until you can get new things." Ioanna gestured vaguely at the wall in the direction of the next guest room. Then her hand fell back down to the soft mattress.

"So you're really a Truthsayer, then? That's not a joke?"

"I wouldn't make a joke about something like that."

"Why haven't you told anyone? People would be very impressed. I'm already very impressed."

"I'm not sure," murmured Ioanna. "My parents didn't want anyone knowing. They always told me if people found out they'd hate me, and I'd be in danger. More danger than usual."

"Why would anyone hate you for that?"

"Reygmadra is the patron of my family and has been for as long as anyone can remember. It's bad enough I don't have her blessing at all. Iolar is very nearly her opposite, and I have the most powerful magic he grants. It would upset people."

"That doesn't make any sense. Being a Truthsayer is—it's one of the most impressive blessings that exists! If I was a Truthsayer, my father would try to make me his heir even over my brother. And he would have a good chance of succeeding because at least half the court would agree."

"Well, my blessing only tells me if someone is lying on purpose," said Ioanna. "So maybe it was only my parents' opinion. Or maybe people in Xytae are different from people in Vesolda."

"Does Netheia know about your blessing?"

"Yes, she realized it when we were both very young. But she's never told anyone, I don't think. Aside from her, the only ones who know are my younger sister Iulia, my grandmother, and the priests of Iolar in Xyuluthe."

"And the Order of the Sun."

"Yes."

Vitaliya sat up and stretched her arms wide. Her upper back made a satisfying noise. "Tell people. Tell everyone. They won't hate you; they'll make you empress. They might make you empress even if your father was a farmer." She paused. "Was that a lie?"

"No. Like I said, it doesn't catch opinions. Or jokes, or figures of speech. I think it's more about intentions than words."

"When someone does lie, what happens?" asked Vitaliya. "I mean, how can you tell?"

"I can feel it in my mind," said Ioanna, touching a finger to her forehead. "Small lies are softer like a pinch. Big lies can feel like being struck in the face. When I hear too many all at once, I start to get sick. That's why I don't like large crowds."

"That's terrible. Blessings shouldn't cause you pain."

Ioanna shrugged. "I don't know. But I understand why most Truthsayers join the Order of the Sun. I'd love to live among people who are forbidden to lie. If this all goes badly, and I don't end up dead, I'll probably join them."

"It won't go badly. Don't think like that," said Vitaliya. "If you've got a blessing like yours, Iolar must mean for you to be empress. There's no way around it."

"And Reygmadra means for me *not* to be empress."

"Oh, who cares what she thinks? We all know Iolar is more important."

"Maybe in Vesolda." But a smile pulled at Ioanna's lips, and she sat up as well.

"Oh!" cried Vitaliya. "There's a *bath* in here!"

"What?"

Vitaliya nearly fell out of bed to approach the enormous square basin in the corner of the room. It was full, and when she dipped one hand in, the water was surprisingly warm—probably heated from below by pipes, something Xytan architecture was famous for. "Was this here last night?"

"No," said Ioanna flatly. "They installed it while we were asleep."

Vitaliya tried to splash Ioanna, but she was too far away for the water to reach, and so it just landed uselessly on the tiles between them. "You're meant to be a Truthsayer! How are you able to lie?"

"My blessing doesn't prevent me from lying."

"Then why are you *called* a Truthsayer if you don't have to say the truth all the time? You should be called..." Vitaliya paused to think up something really good. "Truth...determiner."

"Shall I pass your suggestion along to the temple?"

"Yes, you'd better!" Vitaliya slid one leg into the water. "Oh, this is so nice. How did I manage to not spot this?"

Baths in Xytae were different than baths in Vesolda. Instead of free-standing tubs, they were enormous, sometimes as big as ponds, and usually sunken into the floor. Apparently Xytan people did not care very much about being seen without their clothes on because whole groups of people would use them at once without caring. Vitaliya found this very strange, but the baths in the Imperial Palace had been far more private than the ones in the city, and so she'd taken hers at odd hours when she knew very few people would be around, and never spent too long in them for fear someone might come along. Vitaliya could not really be called modest, and she certainly was not ashamed of her body, but going around in public without any clothes on simply was not *done* in

Vesolda, and she didn't think she'd ever be comfortable with it.

She submerged her head beneath the water, imagining the grime and sweat of the last few days coming loose and drifting away. When she came up again, Ioanna was watching her.

"You should come in too," said Vitaliya. "It's so nice."

"I don't have time."

"Don't have time to get clean? Aren't you supposed to be convincing people you ought to be empress? It will be easier if you're not covered in dirt."

Ioanna gave her a look. "I have time for a bath but nothing else."

"I will sit on my hands," promised Vitaliya.

Ioanna stepped into the bath. She was thin and willowy, a stark contrast to most of the Xytan women Vitaliya had encountered, who were all lean and muscular. Vitaliya supposed this fit with everything she'd heard about Ioanna and her lack of interest in athletics, but she had the sense, though, Ioanna was a little bit unhappy with her body. Perhaps it was just one more thing to set her apart from her family.

Vitaliya's mind went to her own family. She had certainly not forgiven her father, but she would admit he came out ahead of Ionnes, at least when it came to paternal instinct. And while she sometimes felt distanced from her brother, she could say with complete confidence that he had never seriously contemplated murdering her, and if he had, she'd done something to deserve it.

As for their respective mothers...Vitaliya had only caught glimpses of Enessa during her time in the Imperial Palace. This wasn't entirely unexpected since she was essentially running the empire in her husband's absence, but Netheia had barely mentioned her except to complain. Ioanna hadn't said much about her either.

Vitaliya's own mother, Queen Isabetta, died when Vitaliya was fifteen. Her illness had not been a plague or something the priests of Adranus could easily heal. Vitaliya still didn't completely understand it even though the priests had done their best to explain.

They'd kept her alive for as long as they could, burning out the disease wherever they could find it in her body. But nothing could prevent it from rallying and re-growing. In the end, Isabetta had announced she no longer wished for the priests to treat her, for the daily infusions of magic were leaving her just as weak and disoriented as the illness.

Vitaliya could not be angry at her mother for that.

The entire country had mourned her loss, and Vitaliya had always assumed her father would never remarry, or if he did, it would surely be a political alliance because how could he ever love someone the way he had loved Isabetta?

"What's the matter?" asked Ioanna, and Vitaliya realized she'd been glaring at the surface of the water. She looked up and smiled.

"Oh, nothing," she said. "Just thinking too hard. Not about you—about my family."

"Your family?"

"Oh, don't worry about it!" Vitaliya waved her hand. "It's nothing, especially compared to all this."

"I'm sure you'd like to send a courier to your father?"

"No!"

"But he must be concerned—"

"I want him to be concerned," said Vitaliya. "I want him to be sorry."

Ioanna didn't say anything, but Vitaliya could sense she did not quite approve of this.

"Don't *worry*!" cried Vitaliya. "I mean it! My problems are so silly compared to yours. I don't want you to be thinking about them. Really."

"If you insist," murmured Ioanna.

"Shh, let's talk about something else," said Vitaliya. "Tell me what the Order of the Sun wants to do. Are there enough of them to stand against the army?"

"No," said Ioanna. "At least, not under ordinary circumstances. But most of our soldiers are in Masim right now. So long as they're not called back, I think we might have a chance. Knight-Commander Livius wants us to recruit more supporters. Enough to get into the city before the coronation. But it's not enough just to gather an army. We need to be able to feed them, get them weapons, and possibly train them if they've only ever been farmers or laborers in the past."

"Well..." Vitaliya's voice trailed off as she realized she had no idea where one might even begin with that. "How are you going to do it?"

"Grandmother thinks we can get support from some of the lesser noble families. I don't mean to doubt her, but—"

"Families that aren't at court, you mean?"

"Yes, primarily."

"That makes sense," said Vitaliya. "With everything we've seen, I mean. Doesn't it? Everyone in the palace has to act happy with the emperor—or maybe they really are happy, I don't know. But out here, there's no pretending, is there?"

"I suppose not. Still, I can't imagine any of them agreeing. If I fail, they'll lose everything."

"Given how things are going, they're going to lose everything either way," pointed out Vitaliya. "That is, unless they all pick up with Acydon. I still can't believe we met a chaos god, by the way. And I can't believe he was just some man with bad clothes."

"Well, he was only a very little god," said Ioanna. "And his domain was only apathy. I don't expect he'll ever become very influential."

"Do you think you'll send the Order of the Sun after him?"

"I don't think he should be our priority right now. There's so much else that needs to be done. And I know Iolar would hate for those people to go on worshipping him, but maybe it's for the best right now. He didn't lie when he said he's done more for them than the nobility has."

"That's not your fault," said Vitaliya. "You know that, don't you?"

"I know," murmured Ioanna. "But I can't help but wonder, if I'd only known about this before...if I could have changed things. How many of our citizens died of starvation while I sat in a palace?"

"You can't think like that! You're going to make everything so much better. People are going to love you."

Ioanna was the first to step out of the bath, wrapping herself in one of the soft linen sheets that had been left near the edge for drying. Vitaliya watched as she got up and went to the wardrobe to select a new dress. Unlike the one she had been wearing for the last few days, this one was made of fine, light material and had a long skirt that reached her ankles.

Vitaliya pulled herself out of the water with a great deal of reluctance. She did not want to put her old dress back on, given the state of it. Somehow, she had not noticed how awful and stained and dirty it had become when they'd been traveling. But now, she could think of nothing else. She only pulled it on because the alternative was walking around with nothing on, and even though that might have been acceptable in Xytae, she would not be able to bring herself to do it. Then she went to go find Netheia's room.

The first door in the direction Ioanna had indicated was in fact the same one Vitaliya had been shown to yesterday. She hadn't spent much time in it since there were so many other rooms to explore, but the decorations suggested it was Netheia's. Weapons hung from every wall—though even Vitaliya could tell most of them were ornamental and far too impractical to ever use in a real fight.

She opened the wardrobe and began to sort through the dresses. Luckily, Netheia was larger than her sister, or at least not as thin. She selected a midlength dress in pale-blue fabric and was relieved when it fit nicely.

More out of nosiness than necessity, Vitaliya continued to search through the standing wardrobe. She pulled open the drawer at the base and found more folded clothing. As she lifted a few of the garments up, she uncovered a small coin purse and a short dagger in a sheath.

Vitaliya unsheathed the dagger carefully. She thought it might be blunt or rusty since Netheia hadn't mentioned visiting her grandmother recently, but it seemed sharp. And unlike the weapons on the wall, this one was obviously meant to be used. It was small enough she was able to slide it into her shirt. She did not think she would need it inside the former empress's villa, but she'd spent the last few days feeling so vulnerable that she did not think it would hurt to carry it with her.

There was a soft knock at the door, and Vitaliya hurried to open it. Ioanna was waiting there for her.

"Are you ready?" she asked. "I'm sure they've prepared something for us to eat."

Vitaliya hadn't really expected Ioanna to wait for her, especially since it seemed she had so much to do, and so the inclusion warmed her. She liked being with Ioanna, despite their differences, and hoped Ioanna was starting to feel the same way.

The stereotype of the devoted follower of Iolar was not precisely a pleasant one—a person who prized order over compassion and ritual over meaning, obsessed with rules and hierarchies, and generally opposed to having fun. But she didn't think Ioanna fit that image. Yes, anyone could see she had a very strict sense of justice and preferred peace and quiet over noise and chaos, but there was more to her. In fact, Vitaliya suspected her reserved nature had less to do with her devotion to Iolar and more to do with her upbringing, and her fear of what the consequences of expressing herself honestly might be.

And, of course, there was the matter of her blessing. Truthsayers featured in legends far more frequently than they did in reality. Vitaliya paused to examine her feelings on this. Was she afraid of Ioanna? No. Not really. Did she feel as though she must watch her words, or to think carefully before she spoke in her presence? Again, no. Was that foolish? Perhaps. But Vitaliya had no intention of deceiving Ioanna. Keeping track of lies tended to be more trouble than it was worth.

Ioanna led Vitaliya down the halls and into a large dining room, which had been set with food but contained no people, not even Irianthe's servants. They sat down beside each other to eat.

"I wonder how Otho is doing," murmured Vitaliya around a too-large mouthful of bread. "I'll be so sad if he left without saying goodbye."

"He better not have," said Ioanna. "We've got to reward him for his trouble. And I'd feel better if he remained here until this is settled. He could be in danger."

"I don't know if you'll be able to convince him. He's going to want to get back to his villages. Especially at this time of year."

"I know," sighed Ioanna. "But if something happens to him just because he aided us, I'll never forgive myself."

"What do you think might happen?" asked Vitaliya. "None of those priestesses would have any way of knowing he helped us. They'd leave him alone. Wouldn't they?"

"I'm not sure," murmured Ioanna. "I just have this feeling it's not only priestesses after us. Do you remember what Acydon said? That she'd coerced more people over to her side?"

"He was telling the truth?" Even knowing Ioanna's blessing, Vitaliya was skeptical. Surely a chaos god would have lied? Just on principle? "Well, who else would Netheia send?"

"I don't think he was talking about Netheia at all," said Ioanna.

"Who, then? Your mother?"

The sound of sharp footsteps on the cold tile floor cut off whatever Ioanna was about to say. Both young women turned to see Irianthe enter the dining room.

"Finally, there you are," she said. "Ioanna, finish quickly and come to my study. We must begin planning."

"I'll come too," said Vitaliya.

"That will not be necessary," Grandmother Irianthe replied in a clipped, impatient tone. "This matter does not concern Vesolda."

"It's all right, Vitaliya," murmured Ioanna. "It's probably going to be very boring anyway. You should find out where Otho went. And I'll come find you when I'm finished."

Vitaliya was not happy to be excluded, but she decided she would try to cooperate for Ioanna's sake. And besides, while she wanted to be near Ioanna, especially now, she had to admit she was not at her most attentive during meetings of statecraft.

Vitaliya decided to go in search of the stables, for she knew Otho's wagon had been brought there after their arrival. She didn't exactly know the way but decided that trying to find it on her own, rather than asking for help, might be a good way to pass the time while she waited for Ioanna to return.

Vitaliya made her way through the enormous garden, brushing the plants with her fingertips as she passed. She did not press any magic into them, for they would bloom in their own time, but she liked to feel the life pulsing through them and to sense their slow, steady breathing.

As she came to the center of the garden where all the plants converged symmetrically around a large, empty fountain, she realized she was not alone. A woman was sitting on one of the low stone benches, her hands in her lap and her expression distant. From the plain, simple way she was dressed, Vitaliya might have mistaken her for a servant, but she wore no apron or head coverings, and her hands were soft and smooth.

"Hello," said Vitaliya, not wanting to sneak up on the woman. But nevertheless, she startled, rising briefly but sharply from where she was seated.

"Oh!" said the woman. "I'm sorry. I was lost in thought."

"*I'm* sorry," said Vitaliya. "I should have..."

"No, no. It's not my garden." The woman smiled. Something about her face made it difficult for Vitaliya to gauge how old she was. "I don't think I've met you yet. Did you arrive with the princess?"

"Yes, I'm Vitaliya. Of Vesolda." She regretted that second part the moment the words left her, for she did not want the woman to become tense or overly formal. But the woman did not seem surprised. Perhaps she had already been told who Vitaliya was.

"I am Elyne. Of nowhere. Everywhere. Anywhere." Elyne's smile grew wider as though she was telling a joke. "I'm glad Ioanna didn't have to make the journey alone."

"I was searching for the priest who came in with us. I haven't seen him since yesterday, and we're afraid he'll sneak off without saying goodbye."

"The one with all the animals? I saw him earlier. You might be right about him leaving, though. I don't think he's comfortable here. Too tidy."

"I was afraid of that," sighed Vitaliya. "Well, Ioanna and I wanted to give him some sort of reward. If not for him, I don't think we'd have made it here."

"Priests aren't easily rewarded. The good ones, I mean. And Cyne's tend to lean more heavily toward good than some others I might name."

That was a curious observation, but Vitaliya could not quite disagree with it. "Are you with the Order of the Sun?"

"Not precisely. I'm here with one of the paladins, but I'm not a member of the Order."

"Well, don't feel bad. They won't let me in the meeting either."

Elyne laughed. "I'm sure it would put me to sleep. Still, I was hoping to catch a glimpse of the princess. I haven't seen her since she was small."

"Well, she's about my age now," said Vitaliya. "When did you meet her?"

"It was twelve, thirteen years ago, I think? And not for very long. An hour, at most. Her aunt was trying to sacrifice her to a chaos god."

"What!" Vitaliya felt her jaw drop. "She—she *what*?"

"Oh, she didn't tell you?" Elyne didn't sound concerned, though. "Like I said, it was a long time ago. Maybe she's forgotten."

"I don't think that's the sort of thing you forget!"

"It wasn't as dramatic as you're imagining. We managed to get her to safety before anything could happen. The cultists didn't even have a chance to lay a hand on her."

"But why did they want her?"

"Well, she's a very important young woman. She's going to shape the future of this nation. Perhaps even the continent. Not everyone wants the same things she does."

"But she was only...what, five years old? How could anyone—"

"Oh, people will do just about anything when their lives are at stake. And so will gods," said Elyne. "Count yourself lucky that you've never felt such desperation."

Vitaliya sat down on one of the stone benches, her plans to find Otho temporarily forgotten. "I can't imagine," she murmured. "How terrible. And how terrible for Ioanna."

"She's not quite safe yet," Elyne advised. "I'll do my best to keep an eye out, but I'm not sure where to expect an attack from next. Be careful, won't you? Don't trust anyone too easily."

"She, she said something similar this morning. But I don't think Netheia would attack here, do you? Ioanna seemed to think Oredia was a sort of neutral ground."

"Netheia?" repeated Elyne. She sounded confused. "Oh! The sister. I forgot about her."

"She's the one we're *fighting*," said Vitaliya, her brow knotting in concern. "This whole thing is her fault—"

The corner of Elyne's mouth twitched as though she was fighting back a laugh. Suddenly, inexplicably, Vitaliya thought of Acydon, lounging on his fence. *She really doesn't know!* he had marveled, speaking to Ioanna as though Vitaliya wasn't even there. *Why in the world does she think you're out here to begin with?*

"What's going on?" Vitaliya asked slowly.

In that moment, Elyne seemed so indescribably old. Older than her father, older than Grandmother Irianthe, older than the oldest person Vitaliya had ever seen. Her face had not changed, nor had her body. It was something about her eyes.

"The Ten are quarreling," Elyne said. "What you're witnessing between Ioanna and her sister is merely a reflection of what's happening in Asterium. It's been centuries in the making. Don't underestimate the importance, or the scope, of what is happening in Xytae."

Vitaliya did not know what to say to this. Of course, she had never doubted the existence of the gods—how could anyone when they granted blessings so freely? But to hear someone say they were taking an active role in events was a little more difficult to believe. Vitaliya had been taught the gods preferred to stand back and observe and allow Men to live their own lives. And in her experience, people who claimed to know the will of the gods beyond what they'd already mandated to their followers tended to have some sort of ulterior motive.

But Elyne did not give her the impression of a fanatic, nor of someone angling for a political advantage. She was calm and certain like a seer, and Vitaliya got the impression she didn't care very much if Vitaliya believed her words.

"I—I should go," said Vitaliya. "I've got to catch Otho before he leaves."

Elyne nodded, and her eyes went distant once more as though she was listening to something that Vitaliya could not hear.

AS EXPECTED, SHE found Otho in the stables. The stables were not part of the villa; rather, they'd been built outside the high walls just a short walk away so the smell of the horses would not pollute the residential areas.

"I hope you weren't going to sneak away," said Vitaliya as she entered the stable. Otho turned, and she saw he'd already hitched Daisy to the wagon. "Oooh, you were! How rude of you."

Otho gave her a guilty smile and rubbed at the back of his neck. "Princess Vitaliya—"

"Oh, no. Now I'm a princess." Vitaliya struck herself in the forehead, then shifted her hand to see if this had made him laugh. "Are you going to refuse us when we try to give you a reward?"

"There is no need for—"

"I knew it!" Vitaliya considered dropping to the ground dramatically but changed her mind after taking a closer look at the stable floor. "Let me hug the chickens goodbye. I'm not going to hug you, though. I'm very cross with you."

"You don't need me here," said Otho. "I'd only be in the way, and I'm sure the empress mother has no use for me. But if it helps at all, I do believe Cyne guided me to you. And I believe nothing I accomplish in the future will be of greater importance than what I've done here."

"Oh, don't say that!" Vitaliya cried. "You're going to help so many more people—and animals, of course—"

"Certainly, I hope that is the case," agreed Otho. "And I am glad to do it. But I don't think it is an exaggeration to say what is being planned here concerns all of Xytae, and perhaps even lands beyond."

"You won't stay, then?" asked Vitaliya. "Not even for a few more days?"

"My people will worry if I am missing for too long. And I am not meant to remain in such luxury. It is beautiful here, but it's not where I'm meant to be. I prefer the roads and the open fields, and knowing I'm doing Cyne's work."

"At least stay until Ioanna comes out of her meeting," wheedled Vitaliya. "She'll be disappointed if she doesn't get to say goodbye properly."

"Very well, but I sincerely hope she does not try to offer me a reward. I already have all I require, and the temple will provide me with anything I lack. Whatever she might be thinking to give me would be put to better use helping our people."

"Fine! I'll tell her so," said Vitaliya. She climbed into the back of the wagon, where the chickens were already settled and crossed her legs. "But if you ever find yourself in Vesolda, come visit me. Or maybe once Ioanna is empress—I'll make sure they invite you to the coronation. I won't let them forget."

"If it happens in the summer, I may be too busy to attend," said Otho, but he was smiling, teasing. "Some of us must work for our living."

"How terrible. What have you done to deserve such a fate?" Vitaliya took one of the chickens in her arms and held it carefully in the way Otho had taught her with one arm beneath to support the body. She'd never considered whether a chicken might make a good pet, but Otho's were calm and surprisingly affectionate. "Goodbye, egg friend."

"If you're serious about keeping chickens of your own, make sure you get more than one," said Otho. "They're social animals, just like Men. And they're perfectly capable of becoming lonely."

"I'll remember," Vitaliya promised. She'd be the only girl at Bergavenna with pet chickens! Or at least she would be for a week or two until people started copying her. But that was still a long way off. She was still not ready to think of returning home.

THE DOOR TO Irianthe Isinthi's study was under guard when Vitaliya approached it. Two men, both dressed in leather armor, had been posted on either side of it. But they did not draw their swords or even frown at her as she came nearer, so she felt confident enough to ask, "Are they still in there?"

"Yes, Princess," said one. "The empress mother has ordered they not be disturbed."

Could Irianthe still be called the empress mother now that Ionnes was dead? Would she become the empress grandmother when Ioanna took the throne? Vitaliya considered this as she wandered back off down the hall. Surely Enessa would be empress mother then? She had the impression Irianthe wouldn't care very much if Enessa took that title from her.

With nothing else to do, Vitaliya went back to her room, which she could not stop thinking of as Netheia's. Maybe she would take some of the weapons off the wall and swing them around just to see what it felt like and hopefully not cut any of her fingers off. She'd been encouraged to throw a javelin when she'd been among Netheia's friends, but they'd all laughed quite rudely at her first attempt, and so she'd feigned disinterest in the sport ever since.

She examined a sword hanging from the wall. It was a lot larger than the swords the guards outside Irianthe's study carried, and she doubted she'd be able to get it down—and if she did, she certainly wouldn't be able to get it back up afterward.

The room was warm and comfortable, and the bed was still made from yesterday. Vitaliya wondered if the servants had taken note of this and, if they had, what their opinion was. She slid her shoes off and lay down on the soft mattress. Her last, irrational thought before she fell asleep was of home of her empty room at Bergavenna and if anyone was missing her.

Chapter Nine

IOANNA

Knight-Commander Livius had brought two paladins with him from Ieflaria. One was a fellow Xytan, who had left the country with the rest of the Order when Ioanna was young. His name was Vel, and he'd spent a few years fighting dragons in eastern Ieflaria before they ceased their attacks. Following that, he'd remained in Birsgen, prepared to serve if needed but seldom called upon.

The other paladin was a woman, and one Ioanna had met before in childhood. Her name was Orsina, and she was not Xytan, but Vesoldan. Orsina had been responsible for rescuing Ioanna from a chaos cult when she was seven years old. Her mother's sister, Aunt Livia, had invited Ioanna to her home deep in the countryside for a visit. That visit had ended abruptly, with her rescuers turning up just in time to save her.

Ioanna barely remembered Aunt Livia. The woman had vanished afterward, and neither of Ioanna's parents ever mentioned her again, nor did anyone else at court. In a way, it was as though Livia had never existed, as though they'd rather erase her than acknowledge the empress's sister had worshipped a chaos god.

Ioanna frequently wondered if her father had ordered Livia to be executed for her crimes, but lacked the courage to ask.

Orsina was a little bit older now, but her face had not changed too much. Ioanna found she remembered the paladin vividly, unlike Aunt Livia, though their meeting had been short. At the time, she'd seemed so much older and wiser than Ioanna, but in retrospect she'd probably been around the same age Ioanna was now.

Orsina had not acted alone during Ioanna's rescue. Accompanying her was another woman, the one responsible for getting Ioanna out of Livia's house discreetly.

Are you Talcia? she had asked, for something about the woman gave her the impression that she might be. But the woman only smiled and said no, her name was Aelia, and Ioanna had probably never heard of her because she was not very important...

And that was true, but Ioanna had remembered the name and looked it up later, when she was safe at home once more. With the aid of the priests, she managed to locate a single short entry on a very, very long list of everyone the Order of the Sun classified as a chaos god. The entry in question was only a single line long, reading simply, 'Aelia – Goddess of Caprice.'

Aelia had not *seemed* like a chaos goddess. Or at least not what she would expect one to be like given their behavior in stories, legends, and rumors. Chaos gods, Ioanna understood, manifested in awful, monstrous bodies and tricked, bribed, or terrified innocent people into worshiping them. Aelia's body had not been monstrous at all. If not for Ioanna's blessing, she might have passed for an ordinary woman. And she hadn't tried to get Ioanna to worship her or even talked about worshippers at all. She'd been there to help her, to get Ioanna to safety.

Afterward, Ioanna asked Archpriest Lailus if the lists were ever wrong; if the scribes ever made a mistake when they were writing down names. There were so many gods in Asterium, after all, and sometimes they were called different things in different lands. It would only be natural if people mixed some of them up. But Archpriest Lailus said he did not know, and the Order of the Sun could probably give her a better answer. But, of course, the Order of the Sun was gone, and so Ioanna could do nothing but wonder, speculate, and hope.

The one good thing to come out of the entire mess was Ioanna had been able to compose a hasty letter to Knight-Commander Livius. She shuddered to think how naive and foolish it must have sounded to him! And yet, she did not regret sending it. At a time when she had felt so utterly alone, reaching out to the Order of the Sun had given her hope that someday her life might change.

Before now, Ioanna had never been allowed to set foot inside her grandmother's study. Whenever she expressed interest, Grandmother Irianthe would tell her to go visit the Temple of Ethi, for their books were not nearly so expensive. In retrospect, her grandmother probably just didn't want Netheia following Ioanna in and swinging a sword around.

The study was large with a colored marble floor. Some of the shelves had been built to hold books, while others were the square slots meant to keep scrolls organized. At the center of the room was a large table of polished wood, and this was what Ioanna and the others gathered around to discuss their plans. Except they clearly had already discussed things before her arrival because she felt as though it was less of a conversation and more of a lecture.

"We will take advantage of my holdings in Nassai," said Grandmother Irianthe, naming a rural area located west of Xyuluthe. "It is remote enough that we can safely use it as a gathering place for your supporters, but near enough that it will not require an undue amount of resources to march on the capital."

"You don't think it's too near?" worried Ioanna. "If Netheia learns—"

"I'm sure she will, eventually," agreed Grandmother Irianthe. "But by the time she does, it will be too late to call the legions back from Masim in time to intercept us. To help ensure this, I will go to Xyuluthe. I do not think it will require much effort to convince them they cannot risk losing ground."

That was probably true. The Xytan court would view it as a shameful thing to retreat. Especially now, when hatred of the Masimi would be higher than ever following the death of her father.

Ioanna supposed that was their greatest advantage— the fact that, even if Netheia did gain control over the armies, most of their forces were too far away to be of any real use to her.

"I also wish to speak to your mother to understand her intentions." Grandmother Irianthe's expression darkened and her fingers interlocked. "I cannot say I approve of how she is handling this."

Ioanna knew she ought to be grateful people more experienced than she were removing a great deal of responsibility from her shoulders, but for some reason, she was not. She felt like a pawn in their hands, to be moved from place to place for their benefit.

But what choice did she have? She could hardly send them all away and proclaim she'd take the throne from her sister without anyone's help.

Perhaps it would have been easier if she could sense deception, or at least ulterior motives on them. But though the meeting stretched on for hours while they pointed at spots on the map and argued about details, Ioanna felt no signs anyone in the room was anything other than precisely what they purported to be.

Would it be different when she was empress? Or would it all be the same, sitting quietly in a large chair while other people told her what she would do next?

And what's wrong with that? Ioanna asked herself. *What's wrong with taking advice from people who know better than I do?* Refusing counsel out of sheer hubris was the sort of senseless thing she might expect from Netheia. But what if everyone thought her weak because of it?

"Ioanna?" Her grandmother's voice cut through her thoughts. "Are you listening?"

Ioanna blinked and rubbed at her eyes. "I'm sorry," she said. "I think I need to stop. Just for an hour to clear my head. I'm going in circles."

"I think that would do us all some good," said Knight-Commander Livius. He got to his feet, and the other two paladins followed his example. "We have made good progress for now. It is becoming too warm in here."

Perhaps her grandmother wanted to object, but Ioanna couldn't bring herself to care. She hurried out of the room, ahead of all the others. The hall was significantly cooler than the study had been, and a soft breeze blew in from the garden.

Orsina was the last paladin to emerge from Grandmother Irianthe's study, and Ioanna waited behind so she might catch her. They hadn't had a chance to speak at all before Grandmother Irianthe called the meeting to a start, but Orsina had given her a smile that suggested she did remember Ioanna. When she saw Ioanna waiting for her, she smiled again.

"I'd hoped for a chance to speak with you," said Ioanna. "It's been such a long time—"

"I thought you must have forgotten me," said Orsina. "It was so long ago, after all."

"No! Not even a little bit." Ioanna felt herself smile. "Is Aelia here with you?"

"Oh yes, she's about. She's just not terribly good at meetings, so I didn't bring her."

Ioanna nodded. "Can I ask you—"

"Come with me," Orsina said. "I don't want to shout this out for the servants to hear."

They went into the gardens and walked in silence for a time. The day was peaceful and bright, and Ioanna found it difficult to dwell on empires, sisters, and military plans.

"After Kynith and Aunt Livia, I looked at the records," said Ioanna at last. "And they said Aelia was a chaos goddess. But I thought that must be a mistake."

"It is outdated information," said Orsina. "I've made a special effort to have her name stricken from those records, but it is difficult to have it done in Xytae, given that the Order has no presence here any longer."

Ioanna frowned. "So she is a chaos goddess?"

"She was," said Orsina. "Once. Redemption is not only for the mortal races. When you met her, she had only taken the first few steps away from her old domain. That was more than ten years ago...though I'll admit it does not seem so long. It has all gone by very quickly, and we've been keeping busy in the meantime. I'm glad we were in Ieflaria when Knight-Commander Livius received his summons."

"But she changed her domain?" pressed Ioanna. She did not want to be rude, but now she was thinking of the conversation she'd had with her grandmother after her arrival yesterday. *If you believe you can reason her out of her own domain,* Grandmother Irianthe had said of Reygmadra. She'd only said it to point out how absurd Ioanna was being, and Ioanna hadn't been meant to consider it as a legitimate course of action. But the idea was compelling.

"Yes, you've no reason to fear her," said Orsina, misunderstanding Ioanna's interest. "Honestly, even before she shifted, she wasn't one of the more dangerous ones. Whatever awful things you're imagining—"

"I'm not," Ioanna interrupted. "That is, I'm not asking because I'm afraid of her. I'm sure you wouldn't have brought her here if she was dangerous. But I've been thinking of..." Words failed her as she was struck by how *foolish* this line of questioning was. Reygmadra was the goddess of warfare, Eighth of the Ten and one of the most powerful gods in Asterium. She would not be coaxed away from that! Not by one so insignificant as Ioanna!

"Ioanna?" Orsina prompted.

"Never mind," said Ioanna. "Just—just a thought." Persuading a little whisper of a chaos goddess away from the path of evil was certainly impressive, but nothing compared to what it would take to change Reygmadra's nature.

"Are you certain?" Orsina sounded a little concerned. Ioanna nodded. "Well, if you change your mind..."

Besides, even if Ioanna was capable of such a thing, how would she ever communicate her ideas to Reygmadra? She doubted the goddess would listen to her prayers, let alone consent to manifest just so Ioanna could lecture her.

"Don't worry; it was only a passing thought," said Ioanna. "But please excuse me. I should go find Princess Vitaliya. She wanted to attend the meeting, but my grandmother wouldn't allow it." Vitaliya probably wouldn't have been capable of sitting through it if she *had* been allowed in, but Ioanna felt a little sorry for her, nevertheless.

She left the garden and went back toward the house, deciding she'd check Vitaliya's bedroom first. The halls of the residential area were quiet, and Ioanna had a feeling the servants were busy preparing for the midday meal.

Ioanna took a deep breath and knocked on the door that she'd always thought of as Netheia's. "Vitaliya?" she called. "Are you in there?"

"Yes, I'm here!" came Vitaliya's voice, slightly muffled. "Come in!"

Ioanna tried the door and found it unlocked. She entered the room and saw Vitaliya sitting on the bed, her hair in disarray as though she'd been lying down. Vitaliya brightened up at the sight of her.

"There you are! I thought they'd never let you go!"

"I'm sorry. Did I wake you?"

Vitaliya waved her hand to dismiss the sentiment. "Don't worry! I wasn't tired, just bored. I had no idea the meeting would go on for so long."

"I know, I'm sorry. But we're not finished. We've only stopped for a short break."

Vitaliya got up off the bed and smoothed her skirt with her palms. "What did the paladins say? Do they have a plan?"

"We're working out a route I'm to follow to gather supporters," explained Ioanna. "We're still figuring out the details, but we're going to move through the north, then approach Xyuluthe from the west just in time for the coronation."

"That's exciting," said Vitaliya. "When are we going to leave?"

Ioanna hesitated. Then she said, "Perhaps you ought to remain here. Or go on to Ieflaria, or somewhere safer."

Vitaliya pouted, sticking out her lower lip as far as she could manage in the same way a young child might. "We already had this conversation. I'm not going anywhere. I'm staying with you."

"It could be dangerous. It *will* be dangerous. And if you travel with me, people might interpret it as Vesolda supporting me."

"So what if they do? I don't care. Besides, Vesolda *would* support you if they knew what was happening here."

"What if Netheia becomes empress? If she wins, and she decides Vesolda opposed her reign, she might want to take revenge. Your people could suffer."

"I don't, I don't want to leave," insisted Vitaliya. "And besides, who is going to recognize me all the way out here? I'll just go on being Floriana. I'll pretend to be your maid."

"I don't think you would be able to pass for a maid," Ioanna said staunchly. "What will happen when someone asks you to mend something? Or wash something?"

"I'll do my best!" But apparently Vitaliya could tell Ioanna was not convinced by this, so she added, "It's too early to decide anything yet. You don't even know where you're going to go first. And if you leave me here, I'll hold my breath until I faint."

"If you're not going to take this seriously—"

"I can help!" Vitaliya cried. "Think of all the towns and villages you're going to travel through. They'll be low on supplies and desperate. There are not enough priests of Eyvindr in the north. I can make their crops grow. And if we can do that for them, they might be more inclined to take your side. It's easier to think when you're not hungry."

Ioanna had been fully prepared to dismiss any of Vitaliya's arguments, but that last one made her pause. Vitaliya was silly, but her blessing...used judiciously, it could mean the difference between success and failure.

"Perhaps," Ioanna said. "But it truly will be dangerous. I don't want to see you killed because of me."

"And I don't want any more people to go hungry. It's time I contributed to something. Besides, I don't like the idea of you alone with just a bunch of boring paladins for company. You'll get lonely and need someone to talk to. A real person, I mean."

Ioanna reached out and brushed a loose strand of hair out of Vitaliya's face. The gesture was small but vulnerable, and Ioanna hoped Vitaliya recognized the significance of it. Vitaliya reached up to catch Ioanna's hand with her own and pressed it against her own cheek.

"That would be terribly selfish of me," Ioanna whispered. "Bringing you along just for myself."

"You're not, remember? I'm coming to make the fields grow. So your army of ten thousand soldiers has something to eat, so they aren't forced to resort to cannibalism. And so the nobles don't slam the door in your face when you come up to ask for help."

Ioanna gave a tiny smile. "Maybe."

"Oh! And you've got to say goodbye to Otho. He's refusing to stay; I only just barely convinced him to not sneak off. And he won't take a reward either."

"I was hoping he'd stay."

"I know, but he's got people waiting for him. People and sheep." Vitaliya's fingers curled around Ioanna's hand and squeezed it briefly. "How much time do you have before you need to get back?"

"I'm not sure, honestly."

"Let's hurry, then." Still holding on to Ioanna's hand, she began to move toward the door, pulling Ioanna along. Ioanna allowed this, though a small part of her hoped they would not encounter her grandmother or any of the paladins. Surely they would not approve of...of whatever Ioanna and Vitaliya had. Not while she was supposed to be focused on taking back her throne.

"I met the strangest woman, earlier," Vitaliya said. "She came with the paladins, but she wasn't a member of the Order."

"That would be Aelia," said Ioanna.

"What? No, her name was Elyne. She was so odd—not in a dangerous sort of way, I think, just very different. Like a seer, or something." Vitaliya went on chattering, describing the woman she'd encountered. Undoubtably, it had been Aelia. Had she changed her name in order to distance herself from the past? Orsina had not mentioned anything like that—but then, Ioanna had rather monopolized the conversation.

They made their way along to the stables where Vitaliya said she'd already encountered Otho earlier today. As they came in sight of the structure, Ioanna saw his familiar wagon was indeed prepared for departure. Her stomach sank as she realized Otho probably would have left hours ago if Vitaliya hadn't requested he stay, and her selfish desire to see him off personally had robbed him of daylight to travel by.

The fact he wasn't going to accept a reward only made her feel guiltier still. He'd gone to so much trouble to help them, and they'd inconvenienced him every step of the way.

She supposed she could reward the Temple of Cyne once she was empress. Ioanna understood temples never turned down attention from the nobility, no matter what god they were devoted to.

"You're really going, then?" asked Ioanna.

"I am afraid so," said Otho. "I know you'd prefer I remain here, but..."

"I will not order you to stay," Ioanna reassured him. "I understand your people need you far more than I do. I only ask you be careful in your travels, especially with the priestesses."

"I am not completely helpless," Otho said, a smile pulling at his lips. "I promise. But for your sake, I will be cautious."

"For *your* sake, not mine," insisted Ioanna. "And if you feel you are in danger, return to Oredia."

"The temple in Xyuluthe will be enough to keep me safe if things should come to that. Don't think of me. What you're doing is infinitely more important."

"I wouldn't be doing it if you hadn't found us," said Ioanna. "Vitaliya and I were helpless, and I'm certain the priestesses would have easily..."

"Do not thank me; thank Cyne for guiding me to you," said Otho. "Perhaps we will meet again after this is all done. But if we do not—"

"Don't say that!" interrupted Vitaliya. "You've got to come to the coronation at least. Ioanna, you must invite him."

"My coronation may be held at the point of a sword," said Ioanna. "If that is the case, we may not have time to send out invitations."

"Ohh," sighed Vitaliya. "That's too bad. You'll have to hold a second one, then. Afterwards. A proper one. And invite everyone, from everywhere."

Ioanna tried to imagine this but found she could not visualize it with any clarity. Like the plans her grandmother and the paladins had laid out, it all felt unreal and abstract, nearer to fantasy than reality.

Otho was hugged quite tightly by Vitaliya, and clasped Ioanna's hands reverently before climbing into his wagon. With only a soft shake of the reins, he set off down the hill in the direction of the road.

Ioanna and Vitaliya stood there watching until the wagon disappeared from view.

BACK IN HER grandmother's study, Ioanna stared down at the map of Xytae and the path marked upon it with little silver pieces. Nearly all of the places marked were locations Ioanna had never visited before, and she was a bit dismayed to see they would be avoiding every major city in the region.

"Orsina and Vel will accompany you on your journey, and serve as your bodyguards," explained Knight-Commander Livius. "I will be returning to Ieflaria, to gather the rest of the Order and meet your forces in Nassai."

Her forces. Even now, the term felt strange. She still could not imagine anyone swearing allegiance to her. What if she arrived in Nassai with only her guards and a handful of farmers? It would be mortifying.

"As for Princess Vitaliya, she may remain here, or I will have her escorted home," continued Grandmother Irianthe. "I believe the latter would be the most prudent course of action."

"I think it might be better if Vitaliya accompanied me, actually," Ioanna said. "I discussed the matter with her, and—"

"Ioanna, don't be ridiculous," said Grandmother Irianthe, surprising her with how irate she sounded. "There's no place for a girl like her in a military procession. At best, she'll be an unnecessary distraction."

"She may not be a warrior," said Ioanna, fighting down her annoyance that, even now, her grandmother's inclination was to dismiss anyone who could not swing a sword. "But I've seen firsthand what her blessing is capable of. She has Eyvindr's magic—something our people have been forced to do without for far too long. I believe her presence will help us appeal to those who might otherwise be inclined to turn us away out of fear."

Grandmother Irianthe was obviously unconvinced, but Ioanna glanced away from her long enough to see Livius looked very curious. Perhaps if she could win him over to her side, her grandmother would back down.

"There is no strategic advantage to be gained by bringing her with you," said Grandmother Irianthe in a clipped tone, and the lie was so blatant that it nearly knocked Ioanna out of her seat. "Enough of this now. We have far more important—"

"You're lying to me." Ioanna pressed her hand to her forehead to ease the pain. "You don't think that at all. I'm not going to turn away one of our few advantages unless you're able to give me a proper reason."

The atmosphere in the room shifted instantaneously, and Ioanna saw Vel's hand go to his sword before Livius shot him a sharp glare. The paladins were on her side after all.

"I will not discuss this matter in front of an audience," said Grandmother Irianthe. "And you may thank me for that."

"What are you afraid of? Vesolda? You think they'll turn on us if their princess is killed or harmed in a Xytan battle?"

"You're only proving me correct," said Irianthe. "Can't you see it? She's already become a distraction. A liability. Leave her here or send her back to Bergavenna. You can call her back when you've taken Xyuluthe, and then I don't care if you make her empress consort! But until then, I won't allow thousands of lives to be lost because of your infatuation!"

For one brief, awful moment, Ioanna imagined slapping her grandmother across the face. The impulse left as quickly as it had come, but the sick, guilty sensation in her stomach remained behind.

"I do not agree with your assessment," said Ioanna, fighting to keep her voice level. She thought of the way her mother nearly always remained calm no matter how nobles and advisors pushed at her. "And the fact remains that many of those we solicit will not wish to support us unless we have something to offer in return. Something *immediate,* not distant promises. Vitaliya's blessing is extremely powerful, and our people are hungry. It could mean the difference between success and failure for us."

"Ioanna, you are about to embark on the most important military campaign of your life. What happens here will change the course of history. Netheia will look at

Vitaliya and see your greatest weakness. You're a fool if you think she won't seek to exploit it."

"I will not allow that."

"She will not seek your permission first!" snapped Grandmother Irianthe.

Silence descended upon the room. Ioanna looked at each of the paladins in turn, but none of them spoke. Were they waiting to see if she would bend to her grandmother's will or assert herself as empress? Even now, her instinct was to back down and apologize. She did her best to suppress it.

"We're not accomplishing anything with this," Ioanna said at last. "I'm not going to sit here and be shouted at. We'll break for now, and when we return—"

"Ioanna!" said Grandmother Irianthe sharply.

Ioanna ignored her and rose from her seat.

"Ioanna we do not have time for this!"

"I am tired of arguing with you. Vitaliya will accompany me. This is my campaign, not yours. I am grateful for your support, but I will not allow you to overrule my choices. In an hour we will return to discuss our route through the north, and I don't want to hear anything more about Vitaliya."

The expression on Grandmother Irianthe's face suggested she was more confused than angry. Ioanna did not really blame her. Her natural inclination had always been to obey her elders, and she'd spent twenty years trying to compensate for her blessing by being inoffensive and passive.

Ioanna exited the room quickly, not wanting her grandmother to have a chance to order her back.

"Ioanna?" That was Vitaliya, and after a moment of confusion, Ioanna realized she'd been loitering just outside the door either trying to eavesdrop or, more likely, just waiting for the meeting to end. "Are you done? What's—?"

"We are done for now," said Ioanna. "Come on, I need to be somewhere else."

"Did something happen?" Vitaliya frowned, obviously concerned.

"Don't worry," Ioanna soothed. "It's hardly important. Come on, I'm tired of standing here."

"Oh!" Vitaliya's face lit. "Can we see Oredia? The town, I mean. I want to visit!"

"Yes, that's fine." Too late, Ioanna realized this might not be a good idea after all. Her grandmother had mentioned priestesses lurking about. "No. Vitaliya, wait—"

But Vitaliya had never been inclined to wait for anything and rushed in the direction of the garden. By the time Ioanna caught up with her, she was smiling so broadly Ioanna decided it wouldn't hurt to spend a little bit of time in Oredia.

OREDIA WAS A pretty town, located in the shadow of the former empress's estate. Many of the residents were employed by Grandmother Irianthe as servants, and even those who were not supplied the villa with everything it needed. Before her grandmother's arrival, it had been an obscure and not terribly important location. Afterward, there'd been a little bit of an attempt by the nobility to turn it into somewhere worth visiting, but Irianthe herself had resisted these changes, saying she'd left Xyuluthe for a reason and had no intention of replicating it in the peaceful north. Now, it was practically her own personal empire.

When they caught the scent of fresh bread, Vitaliya bolted in the direction of the nearest bakery. Ioanna was fully prepared to do nothing more than stare longingly at the baker's wares, but Vitaliya surprised Ioanna by pulling a coin purse from her pocket.

"Where did you get that?" Ioanna whispered. Had her grandmother given it to Vitaliya? This seemed highly unlikely, and yet it was the only explanation she could think of.

"I stole it from your sister," explained Vitaliya brightly. "She left it in her room, and I've decided I'm owed it for the trouble she's put me through."

Ioanna had not realized how hungry she was until she bit into her roll. She'd been so anxious that she'd hardly thought of it.

Her mind returned to the confrontation with her grandmother. Part of her still could not believe she'd been so assertive. And to her grandmother of all people! Guilt squeezed at her stomach. Would Grandmother Irianthe withdraw her support now? But then, what kind of empress would Ioanna be if she allowed her grandmother to dictate her every move?

She looked around, realizing she'd lost track of Vitaliya. Panic rose in her chest as she remembered her grandmother's claim that she'd twice driven priestesses of Reygmadra from her lands—but then she caught sight of her a minute later, near the banks of the river, investigating some wildflowers.

"Don't fall in," Ioanna called because Vitaliya's sandals were already sinking into the soft mud, and Ioanna could easily envision her losing her balance. "Vitaliya—"

"I'll be all right!" But just as Vitaliya said this, she stumbled, and one of her feet landed in the water. "I'll dry!"

When Vitaliya returned to Ioanna's side a few minutes later, the edges of her skirt were soaked and muddy. But Vitaliya hardly seemed to mind.

"You seemed upset when you came out of the meeting," observed Vitaliya after a period of peaceful silence. "Is everything, you know, all right?"

"Oh." Ioanna shook her head. "It's just my grandmother. Someone's told her your bed wasn't slept in, and now she's cross with me. She doesn't want you to accompany me when I go to gather supporters."

"I'm not that bad!" Vitaliya puffed up a little like a bird attempting to intimidate a predator. "I'm a princess of Vesolda, and if I'm not good enough for her granddaughter, then nobody is!"

"I don't think her objection is personal. I think she just doesn't want me getting distracted right now. By anyone or anything. She said she didn't care if I make you empress consort later—"

"Oh! Don't threaten me!"

Ioanna elbowed her. "Are you even listening?"

"No, I've died of shock. Did she really say that? And in front of the paladins?"

"I'm afraid so. Iolar knows what they must think of me now."

"Did you tell her I only met you a week ago?"

"Stop harping on that! I'm trying to worry."

"You've been worrying since the moment we left the palace!" Vitaliya reached forward with both hands and clasped Ioanna's face. "Please. Please stop for just one moment. I'm not going back to Vesolda, and I'm not staying here and sitting on my hands while you ride around gathering up an army! Even setting aside the fact you need someone to talk to, so you don't get lost inside your own head, there's people starving who need my help."

"I told her you're coming with me." Ioanna turned her face back toward the river, and Vitaliya's hands fell away. "I'm not arguing it with her anymore. This is how it is."

"Good! She's been ordering you around since the moment we got here. Someone should remind her she's not empress anymore."

"Don't be angry with her. Grandmother Irianthe has been very good to me. She didn't need to shelter us or allow the Order to stay on her land. She could have handed us over to Netheia easily. I don't want you to dislike her just because we had a disagreement."

"Your standards are too low," asserted Vitaliya, leaning in to rest her head on Ioanna's shoulder. "Next you'll be saying Netheia was a good sister because she never tried to knife you in your sleep."

"My grandmother has been through a lot. And she realizes Xytae can't go on the way it's been. Nobody else in my family has managed to admit that."

Vitaliya did not reply, but the warmth of her body pressed against Ioanna's side was reassuring. And yet, for some reason, Ioanna could not relax. Despite the beauty and peace surrounding them, she felt uneasy and unsafe.

Priestesses? Could it be more priestesses? Instinctively, Ioanna brought her hands up to hug her upper arms and glanced around. But there was no one near.

"Ioanna?" Vitaliya's puzzled voice cut through her disoriented haze. "What's the matter?"

She'd felt the same way when she'd first sensed Acydon. Something was *wrong*, something was *here—*

Her fingernails dug into her skin. Moments later, Vitaliya was pulling her hands away, stopping Ioanna from injuring herself further.

"Ioanna!" Vitaliya wasn't confused anymore; she was just afraid. "Ioanna, what's the matter?"

"I don't..." Ioanna continued to look around, but all she saw was Oredia, the river, and the familiar road that cut through the middle of town. "There's something here."

"What kind of something?"

"I don't know."

"Let's go back, then," urged Vitaliya. "I'm sure the paladins can—"

"Yes," said a new voice from just behind Ioanna. "You should go back."

Vitaliya yelped in surprise and jumped backward. Ioanna spun around and found herself staring up at a very tall woman.

She was pale, far paler than Ioanna would have expected anyone in this region to be. Her hair fell into large chestnut-copper ringlets, and her eyes were so dark Ioanna could not tell where her irises began and ended, even though they were only inches from each other. She was dressed in a rust-red robe.

But unlike most priestesses of Reygmadra, the robe this woman wore was long, ankle-length, and she did not have a weapon at her belt. That and the lack of obvious armor ought to have been a reassurance, but to Ioanna, it meant she had enough magic that weapons were only a secondary concern.

Ioanna stared at the priestess, and the priestess stared back at her. But she was *not* a priestess. It was impossible to put into words, but Ioanna knew immediately that this woman's body was as much a garment as her robes. It was the same as it had been with Acydon, and the same with Aelia.

This woman, though, was not Aelia. Aelia had been happy, though erratic, and her warmth had shone through her mortal body. Nor was she Acydon, languid and calm and so very, very indifferent. This woman was cold and angry.

"Who are you?" asked Ioanna. She meant to sound assertive, but fear seized at her throat, and the words came out in a whisper. Could it be Reygmadra herself, come to kill Ioanna with her own hands? But if Reygmadra could do such a thing, then surely she'd have done it years ago?

"You don't need to be afraid," said the woman. *Lie.* "I'm not going to hurt you, unless you give me no other choice." That was not a lie, but still hardly reassuring. "All I want is for you to remain here in Oredia. So long as you do, I will not trouble you, and all will be as it should. Will you agree to that?"

"No," said Ioanna. "I won't agree to anything until you tell me who you are."

The woman laughed, a strange and cold sound. "So small," she said, raising one hand as though she was considering clasping Ioanna's chin in her fingers. "So very small."

Ioanna reached for her magic. Even without looking, she knew golden light was gathering at her hands. "Who are you?" she asked again.

"Cytha," said the woman. The goddess of revenge, Ioanna knew from her reading. Like all chaos gods, her worship had been outlawed. But that never stopped Men from whispering her name when they felt they'd been wronged—and that made Cytha more powerful than many of her siblings.

Ioanna knew from the priests, and her reading, that the most practical way to deal with a chaos god was to bind them to their body before destroying them. If she destroyed Cytha's body without performing the binding ritual first, her spirit would be free to return to her plane in Asterium to recover. Then, as soon as she was strong enough, she could manifest on Inthya again.

By binding her to her mortal body before destroying it, Cytha's recovery would be slowed significantly, and it would be months—perhaps even years—before she could manifest again.

Ioanna had never fought a chaos god before, but she was confident she remembered the binding words. She was less confident about her ability to destroy Cytha's body. Immolating it in celestial fire would probably be the easiest way, but Cytha looked so much like a woman that Ioanna wasn't sure if she could bring herself to do it.

It would feel so much like murder.

Cytha must have sensed Ioanna's thoughts because she took a few, drifting steps backward. "I must warn you. If you destroy me, she'll send someone with far less restraint to replace me."

"Reygmadra?"

"Who else?" replied Cytha. "Remain here, if you wish to live."

Out of the corner of her eye, Ioanna caught sight of something—a figure moving toward them. Ioanna turned instinctively to face it, but it paid her no mind, rushing past to stand between Ioanna and Cytha. At first, Ioanna expected to see Knight-Commander Livius, but this shape was a woman.

Just as Ioanna realized this, the woman drew one arm back and struck Cytha in the face, hard enough to send her toppling backward.

"Get out!" screamed the other woman. "Get! Go! Go! Or I'll do to you what I did to Edan!"

Cytha hissed in fury and raised a hand to her nose, which was leaking something dark, but she did not stand back up. Instead, she vanished as though she had never been there. Ioanna stared at the empty spot in shock.

"I'm sorry I'm late," said the other woman. "I'm *always* late."

"Aelia?" said Ioanna.

"Get back to the villa, now," said Aelia, pointing in the direction of Grandmother Irianthe's home. "You can't run off like this ever again. It's dangerous."

Ioanna only nodded rapidly, too shaken to speak yet.

"Here, I'll take us. It'll be quicker," said Aelia. She took Ioanna's hand in hers, then reached out and grabbed Vitaliya as well. Before Ioanna could ask what she was doing, the world around her vanished.

Then, with a sickening jolt, it reappeared. Vitaliya screeched—but the sound weakened and died a pitiful death once she realized they were back in Grandmother Irianthe's garden, surrounded by measured hedges and sleeping flowers. Ioanna tried to take a few steps but stumbled as the ground shifted beneath her feet. Vitaliya caught her, but she stumbled too, and they both toppled to the ground together.

"They're both fine," announced Aelia. "But Cytha's lurking. Seems Reygmadra's talked her into supporting her."

Ioanna lifted her head and realized her grandmother and the paladins were all gathered there with varying degrees of concern on their faces.

"They're just disoriented," explained Aelia. "Give them a minute."

"We'll go after Cytha," said Orsina. "She can't be allowed to—"

"No," interrupted Ioanna, staggering to her feet. "Don't kill Cytha. She said there were others—ones with less restraint—she'll send if Cytha is gone."

"I'm not surprised. Reygmadra's three steps away from being a chaos goddess herself these days." Aelia ran a hand through her hair.

"Do you think she'd come herself?" worried Ioanna. "Reygmadra, I mean. If she wanted to kill me..." If Reygmadra wanted to kill her, nobody would be able to stop her.

"No," said Aelia. "There's rules. If the Ten went around smiting one another's champions from Asterium, nothing would ever get done, and eventually we'd run out of people on Inthya. But they'll both be sending smaller gods in their place to try to tilt things."

"If Reygmadra has Cytha, then who are we getting?" asked Vitaliya.

"Well, you have me," said Aelia.

An uncomfortable silence descended upon the garden.

Someone touched her shoulder, and Ioanna realized it was her grandmother. Her hand was comfortably cool and smooth, far smoother than Ioanna might have expected from a woman who once had Reygmadra's magic.

"Ioanna, I would like you to come with me," said Grandmother Irianthe. "There is something I must tell you."

IOANNA HAD NEVER been in her grandmother's bedroom before, but, unlike the study, she'd never even caught glimpses in the past, nor had she thought to try to get inside. Curiosity overtook anxiety as they stepped through the doorway.

The room was nearly four times the size of the one Ioanna had been given to stay in. The floor was a polished mosaic, and one entire wall was nothing but shelves, which held yet more books and scrolls and writing utensils. In one corner was a bath, not unlike Ioanna's, but this one was twice as large.

"Sit down," said Grandmother Irianthe, and Ioanna sank onto a low stool. "Where were you when you were attacked?"

"I'd hardly call it an attack. She just wanted to warn me not to leave Oredia. But we were in town near the river."

"I'll tell the guards to be more vigilant," said Grandmother Irianthe. Ioanna had a feeling the guards would be helpless against a chaos goddess, but she said nothing. If it made her grandmother feel better, she wouldn't try to stop her.

"I hope you're not too angry with me," said Ioanna. "What happened in the meeting—you know I respect your judgment. I only—"

"I know," said Grandmother Irianthe. "And I feel perhaps I communicated my intentions poorly. If nothing else, understand I am not trying to keep you from Vitaliya because I find her objectionable in some way. Nor is it because I wish to see you unhappy for the sake of strengthening your character. My fear is that, should the worst happen, you will spend the rest of your life mourning her."

"What?" Ioanna had not been expecting any of this and found she had nothing to say in retort.

"What will you do if Vitaliya is captured?" asked Grandmother Irianthe. "If your sister demands your surrender in exchange for her life? Could you put the empire above your feelings for her?"

Yes, Ioanna wanted to say, but the lie would only give her a headache. "I don't know," she murmured.

"I do," said Grandmother Irianthe. "I know you, Ioanna. And I know you'd place the lives of our citizens over the life of a single woman, no matter how much she means to you. My hope was to prevent you from having to make such a choice."

"It might not happen," said Ioanna. "She might never be captured at all."

"She might not," agreed Irianthe. "But what if she is killed in combat? We both know she isn't capable of defending herself against trained warriors. If you fall into an ambush, or if we encounter too much resistance at Xyuluthe...would you blame yourself forever for her death?"

Tears sprang to Ioanna's eyes. Not for Vitaliya and that terrible hypothetical future. Not for any single reason. She had not cried at the news of her father's death. Nor had she cried that first night away from Xyuluthe, hidden away in a forest and listening intently for the sound of distant hoofbeats.

But now all the events of the past week were landing upon her like an insurmountable wave. She leaned forward, bracing her elbows on her knees, and allowed herself to cry.

"I'd hoped we would not have to go through this until you were older," said Grandmother Irianthe, rubbing

Ioanna's back gently. "Much older. It is unfair so much has been placed upon you by Iolar—that one girl is expected to undo centuries of damage. I'd not blame you for running away. I'd be a hypocrite if I did."

"I can do it," whispered Ioanna. Deep down, she had always known it would come to this. She'd been preparing for it for as long as she could recall. Even before Aunt Livia tried to kill her, she'd known she'd have to fight her way to the throne. She'd spent her entire life being regarded with pity and then scorn by her father's court. Too thin, too soft, too weak.

But Iolar wanted her to be empress, and she would not disappoint him. And even if he didn't, things had come into sharp focus over the past week. Xytae was on the verge of collapse. It needed her.

But she needed Vitaliya.

She needed to not be alone anymore.

Chapter Ten

VITALIYA

They left Oredia three days later, just as Vitaliya was beginning to think she might die from boredom. After the confrontation with Cytha, everyone was confined to Irianthe's estate, and Ioanna was so busy making plans with her grandmother and the paladins Vitaliya hardly had a chance to see her.

The carriage they traveled in wasn't nearly as nice as the one Vitaliya had taken from Bergavenna to Xyuluthe, but still significantly more comfortable than Otho's wagon. Vel was disguised as their driver, his identifying tabard stowed in with the luggage as to not raise suspicion, and Orsina rode alongside as a guard, similarly disguised. Within the carriage, Aelia (for apparently her name *was* Aelia, not Elyne) remained with Ioanna and Vitaliya dressed as a maid.

Ioanna would not discuss how she had convinced her grandmother to change her mind about allowing Vitaliya to accompany her on the journey. But Vitaliya suspected she knew the reason for the secrecy: Ioanna didn't want to admit Irianthe didn't think Vitaliya was good enough for her. She probably thought Vitaliya would be offended.

But Vitaliya probably *wasn't* good enough for Ioanna. There wasn't a doubt in her mind about that.

"What sort of things are in Metis?" asked Vitaliya as the carriage rattled along. Metis would be the first community they visited as they attempted to gather supporters for Ioanna's cause. Vitaliya knew it was a midsized city a few days north of Oredia, but not much more. "I mean, what are they famous for?"

"The region primarily raises sheep," explained Ioanna. "And Metis relies heavily on its weaving—or at least, it used to. They've been struggling with the loss of so many workers gone to war and have been forced to reduce the size of their flocks. So, productivity is low."

"And who controls it?"

"The baron and baroness. Camillus and Sabina. I've never met them, or if I have, I don't remember." Ioanna unfolded a bit of paper from her pocket and examined it. "My grandmother says they've felt the effects of the war sharply, and they asked her for aid last spring. I wonder why they didn't go to my mother."

"Did your grandmother help them?"

"Yes, she's put down a list of exactly what she gave them." Ioanna turned the paper to show Vitaliya. The list took up most of the page. "I think she's expecting me to hold it over their heads if they get difficult. But I don't want to do that." She chewed her lower lip. "I know that's silly. I'll have to do much harsher things if I plan to be empress. But they've already struggled so much. I don't want to add to it."

"If they're doing so badly, do you think they'll be able to give you any soldiers?"

"I don't expect too much from them," Ioanna admitted. "But I suppose it's best to start somewhere small, so I can become more comfortable with requesting support. Right now, I'm terribly nervous."

"Don't be!" cried Vitaliya. "You're the rightful empress, and they should be proud to support you. Especially if it means they'll get their citizens back from the front."

"Maybe," murmured Ioanna. "I just can't help but think...if it all goes wrong, it will be my fault if they're arrested or killed."

"You're doing this for them," Vitaliya reminded her not for the first time. "Once you're empress, it will all be worth it."

Ioanna laced her fingers with Vitaliya's and said no more. She'd been so solemn since their encounter with Cytha—even more solemn than usual. Vitaliya wanted to do something to make her laugh. But it was difficult when they were confined to a carriage.

Still, Vitaliya rather liked traveling. Many nobles found it boring, she knew, but she liked to watch the world fly past from her window and daydream. It always made her feel as though she was on the brink of something new. She was glad they were not traveling with a procession of loud, rowdy soldiers who would attract attention and slow them down—though it meant they were more vulnerable to attack.

Vitaliya did not doubt Orsina and Vel were capable fighters, and she could only imagine how fearsome Aelia was when roused, regardless of the impression she gave off. But bringing a few more soldiers along, for strength in numbers, would not have been unwelcome. Especially now that they knew there were chaos gods after them.

As she thought this, she turned her gaze from Ioanna to Aelia—but Aelia was gone. Vitaliya jumped in surprise, for there was no way she could have stepped out of the moving carriage without them noticing. Ioanna made a curious sound.

"What's the matter?" she murmured. From the tone of her voice, she'd been drifting into sleep just as Vitaliya moved.

"Aelia's disappeared," Vitaliya whispered. She reached out and waved one hand over the spot where she'd been sitting, half expecting to hit an invisible torso. But the space was empty.

"Oh." Ioanna sounded more confused than concerned.

"Do you think something got her?" worried Vitaliya. "Cytha, or..." But if something was going to attack them, surely Ioanna would be the target?

Ioanna pulled the door to the carriage open, and Orsina immediately whipped her head around at the sound. "What's the matter?" she called.

"Aelia's gone," said Ioanna. "We didn't see her leave, but she's not—"

"Oh, she'll be back," said Orsina, as though this was the most ordinary thing in the world. "She gets restless. Don't worry."

Ioanna and Vitaliya both looked at each other, equally uncertain. But Orsina's assessment was correct after all because a few hours later, Aelia wandered out from the road ahead, somehow having managed to overtake them despite being on foot.

Overall, the journey from Oredia to Metis was uneventful. No attack came, whether from chaos gods or ordinary soldiers. Every night, they stopped in a city or town and stayed at an inn. Nobody questioned their story—surprising, considering two of the five members of their party were apparently incapable of telling lies, and Ioanna would only do it under duress. But paladins, she'd come to find, were very good at lying without lying. They could evade, imply, and obfuscate.

Vitaliya felt this was against the spirit of the Order of the Sun's code if not the letter. But Orsina and Vel explained paladins frequently went into dangerous situations where revealing all they knew—or suspected—might spell disaster.

Vitaliya had not realized how anxious she'd grown over the last week until she caught herself marveling at the fact everyone they encountered seemed to have no trouble believing they truly were just minor noblewomen on an excursion.

They arrived in Metis late in the day. Vitaliya had been expecting a terrible, run-down place reminiscent of the very first village she'd encountered with Ioanna. It certainly wasn't as wealthy as Oredia. But there were plenty of people around, and most of the fields were clear and well-kept even if they weren't in use. She peered out the window curiously and wondered if the city's good fortune was due to luck, Irianthe's support, or the guardianship of another chaos god.

The baron's villa was set on the edge of the city, surrounded by a low wall. Beyond it were the walls that surrounded all of Metis and past that, rolling hills. Vitaliya was not surprised to see how the city grew quieter and cleaner as they neared the estate.

It was not nearly as large, or as impressive, as Irianthe's home had been. But that was to be expected, given Camillus and Sabina were hardly anyone of note. As she thought this, Vitaliya felt a bit guilty for her unkindness. But they did not hold a particularly prestigious title, and she wouldn't have been shocked to find their situation far worse.

The carriage arrived at the front of the villa where two of the baron's guards approached. Before they could begin asking questions, Ioanna passed over a letter, signed and sealed by the Empress Mother Irianthe. One of the guards hurried off with it to inform his lord and lady, while the other nearly fell over his own feet to help Ioanna out of the carriage.

Like Irianthe's home, the baron's villa featured a large central garden in front of the residential area. The remaining guard led them through it. Vitaliya glanced sideways at Ioanna and thought she seemed paler than usual. Vitaliya wanted to take her hand to comfort her, but such a gesture would probably not be appreciated at a time like this when Ioanna needed so much to appear strong.

"Tell them about your blessing," Vitaliya whispered to Ioanna. "I know you don't want to, but it can only help you!"

"There's no need," Ioanna murmured back, her eyes locked on the colorful tiles below their feet. "I can convince them without bringing it up."

Vitaliya silently cursed Ioanna's parents. How had they managed to convince her that her blessing was shameful? It ought to have been impossible!

Camillus and Sabina were about the same age as Vitaliya's father, which was a little surprising because she'd been expecting them to be nearer to Irianthe's age for some reason. Vitaliya could tell the pair were confused as they approached.

"Crown Princess Ioanna?" Camillus said in disbelief. "Is it truly you?"

"Yes. I have just come from my grandmother's home. I expect you've heard the news from Xyuluthe," said Ioanna.

"We received word of your father's death," Sabina confirmed. "Please accept our condolences. Surely he is fighting in Vailyon now."

Ioanna did not respond to this. Instead she said, "Princess Netheia has driven me from Xyuluthe, hoping she will be crowned empress in my absence. I have found refuge with my grandmother, but I must return to the capital before the coronation. I anticipate resistance, though, and that is why I have come here."

Camillus and Sabina exchanged looks, and Vitaliya had a sinking feeling she knew what they were going to say.

"We empathize with your situation, Crown Princess," said Camillus carefully. "But Metis is struggling. The war has taken many of our residents. We cannot possibly contribute to a second army."

"I'm not asking for an army," said Ioanna. "Nor do I intend to send anyone on a long campaign. I only need to get into Xyuluthe before the coronation to ensure my sister is not crowned. After that, all those who have supported me will be free to return to their homes. Furthermore, once I have secured the throne, it is my intention to bring our war against Masim to an end. Our forces will be ordered to withdraw from Aquiim and the Summer Strait completely."

Camillus and Sabina looked at each other again.

"Tell me your concerns," prompted Ioanna. "Do you believe I am lying?"

"It's a terrible risk you're asking us to take," said Camillus bluntly. "We'd be charged with treason if you fail. I won't deny I want to see an end to the war—who doesn't?"

"Many don't," said Sabina dryly.

"And many do," Ioanna countered. "Their voices have not been allowed at court, but I've seen undeniable proof the war is doing far more harm than good. It is a war without reason, war for the sake of warfare. Even if the Masimi surrendered tomorrow, we would not gain back all we have lost. Regardless of what my father and his generals have claimed, this war has been waged for the veneration of Reygmadra. Any resources gained were only a secondary concern."

"We were unaware anyone at Xyuluthe felt this way," said Sabina. "Least of all one of the princesses."

"The nature of my blessing has put me in the minority," Ioanna explained. "I have never felt Reygmadra's fury—it is foreign to me. My sister believes this makes me unsuitable for the crown. But I have always thought our empire is at its best when the Ten are venerated equally, none above any other."

"In that case, we certainly wish you good fortune," said Camillus. "But we cannot grant you anything more. The risk to our family is too great."

"How much longer will you survive like this?" asked Vitaliya, speaking up for the first time. "Enessa didn't care about your problems, and Netheia will be even worse. Times are already hard. How much longer before you go bankrupt and all your people starve to death?"

Camillus and Sabina both stared at Vitaliya, obviously appalled by her rudeness. But Vitaliya regretted nothing, for *someone* had to ask these questions to remind them that ignoring reality wouldn't work for too much longer.

"She is not wrong," Ioanna murmured. "But there is no shame in it. Many others are in the same position as you, and through no fault of your own. The war has even taken the priests of Eyvindr from our people. I find that unforgivable."

"Perhaps so, but do you truly believe you might have a chance to succeed?" Sabina seemed to be the more courageous, or perhaps simply the blunter of the two. "Xyuluthe is one of the most heavily defended cities on the continent, and you mean to fight your way up to the Imperial Palace with only whatever soldiers you manage to rally in the next few months? You'd be better off accepting your sister as empress."

"If that were the extent of my plan, then I would certainly agree with you," said Ioanna. "But we are not working alone. My grandmother is in Xyuluthe already. She will convince my mother and sister there is no need to heighten security and turn as many as she can against Netheia in secret."

Vitaliya watched Camillus and Sabina's faces carefully. Would the mention of Ioanna's grandmother reassure them or only give them cause to worry?

"My grandmother had words of her own for you, to ease your minds and perhaps help you in your decision," added Ioanna. "It's all in the letter I provided. I do not wish to pressure you into making a hasty choice. Perhaps we can discuss it in more detail after you've taken time to reflect on it. In the meantime..." Ioanna gestured to Vitaliya. "She would like to see to your fields. As a gesture of goodwill."

"Our fields?" Sabina repeated blankly.

"I expect you've had a shortage of priests of Eyvindr?" prompted Ioanna.

"I'm not a priestess—temple life never appealed to me—but I can still help," Vitaliya explained. "If you haven't started planting yet, I can still rejuvenate the soil.

And if you have any orchards, I may be able to coax an extra harvest from them."

Both Camillus and Sabina looked skeptical, and Vitaliya did not think she blamed them. But Ioanna said, "You have my word that no harm will come to your fields. I only wish to offset the damage done by my family."

"We have one priest," said Camillus. "In past years, we had more. When I was a child, there was an entire temple full of them. But they've been called away. First the priests, and then the acolytes too. It is too much work for one man, and we worry he may be exhausting himself."

"I will go to him immediately," said Vitaliya, eager to prove herself. "He can direct me to the areas that need the most aid, and I'll follow his instruction."

Part of Vitaliya had been expecting them to tell her it was too late, that she could go to him tomorrow. But Camillus nodded. "I will have one of our guards escort you to the temple," he said. "If you are successful..." The implication of his words hung in the air, unsaid. Vitaliya's magic would factor into their decision.

She hadn't been expecting her presence to be so crucial to their success but tried not to let her concern show on her face. If Ioanna could ask strangers to commit treason, then Vitaliya could raise a few plants.

The Temple of Eyvindr was located near the middle of town. It was large, fitting with Baron Camillus's account of multiple priests and acolytes during his youth. And unlike many of the structures she'd seen during her time in Xytae, it was clean and well-kept as though the sole remaining priest harbored hope his colleagues might return any moment now.

The guard that was sent along with her was one of the two who had met their carriage upon their arrival, and Vitaliya suspected they only had a handful of guards. Vel had either grown tired of the estate already or did not quite trust this mission because he also joined them.

Both men lagged behind while Vitaliya approached the large double doors of the temple. She suddenly felt very impertinent, offering aid to a priest who was no doubt more learned and experienced than herself by a few decades, at the very least. She thought of the men who'd been brought to the palace to teach her, all of which had been at least as old as her father and as patient as the earth itself.

"Hello?" called Vitaliya cautiously, pushing one of the doors open. "Is anyone in?"

Inside the temple was just as clean as the exterior, but there was something cold and impersonal about it. Vitaliya had never been inside a Temple of Eyvindr that did not contain live plants and enormous basins of water and muddy footprints tracked across the floor. Even the Great Temple of Eyvindr in Bergavenna, where the archpriest lived, was prone to messes. Vitaliya had never minded this for it felt fitting given Eyvindr's domain.

This temple had large urns decorating corners and doorways. They may have once held plants, but now they were all empty. Vitaliya peered into the nearest one and saw the interior was perfectly clean, as though fresh from the potter's shop.

A few troughs lined the walls, and Vitaliya could see pipes that, presumably, had once fed water into them. But they were all dry.

"Hello?" called Vitaliya again. She was just beginning to think that the very last thing Ioanna needed was for her to stumble upon the priest's corpse when she heard a noise from above. She looked up at the low ceiling and realized there had to be a second floor to the temple—maybe a residential area?

The noise was heavy like maybe someone was stumbling around. After a few minutes, a door that Vitaliya had not noticed before opened. A man dressed in the dirty clothes of a country farmer staggered in. In his hand was a crumpled green robe, the sort worn by priests of Eyvindr. His dark hair was messy, and there were dark circles under his eyes.

"Oh, hello," said Vitaliya. "I'm Floriana. Are you the priest here? I was sent by the baron."

"The baron?" The strange man blinked at her, obviously still disoriented. Had he been sleeping? "Why? What's wrong? Is it the north fields?"

"No, nothing's the matter," Vitaliya reassured him. "I'm here to help. Are—are you the priest?"

The man nodded wearily. He was younger than she'd been expecting, probably not too much older than Vitaliya herself. For some reason, that was reassuring. If nothing else, he was likely to be less offended by the insinuation he couldn't do his job properly.

"I've—I've got some magic that can help in the fields. The baron said you were overworked. I hope you don't mind?"

"No. No." The priest shook his head. "I'm sorry. He was right—I am overworked. I can use all the help I can get."

"We can come back in the morning if you need to rest," said Vitaliya. She wasn't going to deprive this poor man of sleep just because the baron wanted quick results. "I don't want you to fall ill." Or drop dead from exhaustion.

"Just give me a moment," he mumbled. "What was your name? Floriana? I'm Kaeso."

"Are you really tending all the fields here on your own?" That might be viable in a small town, but Metis obviously covered enough land that it needed multiple priests unless the sole remaining one was excessively powerful.

"We've got some overwinter crops in the north fields, but most are empty, waiting for the spring planting," said Kaeso. "That will be very soon. I'm trying to pour as much magic into them as I can to increase our yield, but I can only cover so much ground in one day before I run out of power. And I'm also needed to help with the tilling."

"Do you have any orchards?"

"Yes, but those won't be ready until summer. The fields are my priority now."

Vitaliya decided she'd leave the orchards for now. Maybe it could be a nice surprise for later. "Do you want me in the north or elsewhere?"

"I've done all I can for the north fields. Best to work the empty ones before the planting. We're not using all of them this year—not enough seeds, not enough hands. I'll show you which ones."

"Vel, get the carriage," said Vitaliya. "I'm not making this poor man walk all the way out to the fields again."

Kaeso pulled his robe on over his head. "West fields first. How long are you here for?"

"I'm not sure, honestly," admitted Vitaliya. "I just go where they tell me."

"Don't I know how that goes," Kaeso muttered.

It wasn't until Vel brought the carriage around that Vitaliya realized Kaeso would probably leave a fair bit of dirt behind. Vitaliya had never minded that, but she had a feeling Ioanna would, and so would Irianthe.

But that wasn't important. Impressing the baron was. Vitaliya would write home and have them send a new carriage if anyone complained.

Kaeso, for his part, seemed to be too exhausted to realize the carriage wasn't an ordinary wagon. In fact, by the time they rolled to a stop outside Metis's walls, he was sound asleep. Vitaliya decided to let him rest and stepped out alone. The baron's guard, who had chosen to ride in the front with Vel in order to direct him, went to open the gate.

Vitaliya saw the ground had already been turned, which was good—her magic would be more effective if it was added to the soil now rather than before the tilling. She wasn't entirely sure why—someone had undoubtably explained it to her at some point, but it wasn't the sort of information she was good at retaining.

In any case, the field was enormous and would probably take all of her magic to infuse. Vitaliya had done work like this before back in Vesolda, but never without other priests to aid her, and farmers and their families gathered around.

It was a little bit sad in a way. Back in Vesolda, adding magic to the soil was a community affair akin to a local festival. In the morning, there would be black coffee and sweet biscuits passed around. And after the work was done, there was honey wine and herb-wrapped fish grilled over open fires.

She shook herself out of the memories. She would return to Vesolda soon enough. For now, there was work to be done.

Vitaliya knelt down on the edge of the field and dug her fingers into the soil. Closing her eyes, she inhaled deeply and tried her best to clear her thoughts of anything except her own magic.

The magic flowed from her fingertips, and the soft soil absorbed it like rainwater. She didn't know what would be planted in this field—probably wheat if she had to guess, but maybe not. It didn't really make a difference when she was only infusing the soil.

She allowed her magic to spread deep and wide, filling the field in the same way a basin might be filled with water. She knew sometimes the priests would get up and walk to a new area when their magic wouldn't extend any further, but usually there were enough of them spread around that they wouldn't have to go far.

Vitaliya gazed across the field and sighed. It seemed she was in for a good deal of walking.

After a while, her mind began to wander. She thought of Ioanna and hoped she wasn't too bored back at the baron's villa or too lonely. She hoped Orsina and Aelia were keeping her entertained. Ioanna had been alone for such a long time, and so despite everything, Vitaliya was glad they'd encountered each other.

She said she didn't care if I make you empress consort later—

Vitaliya's eyes opened. She liked Ioanna and wanted to stay with her for as long as she was allowed. But empress consort...that was a terrifying title. Even 'princess' was too much for her some days, and she'd been born with that one. Agreeing to become empress consort would be akin to agreeing to walk around with her pockets full of bricks for the rest of her life.

But it wasn't as though Ioanna had offered! Not really. She'd only mentioned her grandmother had mentioned it. Vitaliya took a few deep, calming breaths before she stood up to move to a new area of the field. That hadn't been an *offer*. Ioanna had merely been recounting a conversation.

Besides, they did not know each other nearly well enough to be discussing matters so permanent. Any moment now, Ioanna might realize Vitaliya was selfish and flighty and irritating, and the whole thing would come to an end.

And what about after she became empress? When people would no longer pretend to like her—when they'd genuinely love her. Good people. Wonderful people. People far more worthy than Vitaliya. And of course, there would be princes! Probably from every nation under the sun, flooding the imperial court until there was hardly room to move. And they would be calm and mild and thoughtful, and everything Vitaliya wasn't. Ioanna would be able to talk with them for hours about matters of economics and philosophy and law, and then one day she'd think of Vitaliya and marvel at the fact she'd ever been lonely enough to associate with her.

Vitaliya was having a nice time feeling sorry for herself now. She decided to design Ioanna a husband. Who would she pick? Maybe a Masimi prince, a *sehzade*, in order to cement the peace Ioanna hoped to establish.

She got up and moved to the other end of the field where her magic did not quite reach. Neither Vel nor the baron's guard said anything as they trailed after her. Perhaps they were afraid something might go wrong if they distracted her. But Vitaliya had performed these rituals while surrounded by shouting farmers and singing children and barking dogs. A little conversation would hardly throw her off.

But for once, she did not feel like talking. And that was a little eerie.

The *sehzade* would be dark with striking green eyes, and his hair would have a bit of a messy curl to it—in an attractive way, not a sloppy way. His favorite thing in the world would be mathematics. And riding, of course. His horse would be one of those Masimi ones with the elegant necks and high tails. Black as night—or no, no, pale as a summer cloud! Like Ioanna, he'd have Iolar's magic, and they'd sit in front of the fireplace debating obscure fragments of forgotten rituals...

After a moment of consideration, she added a dog to the scene.

Vitaliya's hands found the soil again. It really was lonely out here, and she pitied Kaeso for having to do it by himself. How many farmers remained behind in Metis? How many had been sent to fight? In Vesolda, ordinary people were only drafted into the army when times were dire. The last recorded instance of this was hundreds of years ago.

People still joined the army voluntarily. Some with Reygmadra's blessing, but some with nothing more than a desire to protect their home or do something with their lives that didn't involve fish or olives or sheep. But there was no enemy to fight. There weren't even any dragons attacking anymore as there had been when she was very, very young.

The light was fading, but Vitaliya was confident that she could have the field done before the sun vanished. She was beginning to grow exhausted but wasn't near to draining herself yet. She doubted she'd have enough power left for a visit to the orchards tonight, but she could return in the morning after she'd rested.

Finally, when she'd expended all the magic she dared, she stood and surveyed the field. The magic would remain until the planting when it would nurture the new seeds and eventually increase their yield at harvest.

"I'm finished, I think," she reported to Vel and the guard. "Let's go. Is the priest still asleep?"

He was. As Vitaliya climbed into the carriage—carefully, as not to disturb him—his eyes fluttered open.

"Are we there?" he muttered. "Let me show you what to do."

The room the baron and baroness set aside for Ioanna was simple. It wasn't terribly spacious and looked rather sad compared to her room in Irianthe's home. But there was no cause for complaint. Vitaliya's room, one door down, was nearly identical. But Vitaliya had no intention of staying in it unless Ioanna ordered her away.

"I think it went well," commented Vitaliya as they prepared for bed. "I mean, they didn't throw us out."

"I'd hoped it would be easier," murmured Ioanna. "But I shouldn't be surprised. What I'm asking them to do isn't a small thing."

"It's more work than starving to death. I'll grant them that."

Ioanna sighed heavily. "I'll give them time to think it over. We have a day or two to spare before we must move on. I don't want to pressure them."

Both young women were too tired from the journey to do anything more than go directly to bed. Vitaliya did not mind this. Being beside Ioanna was comforting and sleeping in a real bed was delightful. It was not long before they both fell asleep.

She dreamed she was home in Bergavenna, watching her mother dress. Her ladies surrounded her, pinning hair and tightening clasps and tying bows. Vitaliya sat on the bed, still in her nightgown, and waited.

When her mother was done, the other ladies all left in a silent flock, filing out somberly. Vitaliya was pleased to see them go, for now she and her mother could talk about anything they wanted.

But her mother was crying. Horror and fury clenched at Vitaliya's heart. Why was her mother crying? Was it something one of her ladies had said? Who would dare?

"Mother!" cried Vitaliya. "What's wrong?"

"I don't want to go to the wedding," said Queen Isabetta, but it was too late. They were already standing in the Great Temple of Pemele in Bergavenna, staring at the altar where her father clasped hands with a shepherd girl. Beside her, her mother sobbed into a handkerchief.

Vitaliya woke with a start as fury flooded her chest. A dream, she realized. A horrible dream. But why would Eran show her that? Eran, God of Dreams and Ninth of the Ten, was generally believed to be responsible for every dream every person ever had. Their priests emphasized not all dreams were visions—in fact, most people could expect to go their entire lives without ever receiving a true vision—but some were signs the dreamer had some matter that needed reflection or resolution.

And some were pure absurdity.

This dream had been so vivid it nearly felt like a vision. But who would send her a vision like that? Pemele? Iolar? Isabetta herself? The dead were not really known to interfere with matters of the living.

As Vitaliya's vision adjusted, she realized the bedroom was filled with a thin silver mist—or perhaps there was merely something in her eyes? She rubbed at them, but the mist remained, illuminated by moonlight. Vitaliya could still make out the nearest pieces of furniture, but it was so strange. Was this normal? Was this abnormal? In that moment, she could not remember.

Even with the knowledge it had been a dream, Vitaliya's rage would not subside. Had she even been this angry when she'd left Bergavenna? Had she ever been this angry in her life?

Vitaliya got up and paced the room, now wide awake and unable to even consider going back to sleep. Her head ached, a sharp and persistent throb. She pressed her fingers to the spot but could not feel any lumps or cuts.

She shouldn't have left Bergavenna. She should have remained behind and made her father's every day an agony until he relented! She hadn't done enough to try to stop the wedding!

Her head ached so badly. She closed her eyes and tried to take a few deep breaths to calm herself. The pain only intensified. Vitaliya imagined it as a bright, cold line that pierced through her brain and traveled downward toward her spine.

The wedding would happen, and it would be *perfect*, and everyone would take it as a sign the marriage was ordained by Pemele. Vitaliya should have been around to ruin it! But instead she'd run away!

Her head ached so badly, and the pain was spreading to her shoulders now. She knew she ought to just go back to sleep and ask for willow tea in the morning. But she could not. How could she even think of sleeping when everything was going wrong?

Vitaliya did not remember picking up the dagger she'd stolen from Netheia's room, but now it was in her hand. Maybe it wasn't too late to ruin things.

They shouldn't have let her leave. There was no telling what sort of trouble she might get up to in Xytae.

Wouldn't her father be sorry if something awful happened to her? He would be so sorry.

Vitaliya's toes curled in satisfaction as she imagined it, and some of the pain in her head lifted as well. He'd receive the news, and *that woman* would reach out to comfort him, but he'd knock her hand away and tell her to get out. It was her fault this had happened, and if they'd never crossed paths, then his daughter would still be alive.

Vitaliya hesitated. Maybe killing herself was a bit extreme? Maybe she should consider another angle. Maybe she could just get herself imprisoned? Her father would have to negotiate with the Xytan Empire for her freedom. Surely the wedding would be ruined then?

Surely...

Pain burned down her arms all the way to her fingertips, and she nearly dropped the knife. But she gritted her teeth and turned toward Ioanna, still peacefully asleep. Moonlight illuminated the curves of her body, cutting through the silver mist. It was her fault Vitaliya was out here. It was her fault she'd never make it back in time to ruin the wedding.

The knife in her hand wavered. She didn't want to stab Ioanna. Did she? Maybe she ought to go back to sleep and reconsider it in the morning.

Maybe just a little stab? A little cut? She'd barely feel it. And in the morning, they'd blame it on an insect, speculate that the baron's linens had not been washed recently.

A little cut. Right behind the ear, maybe?

Her hand wavered again.

Just one little cut! Ioanna wouldn't feel it; she'd sleep right through it! No harm done, not really! Her skin was so pale. So pale under the moonlight. She imagined she could see the pulsing veins beneath Ioanna's skin. What might it be like to spill one open? And then...and then she could go home, directly home.

There was no time to waste.

Still, Vitaliya hesitated. She felt as though she was forgetting something important, some reason why she might *not* want to stab Ioanna. Not stab, not stab! Just cut. Just a little cut across the throat. She'd hardly feel it, and then Vitaliya could go home, and the wedding would be called off, and her mother's spirit would smile at her from Solarium—

The door slammed open and something collided with Vitaliya, knocking the knife from her hands and sending her sprawling across the cold stone floor. Pain shot through her arms as she landed, ripping her from the strange, dreamy state she'd been in a moment before. The mist filling the room vanished, along with the phantom ache in her body. Now wide awake and back in control of her senses, she began to shake as the sickening realization of what she'd been about to do came upon her.

Aelia—for that was who had pushed her—rushed over to Ioanna, who was just waking up from the noise. She sat up and looked around in confusion. "What happened?" she mumbled.

"It's all right now," said Aelia. "You're safe."

The door opened again, and Orsina stepped in, sword drawn. Aelia waved a hand at her, and Orsina lowered her blade.

"What happened?" repeated Ioanna, sliding her legs off the edge of the bed. "Was someone here?" She caught sight of Vitaliya, still on the floor where she'd fallen. "Vitaliya?"

"Someone had her in thrall," said Aelia grimly. "Probably Cytha."

"I, I had a dream," babbled Vitaliya. "I woke up so angry, and I thought—I was so sure if I—but I don't know why, I just—"

"It's all right," soothed Orsina. She knelt down on the ground beside Vitaliya and put a reassuring hand on her back.

"It's not!" cried Vitaliya. "What if Aelia hadn't come in? I could have killed Ioanna!"

"Unlikely," said Aelia. "Even in thrall, it would have been difficult to pull off something like that. You were already resisting."

"But I was going to stab her!"

"You were in thrall," murmured Orsina. "It wasn't your fault."

"I shouldn't have come." Tears welled up in her eyes. "Irianthe was right. I should have stayed in Oredia. I should have gone home."

Ioanna sat down across from her and put one arm around Vitaliya's shoulders. "You didn't hurt me," she soothed. "Not even a scratch."

"But what about next time?" She closed her eyes, and the tears spilled down her cheeks. "What if..."

"If Cytha was able to put you in thrall, it means there was something she was able to entice you with. She deals in revenge," said Aelia. "Vengeance."

Ioanna looked at Vitaliya curiously. "Do you want revenge on me for something?" she asked.

"No!" Vitaliya took a few deep breaths, trying to calm herself, but it had the opposite effect, and she only began to cry harder. "It had nothing to do with you! I was thinking about my father!"

"Your father?" asked Orsina.

"He's marrying a woman. Soon. I thought if I hurt Ioanna, he'd be sorry. Sorry enough to call off the wedding. It doesn't make sense! But it made sense at the time." She shuddered. "Why would I..."

"Well, that explains why you were vulnerable to Cytha's influence," said Aelia.

"Just because I think my father should be loyal to my mother?" Anger flared up in her chest again. Did *nobody* understand how she felt?

"Queen Isabetta died a long time ago—" Orsina began.

"It's only been six years!" Vitaliya wiped at her eyes furiously. "If he loved her, he'd never marry anyone ever again!"

"Is that really fair?" Ioanna asked gently.

"I don't care!"

"Well, that's how Cytha got you," Aelia said bluntly. Orsina frowned at her, but Aelia was unapologetic. "I'm not trying to be cruel. But this is how she works. She gets you fixating on some way you were wronged, and then she convinces you she's got the solution to make them all sorry, but half the time it ends up benefiting nobody but her."

"So what? Now I have to just—just magically be happy my father's getting remarried or else I have to live in fear I'll stab Ioanna?"

"You're not going to stab Ioanna," said Aelia. "Even in thrall, there's limits to what we can force mortals to do. The fact she tried it at all tells me she's getting desperate. And now that she's failed once, it will make it more difficult for her to get you again."

"It shouldn't be allowed," glowered Vitaliya. "She shouldn't be *allowed* to do things like that in the first place!"

"She's not," said Orsina. "That's why she's been classed as a chaos goddess. And next time she strikes, we'll send her back to Asterium. She'll be months regenerating."

The door opened again, and Vitaliya caught a glimpse of Vel before Orsina got up and went to him. She could not hear what Orsina said, for her voice was too low. Then the two of them stepped outside, shutting the door behind them.

"Maybe I should leave, though," murmured Vitaliya. "Everyone here is so good. And I'm a mess."

"I want you here," said Ioanna, gripping her by the hands.

"I don't know," whispered Vitaliya.

"You don't have to decide now," said Ioanna. "It's the middle of the night. Let's go back to sleep, and we'll discuss it in the morning."

Vitaliya got up. "I'm going to my own room," she announced. In the dim light, she could see sadness on Ioanna's face. But this was for the best. "Lock the door behind me. Just in case."

The next morning was clear and bright, but Vitaliya would have much preferred clouds or even a thunderstorm. The good weather seemed to be a mockery of the events of last night. She dressed quietly and slipped out of the room, not wanting a conversation with anyone yet.

The gardens were still a little chilly, and morning dew soaked her sandals as she walked along. She sat on a stone bench briefly but found it was too cold to remain there for long.

She needed to leave. She'd hoped she would feel differently in the morning, but if anything, she was only more certain of her decision. Ioanna's safety was more important than some temporary companionship. Nobody could dispute that.

After a few minutes of aimless wandering, she came upon Orsina, who had found one of the few sunny spots in the garden. She gave a welcoming smile when she noticed Vitaliya and moved over on the bench she was sitting on. Vitaliya didn't really want to have a conversation, but leaving would be rude and probably damage her reputation with the paladin even further.

"I always enjoyed watching the sunrise, even as a child," said Orsina. "Our home was down in a valley, but up at the baron's estate you could see just about forever—or that's how it felt at the time."

"I prefer to sleep late," mumbled Vitaliya.

"Yes, I think most people do!" Orsina paused. "Were you unable to sleep?"

"No, I was fine. Just restless."

"I hope you aren't afraid any of us think any less of you for what happened," said Orsina. "It was not your fault."

"That's not what Aelia said."

"I've seen far too many people to count put in thrall. Young, old, rich, poor...there's very few people who are so detached from worldly desires that they're not susceptible to a single chaos god. Your vulnerability came from a place of loyalty to your mother. Cytha was able to twist that loyalty into something evil, but that doesn't mean there's something inherently evil about it."

"Everyone thinks I'm being selfish," Vitaliya said bitterly. "That I should just let my father have this. That my mother's been dead long enough that it's not so terrible. As if there's a set amount of time that will mean I suddenly don't care anymore."

"I don't think that's exactly it," said Orsina. "Accepting your father's remarriage doesn't mean you'll love your mother any less, does it?"

"It doesn't matter. I'm leaving anyway. I can't forgive him, so Ioanna's in danger from me. Nothing else matters."

"I do not always believe forgiveness is a necessary thing," said Orsina. "If you wish to grant it, then certainly. But sometimes, people will wrong you so badly there is no forgiveness to be had. But that does not mean you need to be angry, vengeful, or obsessed. You simply go on. Without them."

"How?" asked Vitaliya.

"Well, sometimes you can pity them," Orsina said slowly. "Or you can think about how there is so much else in the world to concern yourself with. Good things. Letting go of anger can be difficult, but if you busy yourself with other things—if you let time and distance do their work—one day you might reach for the old hurt and find it's not there anymore."

Vitaliya could scarcely imagine this. "That doesn't help Ioanna now. That doesn't keep her safe."

"Aelia and I have discussed it, and we think it's unlikely Cytha will target you the same way twice," said Orsina. "And even if she does, putting you in thrall won't be so easy the second time around now you know what it feels like."

"I don't want to take that risk," said Vitaliya. "I don't want...I can't. She's too important. To the world and to me."

"I understand how you feel," said Orsina. "But I also think your presence here is important too. I am certain your aiding of Metis's priest has impressed the baron and baroness. I might even go as far as to say Iolar means for you to be here just as much as the rest of us."

"Why would Iolar have any interest in me?" Vitaliya frowned. "I don't even have his blessing."

"Iolar doesn't exclusively care for those who have his blessing," said Orsina. "He cares for all Men, for we are his creation. And even if you don't believe that, you are a princess, so you fall quite neatly into his domain. But what I meant to say was, I think there is something that you, as an individual, contribute to Ioanna's cause. And that is why you're here."

"Plenty of people have Eyvindr's blessing," said Vitaliya. "That's hardly special. Even if most of them are away right now."

"I think your blessing is a small part of things, but not the whole of it."

"What else is there?"

Orsina smiled comfortingly. "There's everything else about you, of course. Take, for example, the fact you care about Ioanna, and she cares about you. Her life has been quite lonely until now, wouldn't you agree?"

"Well, yes. But that doesn't help her build an army."

"It was only an example. Right now, it's impossible for us to truly know what your purpose here is. We might not even realize what it was until long after the fact."

At the sound of footsteps, Vitaliya turned her head instinctively. Aelia was walking toward them, just as untroubled as Orsina. Perhaps she could give some insight to the ways of the gods?

"Is everything all right?" asked Aelia.

"Yes, we're fine," Orsina reassured her.

"I haven't sensed anything else lurking around since last night. I doubt we'll have anything to worry about for a little while, but I'll—"

"I'm going to leave," interrupted Vitaliya. "I've thought it over, and it's for the best. I don't belong here. I'm all risk and no benefit."

"That priest yesterday didn't think so," said Aelia. "In fact, he was glad for your aid. Wasn't he?"

"None of that would have mattered if I'd killed Ioanna last night."

"You wouldn't have killed her. Even in thrall. I feel like I told you this already." Aelia frowned. "I know I told you this already."

"She's afraid," said Orsina. "Don't blame her—it's a frightening thing, to lose control of your mind and body."

"Well, maybe so, but I don't think it's worth leaving over. If it was, I'd be the first to tell you so. I think you're meant to be here."

"Yes! That's just what I was saying!" Orsina sounded relieved. "I'm not sure why, yet. But there must be something. It can't be chance. Not something like this."

"I can't believe that," insisted Vitaliya. "I'm nobody! I'm a princess, but I'm still *nobody*. I can't fight in battles or lead soldiers or...everything you two do. Why would Iolar, or any of the gods, want me here?"

"I have no idea," said Aelia. "But if it helps, I suspect your father met that girl he's marrying specifically because someone in Asterium wanted you to throw a fit and flounce off and be in Xyuluthe to meet Ioanna."

"*What*?" shrilled Vitaliya.

"Aelia," said Orsina flatly.

"Calm down! It's just a guess! I don't know for sure!" Aelia put her hands up in a pacifying gesture. "But I wouldn't be shocked if it turned out to be true."

"Who would do something like that?" Vitaliya's eyes narrowed. Iolar was the obvious answer, but arranging romantic relationships was rather far outside his domain. Pemele or Dayluue? They tended to overlap a little. But what did they care about what happened in Xytae, so long as people went on falling in love or having families?

"Vitaliya," said Orsina gently. "This is not a productive line of thought. It doesn't matter who arranged what. What matters is we're here now, and we all need to do our best to ensure—"

"Of course, it matters!" cried Vitaliya. "It's the worst thing that's ever happened to me! And all for a country that's probably going to fall apart into six hundred smaller countries in a few years anyway!"

"If the worst thing that's ever happened to you is your father remarrying, then I'd say you've had a rather enjoyable life," Aelia commented.

"Aelia," said Orsina again. "You're not helping."

"Well," Vitaliya grumbled, "now I *really* want to leave." She would not pretend like she was not purely motivated by spite now, an innate desire to inconvenience whatever god was responsible for all this.

"That's rather petty, isn't it?" Aelia asked.

"I don't care! Besides, what if my father is in thrall too?" Maybe that was why he'd proposed the wedding. He wasn't in control of his own actions. Someone—maybe one of the Ten, maybe not—was coercing him into it. And if that was the case, she had to get home as soon as possible and make the Order of the Sun or someone else help him break free!

"No," said Aelia. "That's ridiculous."

"Stop it, both of you." Orsina sighed wearily. "We're meant to be fighting Reygmadra, not one another."

"I've got to get home," Vitaliya insisted. "My father's about to marry someone he doesn't love just because one of the gods wanted me to come here! I can't let that happen!"

"That isn't how the Ten work!" cried Aelia in exasperation.

"It might be! *You're* not one of the Ten. You don't know!"

One moment, Vitaliya had been seated on the bench, cold but comfortable. The next thing she knew was she was on the ground, the side of her face pressed into the cold, wet earth and a blunt pain in her neck.

"Listen to me, you spoiled brat!" shouted Aelia. But she got no further, for Orsina leapt up and dragged Aelia off before she could go on. Vitaliya sat up in time to see her kicking wildly at empty air while Orsina held her up around the waist like a particularly rowdy child. "Put me down! Orsina!"

"This is not how we communicate," Orsina said. Her voice was stern, but not angry. Vitaliya got up carefully and stepped back, far enough away that she was out of reach of Aelia's flailing limbs. It occurred to her that Aelia could probably use her magic to get free if she really wanted to, but the goddess did not. Maybe she was out of power. Or maybe she wasn't angry enough to bother. After a rather amusing minute, Aelia stopped her struggling and went calm again, but Orsina did not let her go.

"I can tell you what happened, if it happened at all," said Aelia. "It was all just a guess from the start. It was probably Dayluue. She can match people up perfectly when she wants to. Most of the time she lets you just stumble around and figure it out on your own. But sometimes when she wants someone moved somewhere as quickly as possible, she'll point them at one of their matches. This woman your father has fallen in love with is probably one of his. *Or* it's just a coincidence, and you're getting worked up over nothing at all."

"So...what? You're saying he'll love this woman even more than he loved my mother?"

"I don't know. Was your mother as irritatingly self-centered as you?"

"Aelia! That's enough!" This time, finally, Orsina's voice was sharper. "Go make sure Ioanna is safe."

Aelia's feet touched the ground, and she walked away in the direction of the baron's home.

"I hate this," Vitaliya said bitterly. "I hate all of this."

"I'm sorry." And Orsina did sound genuinely apologetic. "I wish she hadn't told you that way. She—sometimes she forgets—"

Vitaliya leaned forward and covered her face with her hands. "I want to go to the orchards," she mumbled. "I want to at least do some good somewhere before I leave."

Chapter Eleven

IOANNA

Vitaliya did not appear at breakfast that morning, and Ioanna felt terrible for not thinking to check on her beforehand. Obviously, she was more shaken by last night's events than Ioanna herself. She'd hoped Vitaliya's declaration that she had to leave had come from a place of fear, and she would realize it was unnecessary once she'd had a chance to rest.

"Was all well last night?" asked Sabina cautiously. "We heard a commotion…"

"Floriana had a terrible nightmare," explained Ioanna, and this was near enough to the truth that she did not feel any pain. "I apologize for the disturbance."

"Is she still asleep?"

"I presume so. I will go check on her after we've finished if she still hasn't turned up."

"She asked to be taken to the orchards this morning," said Orsina. "Vel brought her out. She finished her work on one of the fields last night but ran out of magic. I think she wanted to do more before you left."

"The orchards?" repeated Baroness Sabina. "What does she intend to do there?"

"I've seen her bring fruit trees to life out of season," said Ioanna. "It's very useful and very impressive."

"I'm surprised the Temple of Eyvindr didn't pursue her aggressively with a blessing like that."

"I'm afraid she would find temple life to be too stifling." Ioanna smiled fondly. "I consider myself fortunate she's agreed to accompany me on this journey. One woman can hardly replace the hundreds of priests that have been called away, but I believe we can at least mitigate a little bit of suffering."

The meal went on in silence. Ioanna wondered if they'd made a decision last night or still needed more time. Or perhaps there would be no swaying them after all, in which case it would probably be best to move on to a new city. It would not be a wonderful thing for morale, to have their first appeal end in failure, but she wouldn't hold it against them.

"Your grandmother's letter," said Camillus at last. "Do you know what she wrote?"

"Actually, I'm afraid I don't," said Ioanna. "She gave it to me after it had been sealed, and only told me to pass it on to you. I hope it wasn't anything unpleasant? If she's threatening you with your debts—"

"No," Camillus said. "Nothing like that. But in her letter, she made a claim I find difficult to believe. No disrespect meant to the empress mother. But it regarded the nature of your blessing."

"Ah," said Ioanna. "Then I suppose we *are* telling people."

"It's true, then? You are—you claim to be a Truthsayer?"

"I would not dare claim such a thing if it was not so," Ioanna explained solemnly. "If we are to be pedantic, I am not a Truthsayer formally, for that requires an assessment by the Temple of Iolar or the Order of the Sun, followed by a declaration of my status. And of course, my father would never allow such a thing to be done. But yes. That is my blessing."

"Why has it been kept a secret?" asked Sabina, leaning forward. "Why was it not shouted from every rooftop the moment it was discovered?"

"My parents never cared for it. Nor does my sister. In childhood, I was led to understand it was shameful. Unsuitable for a future empress. I've only recently come to realize I was misled."

"I can hardly believe it," murmured Camillus. "It seems impossible."

"I expect you'll want a demonstration from me?" said Ioanna. "I can scarcely blame you."

"No disrespect meant—"

"None taken. But I can already tell you that you've lied in my presence once."

Camillus and Sabina both stared at each other in horror. A smile pulled at one side of Ioanna's face.

"Please, don't worry," she said. "It was a little thing. Last night at dinner. The baroness said she didn't know what we'd be having and turned to ask your housekeeper what the cook had prepared. But you did know, didn't you?"

"Well, I—" Sabina's face grew red.

"I was confused as to why you would lie about such an insignificant thing, but then I realized you do not employ enough servants to prepare the meals alone—or at least, not one so large as the one we had last night. You were down there helping them, weren't you? And you were afraid I'd think less of you for it."

"Well..." Sabina floundered, and Camillus glared at her as though she'd done something appalling. "I—I only..."

"Don't worry," Ioanna soothed. "You would not believe the dreadful lies I've encountered at court. Yours was nothing next to those. Is that proof enough, or did you wish to ask me more questions?"

"No—no—" stammered Camillus. "We have no doubt. And we can pledge twenty-five soldiers to your cause. I know it's not much…"

"No," interrupted Ioanna. "I understand how little you have now. I am just as grateful as I'd be if you pledged a thousand."

Vitaliya returned an hour or so later, tired but not drained in the way she'd been after growing figs for the bandit children. Upon her arrival, she said very little but collapsed into bed. Ioanna followed her in, hoping they could finally talk about the events of the previous night.

"Did you visit the orchard?" Ioanna asked.

"Yes," Vitaliya mumbled into her pillow.

"That's good. I'm sure everyone will appreciate it."

Vitaliya did not reply.

"The baron has pledged twenty-five men to me," said Ioanna. "I know that doesn't sound like much, but for a little place like this…well, I'm glad to have them. I was thinking we'd leave at noon today. Our next stop is—"

"I'm not *going*," said Vitaliya harshly. She sat up. "Do you not remember Aelia knocking a knife out of my hands last night?"

"Yes, but that wasn't your fault! It was Cytha!"

"Oh yes, that would have been a wonderful consolation if I'd killed you!"

"Vitaliya," said Ioanna, moving to sit down on the bed beside her. "We can't live our lives in fear of chaos gods. The fact they're going to the trouble to try to stop us tells me we're on the right path. And you're safer here with

Aelia and the paladins guarding us than you'd be if you left."

"Aelia!" Vitaliya flopped down onto her pillow again. "Don't talk to me about her!"

"Why? Did she do something to you?"

Vitaliya huffed. Then she said, "She told me the reason my father is getting married is probably because someone—one of the Ten, probably—wanted me to get mad and run off here and meet you."

"Oh," said Ioanna. "Well that is unexpected."

"It's awful!" Vitaliya turned over onto her side, and Ioanna placed a comforting hand on her shoulder. "It's awful. And she *hit* me."

"Aelia hit you?"

"Yes! And she called me a spoiled brat!"

"Wait. Start over. From the beginning. What happened?"

"Ugh. It doesn't matter. The point is, someone pointed my father and that shepherd girl at each other to manipulate me! I don't know who it was, but I'm not doing *anything* for them, and if that makes me petty, I don't care!"

Ioanna did not say anything. Instead, she began to rub Vitaliya's back in what she hoped was a soothing gesture. They stayed like that for a while until she felt Vitaliya's breathing grow calm once more.

"Well," Ioanna said at last, "I can understand not wanting to do anything for the god who did that to you. But maybe you could do it for me, instead."

They left Metis after the midday meal just as Ioanna had hoped. Their next destination was a city called Pomeria, four days to the west. It was ruled over by Countet Domite who, according to Grandmother Irianthe's notes, had withdrawn from court due to their personal dislike of Ionnes. Ioanna hoped that would work to her advantage when they arrived.

She wondered where Knight-Commander Livius was now. It was probably too early for him to have made it to Vesolda, but he might be in Ieflaria by now. Traveling alone, and on horseback, he'd make much better time than Ioanna and her companions. If all went well, he would be there waiting on her grandmother's land in Nassai by the time they arrived, along with a few hundred paladins.

Vitaliya remained uncharacteristically quiet on the first day of the journey, though Ioanna was never certain if this was due to the magic she'd expended to wake up the fruit trees out of season, or because she was still angry about everything Aelia had told her. But Vitaliya could not stay angry for long, and by the second day she was back to her usual sunny self.

Ioanna was still concerned about Vitaliya's assertion that Aelia had hit her but decided not to bring it up for fear of starting the argument all over again. She only hoped she would not regret it. Ioanna wouldn't tolerate violence from anyone in her carriage, goddess or not. If it turned out that the incident hadn't been a one-time event, she would have to reconsider her choice in guards.

They arrived in Pomeria on a rainy morning. Unlike quiet Metis, Pomeria was obviously doing well. They'd passed extensive vineyards on the way, and as they moved through the city, it seemed to be nearly as busy as Xyuluthe.

"They don't seem to be suffering too badly," Vitaliya observed. "I have to wonder if maybe they've got a chaos god watching out for them."

"I don't sense anything," said Ioanna, remembering how Acydon's presence had pulled at her teeth. "What about you, Aelia?"

"I'm not sure," Aelia murmured. "I think there's someone influencing things here...but not a chaos god."

The carriage rolled to a halt, and a guard dressed in the local uniform of Pomeria opened the door. As she had before, Ioanna passed up a letter bearing her grandmother's seal. After that, they were escorted rapidly up the private road to the countet's home.

It was not as fine as Grandmother Irianthe's villa, but a far sight better than what they'd left behind in Metis. This home had the residential area to the front, and the garden set in the back.

Domite of Pomeria was around Grandmother Irianthe's age, but wore a robe of striking red fabric, fastened with a bright copper belt. They were already holding the letter Ioanna had given to the guard. Domite's eyes flicked from the page, then to Ioanna, then back again. Now knowing what her grandmother had written about her and her blessing, Ioanna could only hope the countet did not declare her a liar and throw her out.

"You don't look like him," Domite said at last. "Fortunate, I suppose. You might have come sooner. I'd be more interested in a fight with Ionnes before his death than after."

Ioanna was not sure how to respond to this.

"It has been my experience that Empress Mother Irianthe is not inclined to lie," continued Domite. "She and I are similar in that—lying is so much trouble, frequently more trouble than it's worth. And yet, I think I might call her a liar now. She claims you are a Truthsayer."

"I have not been assessed by the Temple of—"

But Domite waved a dismissive hand. "I don't care what some old men have to say on the subject. In childhood, I owned a dog. His name was Honey. He died of old age, sleeping in a patch of sunlight. Tell me where the lie is."

Behind her, she felt Orsina bristle. The paladin was about to object to her blessing being treated like a festival game.

"The animal wasn't a dog, but his name was Honey," said Ioanna, speaking rapidly so Orsina couldn't interrupt. "And he did die of old age, but it wasn't in sunlight. It was raining, or nighttime." She closed her eyes, squeezing them shut against the oppressive, distracting light of day. "Wait. I see it now. He was sleeping beside you in your bed. And he was a cat."

Domite did not reply immediately, but Ioanna saw them swallow. After a moment they said, "It's a pity this didn't happen thirty years ago when I was young enough to really enjoy it."

Orsina and Vel were obviously reluctant to leave Ioanna alone with the countet, but Ioanna got the sense Domite was genuinely pleased by her presence and wouldn't require too much more convincing to contribute to her cause.

So, while Orsina, Vel, and Vitaliya were shown to the guest rooms, Domite led her down the halls and into the garden. Domite's home was a busy place, made busier still by the unexpected arrival of so many important guests. Servants rushed here and there, bearing piles of linens, buckets of water, and, on one memorable occasion, a whole live chicken. Ioanna tried to go slowly to keep from colliding with any of them whereas Domite moved easily through the fray.

"Tell me about your cause," said Domite, once they'd made it out to the relative silence of the gardens. The rain was still falling, but lightly enough they could tolerate it. "Where are your soldiers? How many do you have?"

"We—we're establishing a camp. At one of my grandmother's other estates, nearer to Xyuluthe." She was unwilling to give the exact location until she'd got a real promise from Domite. "We're in the process of calling back as many paladins as we can on such short notice. I'm hoping for at least two hundred of them by the time we're ready to march. My grandmother has also contributed some men of her own, and I've already secured a promise from Baron Camillus for a handful of soldiers."

"A symbolic gesture, no doubt." One side of Domite's mouth lifted in a crooked smile.

"But no less appreciated," Ioanna said fiercely. "Their situation is my own family's doing. I will not shame them for giving what little they have."

"Where is your grandmother now?"

"In Xyuluthe."

"How unlike her."

"She's expected there for the funeral and the coronation. And she thinks she can do more for us within the court than in Oredia or elsewhere. I'm inclined to agree. I don't want a long, bloody civil war. I want this done in one day."

"That's a rather ambitious timeframe."

"I can see it no other way. If the conflict drags on to the point that my sister is able to call the army back from Masim, we're finished."

"Well, you're not wrong." Domite paused. "I can assign soldiers to you. But if you let me address my people, I expect you'll have more volunteers—if you will accept the untrained ones?"

"Are you certain? It seems too much to ask. Surely they are needed here."

"I will not command anyone to stay even for Pomeria's sake," said Domite. "You do not need to preach to me; I understand how dire the situation has become. They would have taken up arms soon enough. Perhaps not this year, nor the next, but certainly within my own lifetime."

That was a sobering thought, and Ioanna could not keep the alarm from her face.

"Sometimes I forget how different it is in Xyuluthe," Domite sighed. "I ask myself how the court can be so far removed from the reality of things, but then I recall I was no better in my youth."

"I spent every day beside my mother, and I had no idea." Ioanna shook her head. "I still do not know if she kept it from me, or if the other nobles kept it from her."

"Those who are suffering most would not be allowed to petition your mother directly," said Domite. "Camillus and Sabina, for example, do not hold the rank required to seek an audience with the empress. They would have been forced to entrust their cause to...it is Count Aulus, I think, who controls that region? That they opted to petition the empress mother instead tells me they had little faith in him."

"He would have refused to help them?" asked Ioanna. "Why?"

"His priority would be his own lands, would it not? Resources are sparse. Even if they could pay in coin, he might come to regret it later. Gold is worthless when there's nothing to spend it on. In any case, they weren't offering gold. They were asking for a loan they had no real way of repaying."

"He could have gone to my mother on their behalf!"

"In that case, I expect she would order him to aid them from his own storehouses. Don't you agree?" Domite paused, but when Ioanna did not reply, they pressed on. "I'm sure you've heard her issue such edicts before."

Ioanna had, and at the time, she'd thought them reasonable. How could she have been so oblivious?

They arrived at the center of the garden. The focal point was a life-size statue, depicting a person draped in simple robes. One hand held an empty bowl, carved from the same stone as the rest, and on the other perched a small songbird.

"Who is this?" asked Ioanna, gesturing to the statue. "I don't think I recognize the iconography."

"Isan, neutroi God of Charity. And unofficial patron of Pomeria."

"That's an admirable domain. I'm surprised I've never heard of them."

"They are well known in Aquiim. In my youth, I traveled through Masim and Coplon—long before your father's war, back when our people were welcomed. That was where I first heard their name. When I returned home, I brought a little statuette with me as well as some writings. At first, I kept my veneration private, not wanting to foist an unfamiliar god on our people, but when the war came..."

"Do they have a temple here?"

"No, but only for lack of priests. Maybe if you do manage to end the war, I'll send for some from Aquiim to instruct us in the rituals." Domite glanced down at Ioanna. "Some might criticize me for venerating them over Iolar, but Iolar has done nothing for us for a decade."

A small part of her was horrified by this casual sacrilege, but Ioanna only said, "Times are difficult. We do what we must. And Isan sounds like an honorable god."

"Even so, the harvests have not always been good," Domite admitted. "I won't deny I've been pulling more from our treasury each passing year. You'll have soldiers from me, as many as I can spare. I'd go with them myself if only..."

"Oh, I wouldn't ask that of you!" Ioanna said hastily.

"Nor would my knees, I'm afraid," sighed Domite. "But don't worry. You'll hardly miss me. And if you lose, I expect I'll get my chance to fight at least once. I don't plan to let them arrest me."

"That was easier than I was expecting," Ioanna commented as they got ready for bed that night. "My grandmother never mentioned the countet hated my father so openly."

"Maybe it was meant to be a surprise!" suggested Vitaliya.

"My grandmother isn't the surprising sort. Maybe she honestly didn't know." Ioanna could not blame Domite for keeping their dislike of Ionnes a secret from Irianthe—he was her son, after all. "In any case, they seem like a useful ally."

"Did you see how angry the paladins got when they asked you that question about the cat?" Vitaliya asked. "It was wonderful! I thought they were going to start a brawl."

"That is *not* wonderful," sighed Ioanna. "I'll have to talk to them. I know it's offensive to them, but I can't expect everyone to just take my word that I'm a Truthsayer. It's simply not reasonable. They'll have to set aside their objections until after the coronation."

"I didn't know you could see into the past like that. I mean, when you said it was a cat, and it was in their bed—that was amazing. I didn't know you could do that."

"I can't usually," Ioanna admitted. "It only happens when the emotions around the lie are very strong. Then the truth comes to me even if it's been hidden away. Domite still loves that cat, I think. That's how I was able to tell."

"They seem nice. A bit frightening but in a kind way."

"Yes," agreed Ioanna. "I think I like them."

They lay there in bed together, both staring up at the ceiling, fingers entwined.

"I thought about my father's funeral for the first time today," Ioanna announced at last. "Am I horrible for not caring if I miss it?"

"Don't ask me. I'm biased against fathers right now," said Vitaliya, and Ioanna bit back a laugh. "Honestly, though, why should you care? It doesn't sound like he was a particularly good father to you. And then he went and got himself killed in a duel and left you to deal with his mess."

"Yes, but...he's still my father."

Vitaliya made a rude noise, and Ioanna gave her a little kick under the blankets.

"I know he never loved me," said Ioanna. "He never claimed he did, and I know it was because he didn't want me to feel the lie. And it wasn't as though he was just bad with children because he loved Netheia."

"When you're empress, you can appoint someone to be your new father," said Vitaliya. "And he'll always tell his friends how wonderful you are, commission portraits of you, and remember your birthday. Make it Knight-Commander Livius. He's got the right look about him."

"I think if I were to do that, I'd pick Archpriest Lailus," said Ioanna. "I've known him since I was old enough to speak."

"Who is that?"

"The Archpriest of Iolar here in Xytae. I can't say for certain, but I think he was nearer to being a proper father than Ionnes was." Ioanna breathed in deeply. "I wonder what he's doing now. I wonder if he thinks I'm dead."

"I doubt it," said Vitaliya. "He's probably so faithful he won't even blink when you go riding up to the Imperial Palace with ten thousand soldiers behind you. Never a doubt in his mind. You know how priests are."

"I hope you're right," Ioanna whispered, and Vitaliya squeezed her hand.

Chapter Twelve

VITALIYA

Pomeria was nice, and Vitaliya wouldn't have minded staying longer. But with a promise secured from the countet, Ioanna was already prepared to move on. Far too soon, they were in the carriage and pulling away from the villa. Aelia, who was more restless than usual today, rode up with Vel, leaving the princesses alone in the carriage.

"Maybe you can return, some day," Ioanna suggested, when Vitaliya expressed regret over the brevity of their visit. "I'm sure the countet would welcome you."

"I hope I can," Vitaliya sighed. "I hope we can. Together."

"I can hardly imagine life after this," said Ioanna. "Isn't that odd? Becoming empress and ending the war...I know I want to do it, but when I try to picture it in my mind, it comes out blank like a canvas with no paint yet."

"No, I feel the same way. I just hope you're not too busy being empress to escape now and then."

"I might be, at first. There's a lot to do."

"And there will be suitors too, I expect." Vitaliya thought, once again, of the Masimi prince she'd invented for Ioanna. She'd almost forgotten he wasn't a real person. "Piles of them. You'll need me to help you eat all the chocolates."

"What!" Ioanna burst out laughing. "What are you talking about?"

"You don't think an unmarried empress won't have thousands of suitors? You'll have to put them up in the stables once you run out of guest rooms."

"I'll send them all home, then," said Ioanna.

"You can't do that. They're all very important princes. They'll be offended."

"More offended than if I make them sleep in the stables?"

"Princes love stables," Vitaliya said in the most authoritative voice she could manage.

Ioanna laughed again. "I can't imagine I'll have any time for suitors. I will have quite enough to do already."

"I'll handle them for you. When they come in, I'll rank them on wealth, power, and attractiveness. They'll have to score above a certain number to move on. Then I'll judge the gifts they've brought."

"That is not especially romantic."

"You're empress now. You don't have time for romance. We must be objective about these things. In any case, this can't be news to you. Even as crown princess, I'm sure there were plenty of—"

"Some, but I turned them away the first time they told me a lie. It made for short courtships. And my parents didn't want me marrying a foreigner, so I never had any princes."

"I'm surprised they didn't just pick someone for you."

"I never considered it before, but I suppose I am as well," Ioanna admitted. "Perhaps they thought it would be a waste of time. Seeing as they clearly never intended for me to become empress."

"Well, good. Now we get to decide without their interference. I'm sure they'd have chosen someone dreadful anyway. I'll do a much better job."

A little smile curled at the side of Ioanna's mouth. "Might I make an observation?"

"No, how dare you."

"You seem worried."

"I'm worried we're riding to our deaths, yes," said Vitaliya. Her face warmed. "I thought that was something we had in common."

"I don't think you want me to have any suitors," said Ioanna.

"It doesn't matter what I want! They don't need my permission to turn up on your doorstep."

"I think you're jealous."

"Why shouldn't I be? They'll all be so busy courting you that they'll stop coming to see me, and I'll have to buy my own flowers from now on. I *hate* paying for things."

"You're twisting," said Ioanna. "You think I can't tell? Never lying, but never saying what you mean either. Netheia was good at it too."

"Don't compare me to her!"

"I'll tell them I'm courting you, and they'll leave me alone. Would you like that?"

Vitaliya lapsed into dumbstruck silence.

"What's wrong?" asked Ioanna.

"That's...you shouldn't do that. You're too important—an empress should be with someone powerful and wise and, and besides, they'll all be so much better than me! Once you meet them, you'll forget why you ever liked me to start."

"Where were they when I was alone?" asked Ioanna. "Where were they when I had nothing but a muddy wagon and few paladins? Where were they when Netheia came to arrest me?"

"I'm only here by coincidence—"

"You've had plenty of chances to leave. You don't know what it means to me that you've chosen to stay."

"Don't say that," whispered Vitaliya. "You'll start making me feel like I might be special."

"If you don't already, then I've been communicating very poorly with you." Ioanna leaned forward. "What would you do if I said I didn't want to be empress? That I was going to run away and forget Xytae. Would you go with me?"

"Of—of course," said Vitaliya.

"How many of those princes would say the same?"

"I don't—"

"None of them, I'd think. They'll be coming to court the empress. Without my title, what am I to them?"

"Xytae will need alliances," said Vitaliya desperately. "You can't just, just..."

"An empress can do whatever she likes. Isn't that what you told me?"

"You won't, though," said Vitaliya. "You'll do the right thing. No matter how much you hate it. You'll do what's best for Xytae."

"Don't be so certain," said Ioanna. "Maybe I'll surprise you."

The next town they arrived in was called Enona, but this time their reception was different. As they moved through town, people stopped to watch the wagon go past—which wasn't unusual by itself. But the murmurs and awed faces that followed certainly were. Perhaps Enona was a particularly boring sort of place?

When they reached the baron's home, Vitaliya watched as Ioanna selected yet another sealed letter from her pile. But she never had the chance to hand it over to the guards because the carriage was waved ahead without question.

"Either these guards aren't being paid enough, or we've been expected," commented Vitaliya. "Ioanna, you didn't send word ahead, did you?"

"No," Ioanna shook her head, confused. "Perhaps Grandmother did?"

"I don't think so," commented Aelia, who was currently in the carriage alongside them, and had been for the last hour or so. "I'm surprised, honestly—I knew this would happen, but I didn't think it would be so soon."

"What would happen?" asked Vitaliya. She had not had a real conversation with Aelia since their argument in the garden. Aelia did not seem to be at all angry with *her*, though, and it was difficult to keep up her annoyance with someone who was so cheerful.

"Rumors are spreading about Ioanna. Well, less rumor and more fact, at this point. People are excited."

"Is that good or bad?" worried Ioanna.

"I suppose it could go either way," mused Aelia. "But right now, I'd say it's a good thing."

Outside the baron's villa, they were met by not only more guards, but an assortment of eager servants and even the baron himself.

"Call me wildly optimistic, but I don't think he's going to be difficult to convince," muttered Vitaliya.

"Crown Princess!" he cried in delight before Ioanna even had completely stepped down from the carriage. "It is an honor to have you here." He came forward to clasp her hands. "I'd feared we might not be important enough to expect you as a visitor. I'm glad to see my worries were in vain."

"You have heard of my cause?" asked Ioanna.

"Rumors say you were at Pomeria, and the countet gave their support after you demonstrated your incredible blessing. I hope you don't find us imprudent, but we were hoping—"

"Yes, I know." Ioanna smiled. "I've grown accustomed to proving myself in these past few weeks."

"No disrespect meant—"

"Nonsense. You'd be a fool to take me at my word." Ioanna looked around. "And this is your staff? Quite an impressive reception."

"My father was a member of the Order of the Sun, well loved by our people. He died defending Enona from a wild gryphon—we suspect it was rabid, for they don't usually come down from the mountains. I always regretted his early death, but in later years I came to be grateful he never lived to see what Xytae became." The baron shook his head ruefully. "When news of your blessing came to us, naturally, we were all excited."

"I'd love to hear more stories of your father," said Ioanna. "I had no idea he was a paladin. It's rare for them to marry."

As they were escorted into the villa, still followed by the flock of servants, Vitaliya felt herself smile. People were finally beginning to realize how wonderful Ioanna was. No matter what happened between them in the future, she would not have to spend it alone.

Vitaliya was rather sad to leave Enona the next morning, for everyone had been so cheerful and friendly. They'd suffered through the war with Masim, losing family and resources to the campaign and obviously were tethering on the end of hope before Ioanna's emergence.

Their next destination was Lysera, another small barony only a few days away from Enona, and the journey was uneventful. Like Enona, it was a community that mostly relied on its vineyards, for little else would grow so near to the rocky, colder northern border.

When their carriage rolled to a halt outside the city walls, Vitaliya watched as Ioanna selected yet another letter from her pile. But after a minute, when nobody approached the window or opened their carriage door, Ioanna got up.

Vitaliya watched as she stepped out, still holding the letter in her hands. The carriage was positioned so she could see four guards blocking the way—an excessive number, she thought, for a community so small. She wondered if they were going to get the same reception they had at Enona, but from the expressions on their faces, that wouldn't be the case here.

"The baron isn't able to see you," one of the guards said. "You'll have to move on."

"What?" Vel laughed incredulously. "You can't be serious!"

"I'm afraid so. Please, go. We cannot accommodate you here."

"Listen here, you—" began Orsina angrily, but Ioanna raised a hand.

"It's quite all right," she said. "We don't want any unpleasantness. If the baron won't see us, we'll be on our way. We've many other stops to make."

"But—" Orsina protested.

"No, I don't want to force my presence upon anyone." Ioanna stepped back into the carriage and pulled the door shut behind her. "Let's go. No sense in spending any more time here."

After a moment, in which Vitaliya imagined Orsina and Vel both giving the guards dirty looks, the carriage began to move again.

"You probably could have ordered them to step aside," commented Vitaliya.

"I suppose, but I don't want to have to bully anyone into joining us. It sounds like the baron's already made his choice. Our time would be better spent soliciting those who are still open to my ideas."

"All right, but I'm going to make sure he's not invited to your coronation!"

Ioanna smiled. "I'm not angry, really. I understand why he's afraid."

They made it back to the road without further incident. After a time, the farmlands became woodlands, which was pleasant because the trees shielded them from the worst of the sunlight. Vitaliya closed her eyes and fell into a not-quite-sleep.

She was pulled back into waking when the carriage rolled to an unexpected halt. Vitaliya opened her eyes in time to see Ioanna frown. From outside came the sound of muffled voices.

"What's going on?" asked Vitaliya.

Ioanna opened the carriage door and stepped outside. Vitaliya would have much preferred to remain safely inside, but her curiosity was stronger than her self-preservation, so she followed—though only partway, so she could duck back inside if the situation turned bad.

Over Ioanna's shoulder, Vitaliya could see Orsina and Vel both standing in front of the carriage, their swords drawn. Aelia was still up in the driver's seat, but purple light had gathered around both her hands. All three were facing a group of people who blocked the road. With only a glance, Vitaliya could tell they were bandits.

These were not the children that had waylaid Otho's wagon. They were adults, dressed in hardened leather and carrying swords that looked like they'd been taken off the bodies of real soldiers. Vitaliya tried to do a quick count but lost track after fifteen.

"I'm beginning to really dislike this place," Vitaliya said.

"We just want to talk," said the bandit nearest to the front of the group—the leader, Vitaliya supposed. Neither Orsina nor Vel seemed terribly convinced, but Ioanna stepped out of the wagon's shadow and into the dappled sunlight.

"Wait," she said. Vel looked back at her in horror, but Orsina did not move. "I want to hear what they have to say."

"Probably that this is a toll road. We've all heard it before," said Orsina dryly.

"It usually is, but it happens that passage is free today. It's my birthday," said the bandit woman. Vitaliya sputtered with laughter.

"Both of you get back in the carriage," ordered Orsina. "We'll deal with them."

"I'd like to hear them out, actually," said Ioanna. "We've already stopped. What's a few more minutes?"

"They're saying the emperor's dead," said the bandit woman, speaking hurriedly so that Orsina and Vel might hold off on attacking just a bit longer, "and the rightful heir was chased out of Xyuluthe. Now, we're not ones to get involved in political struggles. What's the difference between one empress and another, right? It hardly makes a difference out here. Except they're saying this princess is different. Saying she's promised to end the war, and maybe even do something about the priestesses snatching children and sending them off to die in the desert."

"You—" Vitaliya had never seen Ioanna so incredulous before. "You want to *join* me?"

"Well, under normal circumstances, we wouldn't get involved. Nobles' promises don't mean much after they've got their end of things, right? Except they're saying you've got Truthsayer magic."

"Yes," said Ioanna. "That's how I know it's not really your birthday."

This got a round of laughter from the assembled bandits, and the woman grinned.

"Everyone here knows how to fight. We've got our own gear, our own food, and you can pay us after the fact plus interest. You can't say yes to those town guards and no to us. I'll be offended and might even take it personally."

"You'd be taking orders from paladins," warned Ioanna. "Could you tolerate that?"

"Nobody mentioned paladins," muttered someone in the group.

"Shut up!" the leader bellowed over her shoulder. "D'you want to break a noble's face or not?"

"I'm not sure if you're in this for the right reasons," said Ioanna. "I find no glory in combat or suffering. If I knew a way to reclaim my throne without bloodshed, I would happily take it."

"We're not monsters, princess," said the bandit leader. "We work the same—always give people a choice before the swords come out, right? That's just civilized. Less mess, less trouble."

"You can't be seriously considering this!" objected Orsina. "We are not so desperate that we need to ally ourselves with common criminals!"

"We're a *little* desperate," said Vitaliya.

"Their intentions are honest," said Ioanna. "And Xytae is their country, so they've a right to fight for it."

"They'll turn on you the moment they get a better offer from your sister! And besides, what will the next noble you visit say when you ride up to his house escorted by a company of bandits?"

"Can't speak to that second one, but I can guarantee we'll not fight for the other princess. Look." She leaned forward and adjusted her sleeve, and Vitaliya realized her arm was a different color than the rest of her body, the color of polished wood—which it *was*, Vitaliya realized. Her arm was made of wood and metal; a bizarre and beautiful piece of craftsmanship.

"I was in Masim," she said. "Lost my arm for the glory of the Empire. They sent me home, and the Temple of Inthi made me this thing. It even moves." She wriggled some of her fingers to demonstrate. "Nice, isn't it? Spent nearly every last copper I had on it. But then the Temple of Reygmadra got word. I already had the papers saying I was released from my service for my injury, but they took it back. Said the new arm negated it. And it was back to the battlefield. Or it would have been if I hadn't made a run for it."

"I am sorry," said Ioanna. "That was unjust—and as far as I know, illegal."

The bandit woman shrugged. "Maybe so, but I had no way to appeal it. And now they say I'm a deserter."

"I promise I'll have your name cleared once I'm empress," Ioanna said. "And anyone else in your situation."

Vitaliya could tell neither Orsina nor Vel were pleased with this decision, but she thought she might be on Ioanna's side with this one. If the woman was telling the truth—and Ioanna would say so if she wasn't—then she would be a helpful ally.

"Crown Princess, with all due respect—" began Orsina.

"I've made my decision," Ioanna interrupted. "What is your name?"

"Modia. And this is the Bronze Boars." She gestured back at the other bandits. "They may not be used to taking orders from paladins, but I'll keep 'em in line, and you can hold me to it if I don't."

"Murderers and thieves. Knight-Commander Livius is going to kill us," muttered Orsina.

"'Us?'" Vel objected. "You're safe! It's me that has no goddess wife for protection!"

"Can we all please calm down?" interrupted Ioanna. "Modia. I'm still in the process of soliciting nobles and will be passing through several more communities. I think it would be best if you went on ahead of us—I can't promise I'd be able to stop any local guards from arresting you, nor do I think your presence would add a great deal of credibility to my cause. But I will write you a letter, so you won't be turned away at Nassai."

"Nassai? Is that where your troops are gathering?" asked Modia.

"On my grandmother's lands." Ioanna nodded. "She is my most powerful supporter, and none of this could have happened without her influence. I only ask you keep the location a secret as you travel. My sister will learn of us eventually, but it's my hope it won't be too soon."

"On my honor, we will tell no one," swore Modia. "Unless they swear to join us."

"Thank you," said Ioanna. "And I'm sorry for what you've been made to endure."

"Wasn't your doing," said Modia, with a wave of her hand. "And look—you're undoing it anyway. That's more than I'd ever expect from a princess. Maybe things won't be terrible forever. I suppose we'll see."

Chapter Thirteen

IOANNA

Word of her blessing was spreading like wildfire. She'd thought their reception at Enona had been an unusual fluke, a combination of lucky timing and the Order of the Sun's history in the area. But when they were stopped in a midsized town they'd only planned to pass through quietly by a crowd of people asking to see the future empress, she had to admit Aelia was correct.

People wanted to see her. They wanted to know if her blessing was real.

It was such a silly, selfish thing to care about, but Ioanna truly could not wait for the day she was formally assessed, and nobody would be able to question her blessing ever again. She was not offended by their skepticism, for she would be equally so if their positions were reversed. But the questions, the endless questions, were beginning to tire her. Now she found she looked forward to the days they spent between towns, regardless of how uncomfortable the tents were compared to true beds.

They never again received a reception as cold as the one at Lysera, but not all the nobles Ioanna solicited agreed to provide support. Some simply had nothing to give, for their situations were too desperate. Others were openly uncomfortable with Ioanna's presence, and though they were never rude enough to order her out, she could tell they wanted her gone and trying to reason with them would be a waste of everyone's time.

One morning, Ioanna woke late and wondered why nobody had come to rouse her. They were meant to be off to the next town as soon as possible, for they'd already been delayed enough. Vitaliya was still sound asleep beside her, and so Ioanna got up quietly to see what was going on.

When she stepped out of her tent, her heart stopped. A group of soldiers in unfamiliar uniforms had gathered in their camp. One was explaining something to Orsina, who had one hand lightly placed over her sword in a way that suggested she was not certain whether or not she believed his words. Ioanna went over to them.

"Dame Orsina. Who is this?" asked Ioanna.

"We have come from Duona, to the north," explained the one who had been speaking to Orsina. Ioanna nodded, for she was familiar with the city. They hadn't planned to stop there, for it seemed unlikely they'd find any support with the count—he was known to be a frequent visitor to Xyuluthe. "We have been sent to aid your cause."

"Count Saverio sent you?" Ioanna raised her eyebrows.

"Yes. I've a letter from him." He reached into his coat and passed it over. "When news of your blessing reached us, he asked for volunteers among the city guard to join with you."

"I see," said Ioanna. She could detect no lies from him or the letter, but she could not help but be a little suspicious. "You truly wish to serve my cause?"

"On our honor, we will see you crowned empress," he said solemnly. "You are the rightful heir, and even if you were not...this war must come to an end before Xytae is nothing but a hollow shell."

"I am surprised," said Ioanna. "I'd no intention of soliciting Count Saverio. I did not believe he would take any interest in my words. Nevertheless, I'm glad he took the initiative to find me. This will not be forgotten."

"Be wary, though," the man advised. "Priestesses of Reygmadra are rare so far from the capital, but we do have a few. Doubtless they've heard of you too. They may already be on their way to report your efforts to your sister."

"I don't doubt it," said Ioanna. She knew she wouldn't be able to keep her movements a secret forever, but she hoped they could at least keep the fact they were gathering on her grandmother's estate hidden for a bit longer.

Knight-Commander Livius should be in Nassai by now, if all had gone as planned. There'd been no communication from him, for such a thing was all but impossible and potentially dangerous. She hoped he was well.

She'd never been more grateful for Vitaliya's presence, a small spot of light and color in a world that was becoming nothing but anxiety and military movements. Perhaps it would have been wiser to leave her in Oredia or somewhere equally safe, but Ioanna thought she might have run away weeks ago if not for her.

She only wished Vitaliya could bring herself to believe it. It was obvious that, even now, she saw herself as unimportant. Ioanna was not sure where the issue stemmed from, nor was she sure how to fix it. She had already tried to communicate Vitaliya's importance multiple times, but it never felt like Vitaliya truly believed her.

When she went back into the tent, Vitaliya was still asleep. She would sleep until noon unless someone woke her. Ioanna sat down beside her and ran her fingers through Vitaliya's hair.

Vitaliya was so certain she'd have countless suitors—and Ioanna had to admit she was probably right about that just because any unmarried regent would be wading through proposals. But she could not muster up any enthusiasm for this possibility. None of them would know the first thing about her, nor would they really care.

The sensible thing to do would be to at least hear them out for Xytae's sake. But for some reason, she did not feel like being sensible. At least, not about this. She'd spent her whole life being calm and reasonable and responsible. She felt she was owed a moment of happiness.

That was, of course, assuming Vitaliya wanted to stay with her. She'd seemed horrified by the prospect of becoming empress consort, which was unfortunately the only logical conclusion to their relationship in Ioanna's eyes. But at the same time, Ioanna was confident Vitaliya did not want to leave her.

Vitaliya's breathing changed, and Ioanna withdrew her hand just as she opened her eyes.

"What happened?" mumbled Vitaliya. "Something's wrong?"

"No. We just slept late." Ioanna paused. "And we have supporters from Duona now."

"Oh, good. Who is that?"

"It's not a person; it's a city to the north. I hadn't planned to go there, but they found us."

Vitaliya stretched, nearly hitting Ioanna in the face. "Good! Better than good. That's wonderful." She continued to stretch, wriggling her shoulders. "I can't wait until we're done traveling. I think I'm tired of tents."

"We're starting southward today," said Ioanna. "It won't be long to Nassai. Assuming we make good time."

"I'm sure we won't. People will be asking to join up every hour, and we'll barely make it out of the mountains by sundown."

"Well, I suppose there are worse problems to have."

Ioanna was looking forward to their arrival at Nassai and taking stock of their forces. Her grandmother's lands there were large, far larger than at Oredia, and it was more rural. Ioanna had only visited it once or twice in her entire life and recalled there'd been nothing to do except read the books she'd brought with her. They hadn't even been allowed to wander through the fields for fear they'd trample the crops.

Vitaliya had reacted with disappointment when Ioanna explained most of the surrounding area was farmland and there were no major cities nearby, but she cheered up a little when Ioanna described the villa there, built to the same standards as the one in Oredia.

Vitaliya reached out for her with both arms, and Ioanna decided she didn't mind being a few more minutes late. The tent was a comfortable temperature, and the fabric was thick enough to keep out the cold, yet still thin enough that it glowed faintly with morning light when the sun rose. And the bedrolls were soft and thick enough that one did not generally feel the ground beneath.

Vitaliya's hands were warm and soft—softer than Ioanna might have expected, given her blessing and her time spent around farmers. But Vitaliya had never been allowed to handle the real tools, shovels and scythes and the like, nor had she been taught to use a weapon. Ioanna found her softness comforting, though, and allowed herself to be pulled back into the blankets.

Vitaliya pressed a kiss to her shoulder. "Is it cold outside?"

"Not colder than yesterday. It will be warmer when we make it out of the mountains."

"It will be warmest if we stay in here forever."

"I don't know if that's the best course of action."

"Of course, it is," murmured Vitaliya. Her lips trailed across Ioanna's collarbone and up to her chin. "Of course, it is."

"That's difficult to argue with," Ioanna whispered back. When Vitaliya smiled, the sight of it was so beautiful Ioanna wondered how in the world Vitaliya could think she'd ever let princes come and court her. "But the sooner we finish this, the sooner we can return to Xyuluthe. And you can get your old dresses back."

"Oh! I'd forgotten about those. Do you think they're still there, or they threw them away?"

"I'm not sure," admitted Ioanna. "Maybe they sent them back to Vesolda?"

"I'd like to imagine everything's exactly where I left it. All over the floor. And after you've stormed the capital and taken back the palace, we'll go in and see everything exactly how it was."

"I'm sure the servants will have at least picked them up—"

"No! This is my fantasy, not yours, and I say they're still on the floor."

Ioanna laughed. "If it's that important to you, then very well. They're still on the floor. And if they've been picked up by the time we arrive, I'll order the servants to throw them back down. Is that acceptable?"

"Oh, she's gone mad with power!" But Vitaliya was laughing now too. "You're going to get a reputation for issuing ridiculous commands, and it will be all because of me."

"Now, I'm curious. What other things were you thinking of asking me to do?"

"I don't have any plans! It's just this suspicion I have. I'll ask for something silly not even expecting you to say yes, but then of course you will because..." Her voice trailed off, and she blinked several times as though she'd lost track of her thoughts.

"What?" asked Ioanna.

"Because...I don't know why." Vitaliya gazed up at her. "It's just what you do. How you are. Going along with all my silly ideas like there's merit to them. And I never really stopped to think about why."

"I like your silly ideas," said Ioanna. "I don't need everything in my life to be serious every moment of the day. And it makes you happy, doesn't it?"

"Yes, but—"

"Then why shouldn't I?"

"I don't know. Most people find it irritating after a while, and so I try not to...but with you, I've never felt like I had to hold back."

"I'm glad. Maybe it means..." Now it was Ioanna who hesitated.

"What?"

"I don't want to offend you."

"I don't think you're capable of saying something offensive. Tell me before I die of curiosity."

"It's certainly nothing worth dying over. I was only wondering if we..." Ioanna struggled to find the correct words. "That is, perhaps I'm not experienced enough to say. Perhaps it's always like this? With...other people?" For Vitaliya had lived a very different life than her, and in the past occupied her time with men and women and neutroi. Ioanna did not think she would ever be capable of taking such a casual approach to love or intimacy, but she understood why it had appealed to Vitaliya.

Vitaliya's fingertips were so soft on her skin. "No," she said. "It's not. Nothing's ever been like this."

"It might not be too much longer," Ioanna murmured. "We're nearly at the end."

"Does it have to be the end?" Vitaliya's eyes were so intense. "Would you let me stay in Xyuluthe with you?"

"Of course, I would," whispered Ioanna. "For as long as you wanted—"

"You'll never be rid of me, then."

"I can live with that," Ioanna whispered into her hair. "Even if...I know you don't want to be empress consort. And you wouldn't have to be—it's just a title; you don't need another one when you're already a princess. And I don't want you to do anything that would make you unhappy."

"Maybe I wouldn't be unhappy." When Ioanna looked down at her, Vitaliya averted her gaze and bit her lower lip. "It's probably too early to say. I don't know. Ask me again in a year or two. If you haven't changed your mind in the meantime."

Ioanna could not keep her smile hidden. Nor did she need to with Vitaliya. "I doubt I will."

"You're in love," Vitaliya whispered up at her, mouth curling into a delighted smile as though she had just won something.

"*You're* in love," Ioanna retorted, picking up one of the extra pillows and dropping it over Vitaliya's face. It was childish, and rather uncharacteristic of her, but in that moment, it was the only thing she could think of to do. Too late she realized it might have been better to kiss Vitaliya or something. Or *anything*. Her embarrassment doubled.

As the pillow landed, Vitaliya laughed and screamed at the same time. Ioanna was afraid everyone would think they were murdering each other—or worse—so she jumped back to her feet.

"Come on, we're extremely late," said Ioanna. "You can stay here forever if you like, but I'm taking the tent."

"How unromantic! We'll have to work on that."

Ioanna wanted to ask what she had in mind but could not find the courage to say the words and spent the rest of the day regretting it.

Chapter Fourteen

VITALIYA

Nassai was just as beautiful as Oredia had been, despite the presence of the enormous encampment set up around Irianthe's villa. As their carriage passed through the neat rows of tents, so meticulously organized that the layout could have only been planned by the paladins, Vitaliya marveled at the sheer number of people gathered there.

"It's amazing!" said Vitaliya, leaning so far out the carriage window that Ioanna, fearing she might fall out, took hold of her dress. "There's so many people here—I had no idea we'd get this many!"

"There's more paladins than I expected," murmured Ioanna. "Significantly more."

"You wanted two hundred, didn't you?" But Vitaliya thought she might agree. It was impossible to count them from a moving carriage, but no matter where she looked, she could see white tabards.

When they arrived at the villa, Knight-Commander Livius was waiting for them. Vitaliya had never seen Ioanna embrace anyone before, apart from herself, but for a moment, she thought Ioanna might be about to hug him. She didn't, though, only clasped his hands and began asking him eager questions about their forces.

"There are currently three hundred paladins gathered at Nassai. Most are Xytan exiles but also some

Ieflarian and Vesoldan as well," he explained. "They came when they heard what was on the verge of happening."

"Then the Ieflarian and Vesoldan branches of the Order are supporting us? Openly?"

"Yes," he confirmed. "Under normal circumstances, I would not expect such a thing. My fear is some will interpret this as a sign the Order intends to continue taking an active role in political machinations."

"Do you think some within the Order will seek to use it as precedent?" Ioanna asked pointedly.

"I don't know," he admitted. "If they did, I would oppose them—I want this to be the exception, not the rule. Else the Order would twist into something I would no longer recognize. But that is a question for much later. We've prepared reports for you regarding the numbers of soldiers here, as well as our supplies, and I'd like to advise you regarding some of the non-soldiers who have joined our cause. If you'll come with me?"

"Of course. Vitaliya..." Ioanna met her eyes. "You might find this dull."

"I'll meet you later." Vitaliya smiled encouragingly. She didn't really want to separate from Ioanna, but she knew this meeting might go on for hours, and it would reflect poorly on Ioanna if she fell asleep during it.

"Do not leave the villa," cautioned Livius. "I'd hoped to keep our location a secret yet, but with the sheer amount of people arriving... I know the news has reached Xyuluthe already. We may even have spies in our ranks."

"Is there anyone you'd like me to question?" asked Ioanna.

"No, but we've twice as many people here as your grandmother expected. It's become impossible for us to monitor them all."

Vitaliya found herself inexplicably overcome with the urge to remain by Ioanna's side. She opened her mouth to say she would stay, but the words died on her lips as she realized this might not be what was best for Ioanna. Perhaps there were spies in the camp, but what good would Vitaliya be against an assassin? Her presence would only add to the chaos, the danger.

Vitaliya closed her mouth and pressed her lips together. Ioanna and the knight-commander were so immersed in their conversation that neither had noticed her about to speak. Jealousy pricked at her but only for a brief, irrational moment. Livius was old enough to be her father. She had nothing to fear from him.

In fact, Vitaliya suspected he still saw Ioanna as a child. He treated her respectfully, of course. She'd never complained he behaved in a condescending manner or tried to overrule her wishes. But Vitaliya sensed he still thought of Ioanna as the little girl he'd known before his exile, not the woman she was now, like a father who could not admit his daughter was grown.

Another paladin escorted her to the villa. As they walked, Vitaliya glanced sidelong at him and wondered if the Order of the Sun would put forward suitors of their own for the new empress.

Like most priests, paladins had to renounce any family rank or titles they might hold before initiating. But that was only a matter of paperwork; there was no changing who one's parents were. And if there were any who came from noble families...

Ioanna will send them away, Vitaliya reminded herself. She would not trouble herself or Ioanna with tedious jealousy for another moment! Besides, would a paladin even be a good match for her? They would have a lot in common, but would Ioanna want to marry someone who revered her, who saw her as nearer to a goddess than a person? That might be enjoyable for a few weeks, but Vitaliya imagined it would quickly grow tiresome.

Upon arriving at the villa, Vitaliya was greeted by Irianthe's servants. They were all cheerful and friendly, but Vitaliya found herself wondering if any of them secretly resented Ioanna for turning their home into a military camp.

But as a servant led her down the halls to her room, Vitaliya noted the villa was actually rather peaceful. There were no paladins or soldiers about. Only servants and the occasional guard. She supposed they were probably all staying in the camp with the villa reserved for only the most important members of the army.

As usual, Vitaliya had no intention of using the room she'd been given, but she appreciated the gesture. Like her room back in Oredia, it had a bath, and Vitaliya wasted no time before stepping into the warm water. Back home, they had to have people with Inthi's fire warm the water for baths. Xytae's pipes were so much more convenient. Some had been left behind in the major cities after Vesolda became independent but had fallen into disrepair. Now there was nobody in the country who knew how to make them work again.

As Vitaliya soaked in the water, she wondered what Irianthe was doing now. Was Ioanna's grandmother safe? She wouldn't normally be worried, for the woman was undoubtably powerful and influential. But if Xyuluthe knew Ioanna's resistance was gathering at Nassai, surely they'd suspect it was Irianthe's doing?

Vitaliya took her time in the bath, and by the time she was done, it was rather late in the day. She was tired from the journey, and part of her considered climbing into bed and hoping that Ioanna came to her in a few hours. But another part of her was curious about the villa and about the people who had gathered to support Ioanna.

The idea of going and talking to members of Ioanna's would-be army was intimidating, though. What could she say to people who were about to risk their lives? Especially since she knew she'd be safely behind them once the fighting started—assuming she was even allowed to go to Xyuluthe.

She and Ioanna had not discussed the matter yet, but she had a feeling when it came time to launch their final offensive, Vitaliya would be forced to remain in Nassai until it was all over.

Well, maybe she could find some fruit trees in the garden and hand out...not oranges, she was sick of those, but maybe pomegranates, cherries, or something else? If nothing else, it would be good for morale, and maybe everyone would forgive her for being useless.

The gardens were peaceful, and the villa's high walls blocked out the worst of the noise from the surrounding encampment. The sun was fading, but it would still be light for a while longer.

She took note of fruit trees as she walked along, deciding she wouldn't wake any of them up until she'd seen all her options. Her hands brushed against the bark instinctively, and the feeling of the wood beneath her hands was soothing. She considered taking her shoes off but decided against it. As nice as it would be to feel the dirt beneath her feet, she had to think of how her actions would reflect on Ioanna.

Would it still be like this when Ioanna was empress? The thought took her by surprise. She was no more confident about becoming empress consort than she'd been the first time Ioanna spoke the words. But regardless of titles, *would* it always be like this—with Ioanna in endless meetings while Vitaliya wandered around and tried not to embarrass her too badly, or at least be useful enough that people would forgive her when she inevitably did?

Perhaps she *should* have attended the meeting with Ioanna. It would not have been fun, but she would pay attention because she cared about Ioanna, and Ioanna cared about Xytae, and so, logically, Vitaliya cared about Xytae too. More importantly, she ought to be informed, so when Ioanna worried about this or that issue, Vitaliya could share her own perspective and give advice or simply commiserate.

But then, Vitaliya was a foreigner. Until her name was on a marriage contract, she could not realistically expect to be allowed to stand beside Ioanna at meetings of statecraft. Perhaps people would be lenient now if she'd asked to go with Ioanna today. But once Ioanna was empress...

She remembered standing in front of the doors to Irianthe's study back at Oredia, waiting for the meeting to end. Would that be her entire life? Perpetually standing outside, counting the seconds until Ioanna returned to her?

No, she would not allow that. She would find *some* way to be useful—whether raising crops or just throwing parties until the court forgot why they hadn't supported Ioanna from the start.

The sound of shouting caught her attention, drawing Vitaliya back to reality. She turned away from the plants, curious but not concerned yet. Were they under attack? Or were the soldiers fighting amongst themselves as soldiers were sometimes known to do when they had no one else to direct their aggression toward? But most of the soldiers here were paladins, so that seemed unlikely.

Perhaps it would have been wisest to remain where she was, or even return to the house, but Vitaliya could not help but follow the noise. Surely she was in no danger now that she was in the villa surrounded by guards?

The noise was coming from the other side of the wall, toward the camp that surrounded them, and Vitaliya began to walk toward the entrance. Just as she came within sight of the wide opening, two maids rushed to her, their faces red and sweaty.

"Oh, hello!" said Vitaliya, surprised. "Is everything all right?"

"You must come with us immediately," said one of the women, stepping forward. "A chaos goddess has attacked our soldiers."

"What? Which one?" Cytha? Would she be foolish—or desperate—enough to attack a few hundred paladins? Or maybe Reygmadra herself, fed up with incompetent underlings? "We need to get Ioanna first—"

One of the servants grabbed her by the wrist. Her grip was surprisingly firm. "Come with us; we'll get you to safety."

"Yes, but—" Still disoriented and panicked, Vitaliya allowed the woman to pull her along. "What about Ioanna?"

"The paladins will protect her."

"Wait." Vitaliya dug her heels in to the soft ground, grateful she'd kept her shoes on after all. "Wait. I'm not going anywhere. Tell me what—"

The servant released Vitaliya's wrist and sighed heavily. "Do it," she said.

Before Vitaliya could ask what she was talking about, something struck her in the back of the head. The blow was like nothing Vitaliya had ever felt before. The world tilted, and went black before she remembered hitting the grass.

Reality faded in and out, but she was aware someone was holding a waterskin to her mouth. She drank without thinking, but the wine was strange and bitter like it was tainted with something...a poison?

But what would be the point of waiting for her to wake up just to poison her when they could just as easily have killed her in her sleep?

Her vision cleared somewhat, and she realized someone was kneeling in front of her. It was one of the servants from the garden, except she wasn't wearing a peasant's dress anymore. She was dressed in light leather armor, and her hair was pinned in a coiled braid.

"What happened?" Vitaliya mumbled. They were in the middle of a forest, and two horses had been tied to a tree not far from where she sat. She tried to move, but her hands and ankles were bound by rope.

"Be quiet," ordered the woman, and Vitaliya considered screaming just to spite her. But she was already growing drowsy again, so drowsy she thought screaming would be more trouble than it was worth.

She had to think of a way to escape, to get back to Ioanna, and to warn her that her camp had been infiltrated...

But it was so difficult to think when she was so tired.

Vitaliya closed her eyes and resolved to come up with a better plan after she'd rested.

Vitaliya opened her eyes and took in her surroundings. She was on a cold floor, in a box—a cell, she realized. The sort that prisoners were sent to. The back wall was made from plain stone while the other three were iron bars. She tried to get up, but the world shifted as though she were on board a ship.

Vitaliya managed to stagger over to the door's bars, which was sealed with a heavy, ugly lock. Surrounding her were more cells identical to her own, all empty.

Vitaliya took a few deep breaths and tried to assess what had happened to her. The attack on Nassai was clearly meant to be a diversion, so she could be kidnapped. But why her and not Ioanna, who was so much more valuable?

Or perhaps Ioanna was already dead, killed by whatever goddess had been sent.

No. That was impossible. There were hundreds of paladins at Nassai. No chaos goddess would be able to get within arm's reach of Ioanna, let alone kill her.

Somewhere nearby, but beyond her line of vision, a door opened. As footsteps approached, Vitaliya realized she might not want to see whoever was coming, and she backed away from the door. A moment later a figure rounded the corner, and Vitaliya saw it was Netheia.

The last few months must have been difficult for the princess because she had a haggard, haunted look in her eyes. Vitaliya would have been expecting her to be pristine and finely dressed so near to the day of her coronation, but she wore a dress that was stained and torn as though she hadn't changed in many days—and had been spending a great deal of her time sparring. There were dark circles under her eyes, made darker still by her pale, sickly complexion.

"Netheia," said Vitaliya, unable to stop herself. "What happened to you?"

Netheia did not reply. Instead, she pulled a ring of keys from her pocket and unlocked Vitaliya's cell. It occurred to her to try to run, to bolt past Netheia and try to make it to wherever the exit was...but before she could take a step, the door swung shut behind Netheia.

"I was sure you'd have run back home," said Netheia. "Anyone with sense would have."

"This..." Vitaliya's throat was dry, and she coughed a few times to try to clear it. "It's just a misunderstanding. There's been a mistake."

"There's no mistake. You tried to warn Ioanna I was coming for her, you fled to my grandmother's estate with her, and you've been traveling around the north gathering up an *army* with her for the last two months!"

"That's not true. I was, I was kidnapped! She forced me to go along with her! She has a powerful blessing! I couldn't get away from her!"

Netheia hesitated, and for a moment Vitaliya thought she might have believed the lie. Then her eyes went distant, and she frowned a little as though listening to a voice that only she could hear.

"You're *lying*," she spat. "And you're not even good at it. I almost hope she doesn't come for you, just so I can kill you."

"Well, good news, then," said Vitaliya. "She's not coming, and I don't know why you ever thought she might. She'd never put one life above the rest of the empire."

"Above her crown, you mean!"

"No," said Vitaliya. "Above your sad, crumbling empire with dying fields and starving children and veterans forced into banditry. Maybe you should get out of your palace more often because from what I've seen, nobody with any sense would want to rule a country like this!"

Netheia struck her across the face. The blow didn't seem like one that should have hurt too badly, but from Netheia it was enough to knock her to the floor. Vitaliya landed on her hands, and pain shot through her arms.

"Maybe I should just kill you now," Netheia said. "If she's not coming to turn herself in, maybe I should just get it over with."

"Wait," said Vitaliya, pushing herself back up. "Wait. Listen—you don't know what I've seen. Nobody in Xyuluthe knows how bad it is, or if they do, they've kept it a secret. Xytae is falling apart. Your people are starving because you sent all the farmers to Masim and all the priests of Eyvindr to the Imperial Fields. It won't matter if you become empress because Xytae won't last more than a few years before—" Her words ended in a shout as Netheia kicked her in the stomach, and she doubled over in pain.

Netheia's hand gripped a handful of her hair and dragged her upward again. Vitaliya tried to pull away, but Netheia was absurdly strong. She slammed her fist into Vitaliya's face—once, twice, three times—and her vision blurred. Vitaliya put up her hands to protect herself, but Netheia barely seemed to notice as she drove her knee into Vitaliya's ribs.

This was what Netheia had meant by killing her now, Vitaliya realized. There would be no quiet, dignified execution. Just the blood rage. And a war with Vesolda would surely follow once the news reached home.

And her father would never know she did not hate him.

"That's enough," said a new voice. It was not particularly loud, or forceful, but Netheia froze immediately. Though her eyes were streaming with tears, and one was swelling to the point that she could barely see, Vitaliya could make out the shape of a woman standing just inside the cell—though she had not heard anyone enter.

Netheia released Vitaliya's hair, though there was still quite a bit of it left behind in her hand as Vitaliya slumped to the ground.

"Ioanna isn't coming," said Netheia bitterly. "I should have known. It was a ridiculous idea from the start."

"No," said the other woman, her tone cool and dispassionate. "For this one, she will order her army to surrender."

Vitaliya studied the strange woman. She was tall with long, messy hair, and the only ornamentation she wore was the smear of red paint across her eyes. She was dressed in plain, battle-damaged leather armor—an odd choice given there was no shortage of intact armor in the city—and carried a sword at her side.

"Ioanna doesn't think like that," objected Netheia. "It's not how she is. She won't put one person above her whole army."

The red lady—for there was indeed something intangible about her that Vitaliya could only describe as "red"—did not reply. She only stared at Vitaliya, one side of her mouth curling into a smile that seemed more predatory than pleased. "Do not kill her. Do you understand me? Ioanna *will* accept your terms but not if you've only a corpse to trade."

Netheia looked about as skeptical as Vitaliya felt, but the red lady paid her no mind. Instead, she crouched down so she was at eye level with Vitaliya, her brow furrowing as though Vitaliya was a puzzle she could not quite work out.

"Almost *too* perfect," she murmured. Her eyes were so dark, so cold. "Who moved you here? Dayluue? But why?"

Vitaliya glanced over at Netheia, wondering if she had any idea what the other woman was talking about. But Netheia just stood there, stone-faced and awkward. The red lady tapped her fingernails on the stone floor, considering.

"*You* don't know, do you?" she asked.

Vitaliya could not tell if the lady was mocking her or not, but she shook her head—only to regret it as the entire room tilted dramatically. "Know what?" she rasped, swallowing a few times to keep her stomach under control.

"Why you're here."

Vitaliya recalled her conversation with Aelia, and the rage-inducing suggestion that Vitaliya's father had met his future bride only because someone had wanted Vitaliya to go to Xytae. She had a feeling the red lady was talking about that. "I don't know. I'm not important. It, it might have already been done. When Ioanna and I escaped, when Netheia came to arrest her—she didn't know what to do. If I hadn't been there, she might not have made it out of the city."

And that was truly Vitaliya's only guess. She'd hoped by now she'd have a little more clarity, but the lack of any sort of answer on the subject led her to believe she'd served her only purpose months ago.

In that case, she should have gone back to Vesolda as soon as she'd had the opportunity.

Tears sprang to her eyes at the realization that, if this woman was correct, she would be the cause of Ioanna's downfall. The red lady made a disdainful face.

"That can't be it," she said scornfully. "That's nothing. Anyone might have done that. A servant, a priest...nobody moves a princess to the site of a civil war without a very, very good reason. And you—you're nothing but a weakness, a vulnerability to exploit. Dayluue is meant to be on Iolar's side, but she only gave Ioanna a new weakness when she called you here, and I want to know *why*."

"Maybe she's not on Ioanna's side, then," said Vitaliya emptily. "Maybe she's on yours."

The expression that came over the red lady's face was difficult to describe. At first, it resembled confusion, but then it gave way to scorn and disgust, which was followed by dark, ugly fury.

"You stupid, worthless insect." The red lady's voice was as cool and level as ever, but Vitaliya could sense something about the suggestion had shaken the woman. She rose to her feet and walked out of the cell, leaving Vitaliya there on the floor. "It hardly matters, I suppose. It's nearly finished." She paused to acknowledge Netheia only briefly. "Do not kill her. She will be worthless to us if she's dead."

The woman left, and Netheia followed her. Alone once again, Vitaliya lay her head on the cold ground and tried to find a position that did not send pain shooting through her body.

If only the floor were dirt, not stone. She doubted there'd be any seeds for her to coax life from, and if there were, they'd hardly be of any use, but at least she could listen to the world's heartbeat and allow it to soothe her.

She thought, again, of her father. She did not hate him; she never had. She loved him just as she loved her mother, and now she deeply regretted she'd never written to him to say she was safe, and sooner or later he'd learn what had happened to her.

She only hoped he did not think she'd died hating him.

Perhaps she'd be allowed to visit him in a dream from Iestil and tell him so.

Though only marginally successful in finding a comfortable position, eventually she managed to drift off to sleep.

She dreamed she was in the sun, her head rested in Ioanna's lap and the scent of fresh flowers in the air. But when Ioanna leaned down to kiss her, Vitaliya realized she was someone else, someone different...

"Don't worry," said not-Ioanna. "It's nearly finished. It's nearly finished."

Chapter Fifteen

IOANNA

As they made their way through the camp, Knight-Commander Livius explained the situation at Nassai in great detail—the resources they had, how many people had joined, and how long Ioanna could realistically afford to feed them for.

"How soon can we leave for Xyuluthe?" asked Ioanna as they walked. "If Netheia knows we're gathering, then we can expect she's already issued an order for troops to return from Masim. I don't want to waste a single day."

"I've received word from the Empress Mother Irianthe that an order was issued several days ago," said Livius. "But she tells me it will be weeks before the nearest of them make it back."

"Then we should move out immediately," said Ioanna. "We're only using up supplies by sitting here and risking infiltration by spies or saboteurs."

"I agree, but we've been training those who have no experience in combat. A few more days would benefit everyone."

Ioanna frowned. "I don't want to send anyone away, but I don't like the idea of farmers fighting the city guards. Even if we can get them proper equipment, they're at a disadvantage. Could we feasibly leave them here?"

"We don't know what will happen in the capital," Livius reminded her. "We need every bit of support we can get. But we will see to it those who have never fought before are not stationed near the front."

Ioanna gazed out across the camp. Everyone was watching her, and she was sure they'd approach her if she hadn't been ringed by paladins. Ioanna did not know whether she wanted to invite them to approach her or not. They deserved her gratitude for risking everything to support her. But her confidence wavered as she recalled how the nobles back home always sneered when she spoke up. Perhaps it would be better to remain silent, rather than risk saying something foolish and making everyone regret coming.

She smiled briefly at the gathered soldiers, trying to meet as many of their gazes as she could, trying to convey without words that she valued each of them and understood what they stood to lose. Fortunately, Livius was talking again, giving her an excuse to remain silent. She could not wait to see the expression on Netheia's face when she rode back into the city with an army. She could just imagine herself on a warhorse, sword in hand, running down every noble who had ever sneered at her approach—

No!

Ioanna shook herself. Where had *that* come from? It was the most uncharacteristic daydream she'd ever had in her life! She did not want to hurt Netheia or any of the court. Yes, talking sense into them was probably a childish fantasy, but she had no desire to kill them, especially not by her own hand.

Besides, she hardly knew how to use a sword.

"Crown Princess?" asked Livius, and Ioanna realized she hadn't been paying attention. "Are you all right?"

"I think so," murmured Ioanna, but now he had a hand to his sword. "Do you sense something?"

He did not reply, but he did not need to. The expression on his face was answer enough. Ioanna had just enough time to wonder which chaos god was foolish enough to attack an encampment of several hundred paladins before rage washed over her.

How dare Netheia drive her from her home? How dare Netheia try to rob her of her birthright? How dare their parents deceive her into believing her blessing was shameful, rob her of a proper childhood, bring her into such a tainted world—

Ioanna ripped herself out of thrall, landing on her knees in the process. She had *felt* Cytha's hold on her, heard the thoughts that were not her own, but they'd been so antithetical to who she was that they could only hold her for a moment.

"Get her out of here!" Livius barked at one of the other paladins. The nearest one took her by the arm and began to pull her in the direction of the villa. Ioanna was not certain whether to cooperate with him or join in the fight against Cytha.

But Cytha had not manifested yet, or if she had, she was hiding somewhere unseen. Maybe she would not manifest at all? She hadn't when Vitaliya was in thrall all those weeks ago.

Then, distantly, Ioanna saw one of her would-be soldiers pick up a sword and stab one of his companions through the chest.

Livius saw it too, but other paladins were nearer and reached him first. Within minutes, they held him by the arms, and Ioanna saw one draw his own sword.

"Don't kill him!" Ioanna cried. "He's in thrall!"

Belatedly, Ioanna realized she might be incorrect. The man might just be a spy. But what sort of spy would kill exactly one man in plain view of everyone? She decided she could question him later. For now, she would accept the risk if it meant saving his life.

Something tightened around Ioanna's arm, and she looked up into the face of the paladin who had been ordered to take her away. She expected him to tell her they needed to leave, but instead he looked at her very strangely and said, "It's your fault we were cast out of Xytae."

Ioanna did not think. She called her magic to her free hand and blasted the man back, knocking him off his feet and sending him flying in the opposite direction.

"I'm sorry!" she cried after him.

Aelia had not been beside Ioanna a moment ago, but now she was. "She's manifesting," the goddess murmured. "Once she does, I can guide you to her."

Ioanna scanned the camp again. Everyone she saw had a sword in their hand, but that only made her heart sink.

"Come on!" Aelia cried. "Let's finish this! You know I hate waiting for things!"

All was silence for a moment longer. Then mist began to gather in front of them, shaping into a woman. When it was done, Cytha stood there before them, looking just as she had when they'd faced her back in Oredia.

"What are you *doing*?" asked Aelia incredulously. "You can't be this desperate."

Cytha's eyes went from Aelia to Ioanna. Though her body showed no signs of exhaustion, something about her gave Ioanna the impression she was very, very tired. Ioanna waited for her to attack, but she did not. She only stared at them as though she'd just woken up and could not recall why she'd come here.

"Cytha?" prompted Aelia. "Come on. Are you going to call me a traitor, or do I have to do it for you?"

Behind Cytha, Livius was approaching rapidly. He was saying the binding words that would trap her in her body and allow them to kill her, albeit temporarily. Cytha waved a hand without even glancing back at him, and a gust of blue-white magic struck him in the chest, sending him down to one knee.

"You don't have to do this," said Aelia. "You don't have to destroy yourself to be free of her. You could just tell her no."

Cytha laughed. "Oh, could I? And what do you think she would do in return?"

"I can help you," said Aelia. "We can help you."

"Twist me into something new, you mean?" asked Cytha. "And when Men whisper my name, I'll just tell them, 'No, I'm sorry. I don't do that anymore. Solve your own problems'? It was so easy for you to run away from your old domain because nobody wanted you to start with. I am not so worthless."

Aelia ran her fingers through her hair casually, but Ioanna saw her swallow. "I forgot how miserable you are," she said. Her tone was light, but the lightness was a lie, even if the words were not. "All right. Let's get this over with, then."

Other paladins had gathered around Cytha, but most of them would not need to do anything more than stand there to prevent her from escaping. Not that Ioanna thought she would try. Cytha was so resigned. How terribly was Reygmadra treating her that she would take death—even a temporary one—over being her ally?

When Livius got back up and approached Cytha with his sword, Ioanna averted her eyes.

She allowed one of the paladins to steer her into the largest tent in the encampment. It was sparse inside, despite its size, and Ioanna sank down into the nearest chair, her legs trembling. Someone put a cup of water in her hands.

The minutes dragged on, but her heartbeat would not slow. Ioanna closed her eyes, and all she could see was that soldier, the one who had been killed when the first man was put in thrall.

Could she have stopped it? If she had been just a little faster, she might have put a shield up between him and his victim.

"Crown Princess," said a voice. Ioanna opened her eyes and looked up at Livius. Orsina was just behind him. "Are you all right?"

"Yes, I'm fine," Ioanna murmured. "I, I attacked one of the paladins. He was in thrall. I should apologize—" She began to stand, but Livius pushed her firmly back down into the chair.

"It's nothing," soothed Orsina. "He's more embarrassed than you are."

"I wasn't angry at Vitaliya for being put in thrall, and I'm not angry at him either," said Ioanna. "Can you tell him that? I don't want him to think I hate him." She thought of his accusation that her father had ordered them out of the country because of her. Surely that was not true? The Order of the Sun was not responsible for the blessing Ioanna had received, and her father would not blame them for it.

But he might seek to punish them for lack of another victim.

Ioanna forced herself to breathe deeply. Even if that was the case, the blame lay solely with her father for the choices he'd made, not with Ioanna for existing.

"Someone—someone check on Vitaliya," said Ioanna. "Someone make sure she's all right."

"I'm sure she's fine," soothed Knight Commander Livius. "She's still at the villa; she was nowhere near—"

"I'll go," said Orsina quickly. "Better to be safe."

"That was Cytha?" asked Livius once Orsina was gone. Ioanna nodded.

"She's more powerful than some of her siblings, but she should still be weeks regenerating," he said. "At least we won't have to worry about her until after we take back Xyuluthe."

Ioanna nodded again and stared down at her feet. How many of her soldiers would flee the camp after what had happened? She should address them, try to assuage their fears.

Her thoughts returned to Cytha. This had been little more than a suicide mission. She'd obviously known how attacking Nassai would end for her. There had to be more to her plan than just desperation.

"I want to talk to the soldiers," said Ioanna. "They signed on to fight my sister, not chaos goddesses. I need to get ahead of any rumors that might pick up now. Or else they'll frighten themselves into deserting."

"I don't think they will with so many paladins here," said Livius. "But there's no harm in addressing them. Take some time to prepare what you want to say, and we will have them gather tonight."

"And if any of them do try to desert, let them go," said Ioanna. Livius opened his mouth to object, but she shook her head vehemently. "No. I won't force anyone to stay after that. Netheia surely knows what's happening by now, so there's no useful information they can pass on to her. My father forced people into armies. I won't be like him."

"You are already nothing like him," said Livius.

She supposed she ought to be proud of that, but the only emotion she could muster up right now was exhaustion. "You killed Cytha so easily."

"That is why I am here, Crown Princess."

"Yes, I know." Ioanna hesitated, trying to decide how to describe what she was thinking. "When we go to Xyuluthe, Netheia will certainly confront me, or try to. I, I don't want her killed."

"Crown Princess—"

"I don't want her killed," repeated Ioanna. "She can't help the blessing she was given. She can't help how our father and the priestesses raised her. Promise me— promise me—"

"No."

Ioanna stared up at him, and she must have appeared sufficiently distraught because Livius relented.

"We will try to take her alive, if possible," said Livius. "But it may not be. And I would rather have your hatred for the rest of my life than see you dead by her hand."

Ioanna realized she could not expect any paladin to prioritize their enemy over herself. There was a very real possibility one of them might even defy her orders and go after Netheia deliberately, reasoning that any punishment Ioanna might issue was more than worth the cost of seeing her greatest enemy dead.

"My mother's blessing isn't strong," Ioanna said slowly. "She doesn't fight when she can't win. My sister Iulia, she's only ten, and she has Reygmadra's magic, but she's not like Netheia at all. She's happy—"

"They will not be harmed," confirmed Livius. "So long as they do not attempt to harm you."

"The servants are innocent—"

"Ioanna." He leaned forward and took her by the hands. "We are not mercenaries. We do not want to see bloodshed any more than you do. The Order will do their utmost to preserve the lives of your people. I cannot promise there will be no tragedies in the heat of battle, but we take no joy in killing."

But not all her soldiers were paladins. Some were farmers, city guards, or ex-soldiers like Modia and her bandits. Could she trust them to show restraint? Could she even ask that of them, or would they think her a foolish, idealistic child?

She would have to say something about it when she addressed them. Urge them to think of the citizens of Xyuluthe as their allies, not their enemies. The residents of the city were their countrymen, and most of the palace residents were harmless or at least thoughtless courtiers. Most would turn and run once they realized what was happening—Ioanna hoped. If nothing else, she would make it clear she would not tolerate pillaging. The very thought of it made her heart burn with fury.

Someone else entered the tent, and Ioanna looked over to see Orsina standing there with something in her hands. A letter, Ioanna realized. It was open, but the wax seal was still stuck to one end of the paper—dark red, but not so dark she could not see her own family's insignia. Her face was solemn as she passed it over to Livius.

"Is that from my grandmother?" asked Ioanna. She rose partway in her chair, trying to see what was written, but they were both so much taller than her.

"No," Orsina said.

"Did you find Vitaliya?"

"No."

"What is that letter?" Ioanna got to her feet, impatient now. "What's going on?"

"It is..." Orsina looked at Livius helplessly. "It is a ransom letter."

Truth.

How strange. Her blessing had never detected truth before, only lies. But the word chimed in her head like the ringing of a bell, strong and smooth.

"Where is she?" Ioanna could hear her voice shaking. "Where—"

Vitaliya was fine. She had to be. Maybe she'd woven herself a grass bed and slept in the garden? Ioanna leapt to her feet and tried to push past them, but Livius caught her by the arm and refused to release her.

"Listen to me, Ioanna," he said. "You must remain calm. This is what Netheia wants you to do—she wants you to panic, so you'll stop thinking clearly and make mistakes."

Ioanna ripped her arm out of his grasp, and it was only then that she realized her hands were glowing with golden light, even though she could not recall summoning her magic. Despite the warmth of it, she only felt very, very cold.

"Ioanna?" said Livius, but his voice was oddly muffled like it was coming from somewhere far away.

Ioanna opened her mouth to reply, but something was caught in her throat, and she coughed. A bit of phlegm, or something. Ioanna had never spat in her life, but she did now—and what landed on the ground before her feet was strange and glowing gold. It pulsed for a moment before dissipating into the dirt.

"Oh," said Ioanna, now thoroughly convinced she was dreaming. She rubbed at her eyes, and more gold light stuck to her hands—it was streaming from her eyes.

"Ioanna?" There was panic in his voice, and if Ioanna hadn't been in the process of coming untethered from her own body, maybe she would be worried too. "Ioanna! Can you hear me?"

"Yes," said Ioanna, but even her voice felt distant, meaningless. "Don't yell. Please."

"What's happening to her?" Livius asked, and Ioanna realized he was addressing Aelia, who had once again appeared among them. "What is this?"

Aelia was interesting to see. Ioanna could see her mortal body, the vessel of water and meat that she wore every day so she could live beside Orsina. But beyond that was something else, something beautiful and terrible that existed simultaneously within arm's reach and at an insurmountable distance.

Ioanna saw it—and it saw her. She would not have imagined that a creature made of pure energy would be able to look surprised, but it did.

"She's not a woman at all; she's just purple," Ioanna tried to explain for the benefit of the others, but the words came out strange and slurred. It was like being drunk, but she did not feel tired. She felt invigorated. She felt as though she would never need to sleep again.

"Have you ever seen this before?" Livius asked Aelia.

Aelia exhaled through her mouth. "Not in a very long time."

"What should we do?"

"Point her at Xyuluthe. And then stand somewhere out of the way."

"Xyuluthe," Ioanna mumbled. Xyuluthe was the source of the corruption in this tainted land, spreading misery and fear like a poison. And it was where Netheia had taken Vitaliya.

You'll do the right thing. No matter how much you hate it. You'll do what's best for Xytae.

Who had said those words to her? Her grandmother, warning her of this exact scenario, as though she had foreseen it?

No, it had been Vitaliya.

Maybe I'll surprise you, Ioanna had said.

Maybe she would surprise everyone.

"I need to go to Xyuluthe now," said Ioanna. "Goodbye." She pushed her way out of the tent and tried to remember what horses were in the stables and which ones were the fastest. It would be days, perhaps even a week, if she brought the entire army she'd amassed. But alone, on horseback, she might make it before tomorrow night...if she did not care whether her mount lived or died.

"Ioanna, *wait*," said Livius. When Ioanna did not wait, he hurried to keep up with her. "Listen to me! This cannot be Iolar's will! We've raised an army—larger than any of us ever dared hope! We can take back Xyuluthe in the way we planned."

"And Vitaliya will die," said Ioanna. The gold light tasted so strange in her mouth—simultaneously sweet and bitter. She wiped at her lips. "No. I will not be alone again."

"You can't put her life above the rest of this country!"

"Do you think I'm going to surrender?" Ioanna tilted her head curiously. "Do you think I intend to turn myself in?"

"I've no idea what you intend," said Livius. "At this moment, I'm not even sure *who* you are. If I didn't know better, I'd say something had you in thrall!"

Something about that sentiment struck her as hilarious, and she laughed. But the laugh was not entirely hers. It was like the ringing of a bell, pure and powerful. She turned away and continued walking. Behind her, she could hear their conversation as they followed.

"Should we try an exorcism?" muttered Orsina, not as quietly as she'd probably intended.

"It won't do anything; it's Iolar's magic on her," said Aelia.

"I refuse to believe this is his will," insisted Livius. "This is—this is not his way."

"No, you're right about that. Someone else pushed her to this." Aelia exhaled loudly. "Someone who didn't trust Iolar could get it done properly."

Part of Ioanna—a very small, very quiet part—was curious about what they were saying. But it was stifled by the much larger part, which was suggesting they tear the Imperial Palace apart, stone by stone, until Vitaliya was safe once again.

"Why is this happening?" asked Orsina. "*What* is happening?"

"I can try to explain it, but mortal languages aren't designed to describe things like this," warned Aelia. "I can't promise you'll understand."

"Tell us whatever you can," instructed Livius. "Anything helps."

"Ioanna has an ordinary blessing within her body, just as you and Orsina do. It's how she uses her shields. But her Truthsayer magic is not part of that, it's separate...and it's kept within Iolar himself. She is tethered to him."

Truth.

Ioanna paused and glanced back over her shoulder at Aelia. If she was feeling more like her usual self, she was certain she'd have thousands of questions. But now, she could only muster up a little twinge of curiosity.

"Truthsayer magic is always active, always waiting, always drawing power." Aelia met Ioanna's eyes. "If it was kept within you, you'd have died when you were only a few days old; you'd have drained yourself by just existing."

"How can we get her back to normal?" asked Livius.

"I understand why you're asking, but I think it might be best to let her do what she wants." When he opened his mouth to object, Aelia added, "Someone went to a lot of trouble to set this up—someone significantly more powerful than me. There's got to be a reason they want her to do this instead of following our original plan."

"How do we know the one who did this to her is benign?" he asked. "How do we know it wasn't meant to be a way to get her to Xyuluthe without our protection? What if it was Reygmadra herself?"

"It wasn't Reygmadra," asserted Aelia. "I, I think it was Dayluue. I *know* it was Dayluue. She's had her hand in this from the day Ioanna was born. Vitaliya and Ioanna crossing paths was her doing. I've spent weeks trying to figure out why Vitaliya was sent up here. But now I think I've got it. Dayluue knew Reygmadra would see Vitaliya as a weakness to exploit...and when she did, Ioanna would lose control of her blessing."

"How do we know Dayluue isn't aiding Reygmadra?" pressed Livius.

"Because Dayluue is the reason Reygmadra wasn't able to give Ioanna a blessing from the start," said Aelia. "And Reygmadra's never forgiven her for it."

Ioanna was tired of this conversation. Vitaliya needed her, and every minute wasted was another minute that Netheia might decide to kill her out of pure spite. She turned away again and continued her walk to the stables.

"Ioanna, wait," said Livius. "We'll go to Xyuluthe, but you cannot go alone. Even if you do manage to rescue Vitaliya and defeat your sister, you don't have enough supporters within the city. What if your mother turns on you? What if the other nobles refuse to support you?"

"I don't care." *Lie.* Ioanna paused, surprised. She *did* care? Yes, yes, she did. Or at least, that little piece of her that was still curious and afraid and soft did. Maybe she ought to listen to it? But there was no time. She'd spent the last twenty years doing nothing except being inoffensive and invisible. Now it was time to act, to fight, to purify—

"Let us come with you," coaxed Orsina. "Aelia and me and some of the other paladins. Enough to protect you but not slow you down. And we'll arrange for the rest of your forces to follow behind. They'll catch up with us in a few days, so if the worst happens, we can hold out until more support arrives."

Ioanna warred with herself, the large and loud part of her that could not care less about strategy and empires and anything that wasn't Vitaliya against the small, soft part of her that cared very, very much. Finally, when the headache was too much to bear, she muttered, "Fine."

"It won't be long," Livius promised her. "Just be patient. We'll leave before dawn."

Ioanna nodded, reluctantly. Perhaps sensing she needed reassurance, Aelia placed a hand on Ioanna's shoulder.

"Don't worry," said Aelia. "We'll get her back."

It was not a lie, but it was an opinion, so it did not count as the truth either.

The journey to Xyuluthe was tedious, made all the more so by the fact they were stopping constantly to rest, eat, and give the horses water. When Livius insisted it was too dark to go any further, and they had to stop for the night, Ioanna wanted to scream.

Aelia irritated her too. Every so often she'd ask Ioanna her name, where she was born, how old she was, and other questions that served no purpose. When Ioanna finally snapped at her to stop, Aelia said, "I need to make sure you're still in there."

Ioanna did not sleep at all. Each of the paladins took a guard shift, watching the camp or perhaps watching her. She never was certain. In the darkness, her skin glowed with soft golden light—too faint to see in daylight, but a beacon at night. Perhaps this ought to worry her, but she found it difficult to muster up any emotions more complex than righteous fury.

The moment the eastern sky began to show the slightest tinges of gray, Ioanna leapt to her feet and went to the horses. The saddles that had always been too heavy for her to handle were now strangely light, and she placed them onto each horse's back with no struggle, save for the unfamiliar and complicated straps she'd never learned to do properly because Vitaliya was so much better at it.

Was she dead by now?

By the time the eastern wall of Xyuluthe came into view, Ioanna felt all but certain that they were too late and Vitaliya was lost—despite everyone's constant reassurances that killing her would defeat the purpose of taking her prisoner to start with.

"All right, we need to approach this carefully," announced Livius. "If we're fortunate, we might be able to get Ioanna into the city by claiming she's a visiting noblewoman, and we're her guards. Orsina and I will—"

But Ioanna found she had no interest in what he and Orsina intended to do. She dug her heels into her mount's side and pointed it toward the city, leaving Aelia and the paladins behind. Shouts of alarm and horror rose up from behind her, but she ignored them. She had tolerated their meticulous plotting for long enough.

It was time to act.

She might have entered the city through the east gate—it was certainly the closest entrance. But the gates were always so crowded with people. It would be far more efficient to just make her own gate.

Ioanna guided her mount, following the eastern wall northward until she could see the highest tiers of the Imperial Palace over the edge of it. When she was satisfied, she dismounted and began to walk toward the wall.

She called her blessing up, but this time it did not stop at her hands. She allowed it to overtake her entire body, trailing up her arms and across her chest, engulfing her face, her torso, and her legs. When she looked down at herself, her body appeared to be made of pure light. She grasped a lock of her hair in her palm and took a moment to marvel at the way even her curls had gone strangely translucent.

"Ioanna, wait," began Livius, but Ioanna was done waiting. She would never wait for anything ever again! As she rushed toward the wall, she could hear their shouting behind her—and then all was silence as she murmured the prayer for celestial fire and pointed it at the ancient wall.

Stones struck her body—some of them quite large—but she hardly felt them. People were screaming, running...but Ioanna could not bring herself to care. She had no desire to kill her own citizens, and hoped they'd have the sense to stay out of her way.

She was not far from the palace—she could see its wall. She stepped out from the side street she'd forced her way into and began to walk toward it, only vaguely aware of how everyone fled at the sight of her. Of how even guards dropped their swords and backed away as though lacking the courage to address her.

She walked past the familiar temples, the ones she'd been forbidden to wander beyond in childhood. Just ahead were the enormous palace gates...closed, oddly enough. They were usually open during the daylight hours.

There were four guards at the gate, and one of them bolted outright as Ioanna approached. Two of the others drew their weapons while the third looked like he was considering going after his wayward colleague.

"Get out of my way," said Ioanna, aware of the light that streamed from her mouth as she spoke. When they did not move, she pulled one arm in toward her chest and then swept it outward, sending a wave of warm golden light at the trio. They were not evil, so the light did not burn them—but the force of it was enough they all collided with the gate with enough force to splinter the thick, ancient wooden door.

Ioanna decided to be merciful and give them time to scramble out of the way before she blasted it open. Unlike the wall, it did not crumble but swung open, the barring mechanism on the reverse side coming free.

Ioanna paused to take in the sight of the palace that had been her home for her entire life. Perhaps she ought to have felt some stirring of homesickness, of remorse, of nostalgia...

But all she felt was disgust.

Tear it down.

The suggestion was soft, but insistent. The palace, and everything it represented, was an affront to civilization, to order, to justice. Yes, why not tear it down? With her own hands, even? What better way to begin her reign? Why not cast every stone into the sea and cleanse the foundation with purifying fire until all the corruption was scoured away?

I can't do that. There are people inside. Innocent people. Servants. Children. Iulia. Vitaliya...

Thinking of Vitaliya brought her back to herself. She had not realized how far she'd drifted into...into whatever this was. Yet the idea of simply *blasting* her way into the palace was seductive in its simplicity.

Ioanna walked through the gates, through the front gardens—and the few nobles who had made the decision to spend their morning in the sunlight fled at the sight of her. She ignored them. They would answer to her later.

She walked up the stairs, through the familiar columns, and into the main foyer of the palace.

"*Netheia!*" she shouted. Her voice echoed up to the distant ceiling. When there was no answer beyond the sound of retreating footsteps, anger overcame her, and she sent a wave of golden magic at the nearest wall. It collapsed, gloriously, the ancient stone cracking and crumbling as it smashed to the floor.

"Ioanna!" That was Livius. She'd completely forgotten about the paladins behind her. "What are you doing?"

She had no response for him.

"You need to get yourself under control." But he sounded more confused than angry. "If you bring the palace down, you'll kill innocents. That's not why we're here."

Nobody is innocent.

"Ioanna?"

She turned away from Livius at the sound of her own name. Someone was peeking around the doorway—Iulia. Her youngest sister. The majority of her body was hidden behind the wall like she thought it might be able to protect her from another wave of magic.

"Ioanna, is that you?" she whispered.

"Where is Netheia?" asked Ioanna. "*Where is she*?"

"I'll go get her!" squeaked Iulia, and she fled. It was a lie, but Ioanna could not bring herself to be angry at Iulia. Iolar hated liars, but Ioanna had a soft spot for Iulia, so she would be allowed to live.

More footsteps, more guards. Ioanna frowned, disappointed. She would fight them if she had to, but she wanted Netheia. Everyone else was unimportant. But before any of them could raise their sword, someone pushed through the center of their group.

"Ioanna?" Netheia sounded more concerned than frightened. "What—what's happened to you?"

Ioanna paused to take in her sister's new appearance. She did *not* look well. It was as though she had not been eating, sleeping, or combing her hair. Netheia was not the sort of girl to spend hours in front of her mirror, but Ioanna could never recall seeing her so unkempt before.

Kill her, suggested Ioanna's blessing. *Impure. Corrupt. Kill her before she kills.*

"That can't be her," said another voice. Decima. She was just behind Netheia, one hand on her own sword. "That's—I don't know what that is. A demon, or something. That's not Ioanna."

"Fight me," said Ioanna. "That's what you're always saying, isn't it? Fight you, and prove I deserve to be empress. I always thought that was such a childish sentiment. But now I'm inclined to accept your challenge."

Netheia shook her head. "You can't be Ioanna. This is impossible—"

Ioanna moved forward and seized her sister by the collar. Netheia screamed in pain as Ioanna's golden magic touched her skin, but Ioanna found she could not care less.

"Fight me, you coward," Ioanna hissed. She threw Netheia to the ground with all the force she could muster, and raised her hands, preparing to strike out when Decima or the guards came to Netheia's defense. But Decima did not move, and neither did the soldiers. They remained rooted to the spot, eyes wide and incredulous.

Kill her.

What a good idea. Why had Ioanna never thought of that before?

Ioanna moved forward to attack again, but Netheia had finally realized it was time to fight. Rust-red magic began to flow over her body in the way it had that day so long ago when their mother had told them their father was dead.

In the same way Ioanna was bright with golden magic, Netheia's body glowed red. Last time she'd been in this state, she had punched through Ioanna's shield. But she'd been weak to celestial fire...which made no sense because it was only meant to hurt chaos gods and other evil things...

Reygmadra's three steps away from being a chaos goddess herself, these days, Aelia had said.

Ioanna called up the purifying fire and aimed it at Netheia. Netheia must have realized the same thing, because she sprang out of the way just in time. Then, without slowing, Netheia lunged at her, slamming Ioanna into the wall.

Stone and plaster crumbled, but she ignored it. Now Netheia was squeezing her throat, but that only meant there was nothing she could do to defend herself when Ioanna grabbed Netheia by the neck, searing burns into her skin. Netheia screamed again and staggered backward. Ioanna struck again with another wave of magic, but it went wide as Netheia shoved her arm away.

A pillar fell, taking down two others with it. Ioanna called up a shield to protect herself from the falling stone. Something shattered on the golden surface above her head, and Ioanna realized it was a piece of the ceiling—the ceiling was falling.

It was difficult to see through her shield, and she'd lost track of Netheia. Rage bubbled up within her again. Netheia would *not* be allowed to run away. She'd spent twenty years challenging Ioanna to duels, and now it was time to stand by her words!

Ioanna climbed over one of the fallen pillars and spotted Netheia crouched behind a piece of the wall—or maybe the ceiling, it was hard to say. One of her hands massaged her burned neck while the other gripped a sword that seemed to be formed by pure magic in the way Ioanna had seen Talcia's priestesses do when they were called to spar. Blood poured from a large, open wound on Netheia's forehead.

Ioanna leapt down, tackling her sister. Netheia brought the magical sword around, and to its credit, it sliced through Ioanna's shield like it was made of paper. She felt it pierce her shoulder, but it did not hurt as much as it ought to have. Perhaps later she would feel the wound, but for now it just seemed like an inconvenience.

Ioanna aimed her fire at the sword, hoping maybe she could injure it in the same way she injured Netheia. Netheia leapt to her feet and ran, clearing enormous pieces of stone with effortless jumps. Ioanna aimed her magic at one of the still-standing pillars, knocking it over and blocking Netheia's escape.

Kill her.

A piece of the ceiling crashed to the ground only a few inches from Ioanna, distracting her long enough for Netheia to bolt around the pillar and take off deeper into the palace. Irritated, but certainly not ready to give up, Ioanna followed her.

Nothing about the palace had really changed in her absence. It was as though she'd only been gone for a few days. But then, very little changed at Xyuluthe unless it was forced to. Ioanna threw a few waves of celestial fire at her sister, but they all missed as Netheia dodged and wove through rooms and behind furniture. On and on they ran, heedless of the destruction they left in their wake.

Ioanna finally caught up with her sister just outside the throne room. Something was wrong with Netheia's leg, Ioanna realized. She'd twisted her ankle, and it was slowing her.

Ioanna struck at her sister with one last wave of celestial fire. Netheia screamed and crumpled to the floor. Behind them, the door to the throne room opened, but Ioanna did not look up to see who had just exited. It wasn't important.

Ioanna advanced on her sister, wondering if the celestial fire would be enough to kill her or if she'd have to do it with her own hands. Netheia was trying to stand, struggling to push herself back to her feet, but her injured leg was no longer cooperating. She stared up at Ioanna, her eyes wide.

Kill her. It is the only way to be certain.

Ioanna thought of her miserable, lonely childhood. Of how her parents had always loved Netheia more...of how her father had never loved Ioanna at all.

"Ioanna."

Ioanna looked up at the familiar voice and saw Grandmother Irianthe standing in front of the door to the throne room. Just behind her was Ioanna's mother, her face pale and eyes wide.

"Ioanna," said Grandmother Irianthe again. "This is not what you wanted."

Ioanna stared at her grandmother blankly. Not what she wanted? All she wanted was to purge the corruption from her nation, and how could she ever expect to do that if Netheia still lived?

"Ioanna, look around you," said Grandmother Irianthe, gesturing to the crumbling walls and smashed pillars. "You've won. You've proved your point. There's no need to kill your sister. You do not want to kill your sister. The voice screaming in your ear might, but *you* do not, and you are the one in control here."

Truth.

Ioanna stared down at her sister. It occurred to her that she'd never seen her beaten in a fight before. The sight should have been thrilling, satisfying...but it was not.

She was just tired, and a little bit ashamed.

"Where's Vitaliya?" she asked.

"The—the dungeons—" stammered Enessa. "Ioanna, what's happened to you?"

Ioanna ignored the question and dashed away, desperate to see Vitaliya now.

She had only been down in the dungeons once or twice in her life as a child, exploring the palace with Netheia. Ioanna could have probably lived without ever seeing them, but Netheia found them morbidly thrilling.

They were usually empty, for it was a bad idea to keep dangerous criminals in the Imperial Palace. Sometimes, when parties got out of hand, Enessa would threaten to throw everyone in the dungeons, but usually did not honor her word unless something expensive was broken. Occasionally a high-ranking political enemy would be held there before execution, but that was even rarer.

When Ioanna threw the doors open and sprinted toward the cells, she saw only one of them had an occupant. It was Vitaliya, curled up on the floor asleep. But at the sound of Ioanna's footsteps, she woke—and recoiled, eyes wide with fear.

"Ioanna?" she asked tentatively.

Ioanna gripped the cell door in her hands and, after taking a moment to ready herself, tore it from its hinges. Vitaliya screamed, though Ioanna was not certain why— she'd not been harmed in any way from the removal.

But she *had* been harmed. Her face was horribly bruised, so badly that Ioanna could barely find an unmarred spot to kiss. She had a wound on her face, which leaked blood, and it looked like her nose had been bleeding too, and she'd had nothing but the fabric of her own dress to staunch it.

"I'm sorry," whispered Ioanna, kneeling down to cradle Vitaliya's face in her hands. "I should have protected you—I should have known."

"*I'm* sorry," Vitaliya rasped. "I should have been more careful."

"No." Ioanna pressed their foreheads together. "No. Don't be sorry. Please. I love you."

"I—" began Vitaliya, but her words ended in a scream as Ioanna was wrenched from her arms. Ioanna struggled to break free from whoever had grabbed her, but the person was strong, even stronger than Netheia had been.

Ioanna looked up into the face of a woman she had never seen before. For a moment, she thought it might be one of Netheia's friends or a palace guard. But then she realized the woman was not a woman at all. Like Aelia, she wore a body in the same way Ioanna would wear a dress. Her true self was something else—something angry, something powerful, something that glowed rust-red.

"Did you think you'd won?" asked Reygmadra. "Did you think I'd just accept defeat and walk away? Iolar has convinced you that you're clever and powerful, but he doesn't care enough to stop me from snapping your neck!"

She could not win, not against Reygmadra, but she might be able to leave a few marks in her avatar before she went to Solarium. Ioanna twisted like a wildcat, lashing out with both magic and teeth. But Reygmadra seemed to feel neither, for she only laughed and wrapped her fingers around Ioanna's throat, lifting her clear off the ground so that she could only kick uselessly at the empty air.

"Put her down."

Reygmadra froze and her hand opened, sending Ioanna sprawling on the ground unceremoniously. When Ioanna looked up to see where the voice had come from, she realized another woman stood just behind Reygmadra.

She was beautiful, breathtakingly and impossibly so. It was as though she'd been a statue brought to life, for surely such perfect features could not exist without the use of magic. Her hair was long and thick, reaching past her waist, and she wore a short white dress in the Xytan style and no jewelry except the silver belt around her waist. But flowers had been woven through her hair, enormous white roses and tiny purple blossoms Ioanna couldn't identify.

And beyond that, Ioanna could see the truth of it, just as she had with Reygmadra and Aelia. The body was just a puppet, and the creature that pulled its strings was made of light and magic. But unlike Reygmadra, this being was warm and gentle and so very, very joyful.

"We all agreed that we would not directly harm each other's champions," said the beautiful woman. "You'll follow the rules, or you won't be included next time around."

"Dayluue," Reygmadra snarled. It seemed she had forgotten Vitaliya and Ioanna entirely as she stalked toward her fellow goddess. But if Dayluue was meant to be intimidated by this, it did not work. There was barely a hand's width of air between them, and Reygmadra towered over Dayluue—but Dayluue only smiled up at Reygmadra like she was a lover approaching for a kiss, her eyes soft and affectionate.

"This was all your doing," Reygmadra hissed. "You kept me from giving a blessing to Ioanna until it was too late. You tricked me into taking Vitaliya hostage. I can hardly imagine how you could have done *more* to hurt me."

"I did not do any of it to hurt you. My priority has always been the mortals that trust us to protect them—"

"Spare me the sanctimonious lecture. I've no patience for your words today."

Dayluue reached up and clasped Reygmadra's face in the same way Ioanna had done to Vitaliya only minutes before. "I love you."

Ioanna saw Reygmadra hesitate, her face softening for the briefest moment before it twisted back into an expression of scorn. She ripped free of Dayluue's hands as though they had burned her.

"Is that meant to impress me?" Reygmadra spat. "Who *don't* you love?"

"You're being cruel."

"What else should I be when my siblings craft each new world to be gentler than the last? If I sat back and allowed you to do as you pleased, I'd have faded out eons ago! You say you fight for mortals, but I fight for my very existence!"

Ioanna turned back toward Vitaliya, still on the ground with her arms wrapped around herself. Ioanna went to her, shuffling forward on her knees, trying to move quietly as to not catch the attention of the quarreling goddesses only a few meters away. When she reached Vitaliya, she pulled her close as gently as she could, trying not to further aggravate any of her wounds. Vitaliya curled into Ioanna's chest, her breath soft and gasping.

"You can change." Dayluue reached her hands out for Reygmadra again as if longing for an embrace. "There are other domains you can claim. Sustainable ones. There's no shame in it. Honor. Glory. Valor. Why won't you at least consider—"

"Who do you think my replacement will be when I can no longer hold my place in the Ten?" demanded Reygmadra. "Cyne, who smiles so gently? He seems the most likely one. Or maybe Nara—at least she'll not do me the dishonor of feigning friendship as she stabs me in the back."

"Reygmadra," pleaded Dayluue.

"Adalia? She's been growing in power these past few centuries, creeping up on Adranus's domain. There's no telling what she's capable of now."

"You will not be replaced. I'll never allow it."

Reygmadra laughed bitterly. "As though you could stop it."

Dayluue looked at Ioanna, and Ioanna tightened her arms around Vitaliya instinctively. But Dayluue meant them no harm—she had interfered in order to save them. After a moment, she turned back to Reygmadra again.

"Come to Vanya with me," she coaxed. "We can talk there. I've missed you so much—"

"That was your own doing!"

"And I'm sorry!" It was a lie. But a soft lie, designed to comfort, not hurt.

"You're not," sneered Reygmadra. "But you will be once the Outsiders come, and I'm too weakened to protect Inthya. I only hope there's enough of me left to see it."

Dayluue began to object, but before she could say more than a few words, Reygmadra disappeared from the dungeon as if she'd never been there at all.

Dayluue turned back to Vitaliya and Ioanna, and there was such sorrow in her face that Ioanna felt compelled to say something reassuring. But what could she possibly say to reassure one of the Ten?

"You can let go now," Dayluue murmured to Ioanna. "Your part is finished."

She was all alone in her grandmother's study at Oredia, which would normally be a rather exciting prospect. But something was not quite right. Whenever Ioanna removed a book from the shelf or unrolled one of the scrolls, the writing was all in a language she had never seen before. It was beautiful to look at but utterly incomprehensible. After twenty years of curiosity, this was a bit of a disappointment.

"What are you doing?" asked a voice from behind her. Ioanna gave a little jump and turned, expecting to see her grandmother there ready to scold her. But a man stood before her.

Ioanna held a book out to him. "I can't read this," she complained. Her voice was high and thin, the way it had been in childhood, and when she glanced down, she realized her hands were small as well.

"You will learn," said the man. "Someday. But you have a great deal to do before then, don't you?"

Ioanna put the book back on the shelf in the exact spot she'd taken it from. Nobody would ever know she'd touched it.

"Do you wish to remain a Truthsayer?" asked the man. "I understand it has been more burden than blessing to you. Now that your most difficult task is complete, I offer you the chance to be free of it."

"I'd like to keep it. Unless..." Ioanna frowned. "Do you need it back?"

The man laughed, softly. "No. I do not need it back. I am asking for your sake, not mine."

"Then I'd like to keep it."

The man nodded, and she thought he looked proud of her. "You can go, then," he said. "We can talk again later once you've finished what needs to be done."

"I wish you'd spoken to me earlier." Ioanna regretted the words the moment she said them—what horrible hubris! But the man did not look angry. He looked tired and sad but not angry, and Ioanna found the courage to go on. "Why didn't you? I was so alone, I—"

"You will learn," said Iolar again. "Someday."

Ioanna opened her eyes and found herself staring up at a perfectly clear blue sky through a rather large hole in the ceiling. All around her, people were shouting and arguing and even sobbing, but Ioanna felt strangely disconnected from everything until a familiar face appeared in her line of vision.

"I have good news and bad news," said Aelia. "What do you want to hear first?"

Ioanna blinked up at her.

"The good news is you're the Empress of Xytae." Aelia paused, but when this got no reaction, she went on talking. "The bad news is you took down nearly the entire south face of the palace."

Ioanna's eyes flicked away from Aelia's face and back to the sky above. Why had destroying the palace seemed so important? She couldn't really remember. Something about corruption, something about purity...but the palace was just a building. It was neither pure nor impure. It was just stones.

All she could say was that it had made sense at the time.

"Netheia—" Ioanna began. "Where—"

"She's been arrested, but they didn't put her in the dungeons. She's confined to her rooms. You can probably get that changed if you insist, but..." Aelia shrugged.

"No. It's fine, I'm sure." If her grandmother wasn't objecting, then Ioanna would not either. Ioanna rubbed at her eyes. She was so dizzy, and so hungry. She struggled to sit up, and Aelia helped her.

"What's an Outsider?" murmured Ioanna.

Aelia's mouth fell open. "Wh—where did you hear that word?"

"Reygmadra said it. To Dayluue. She said, she said you'd all regret weakening her once the Outsiders came—"

"Here, look at this," said Aelia, holding up her hand. Purple magic glowed at her fingertips, but before Ioanna could ask what she was doing, she snapped her fingers and Ioanna's mind went blank for the briefest moment. When her thoughts returned, she could not remember what she'd been about to say.

"Sorry, what was that?" asked Aelia.

"I..." Ioanna searched her memory, but for the life of her, she could not recall the question she'd been about to ask. Something about Reygmadra, Dayluue, and...? "I'm sorry. I lost track of—"

"Don't worry, you've been through a lot today," said Aelia. "Let me know if you remember later. Did you want to see Vitaliya? She's with the healers."

"Yes!" Ioanna pushed herself upward, and pain shot through her shoulders all the way down to her fingertips. The wound her sister had given her during their fight was still there, and now she could feel it. Someone had wrapped it with a bandage, but pain still radiated from the source. "Is she all right?"

"She's fine, she—" But Ioanna did not hear the rest of the words as she took off running.

She found a group of white-robed healers in the next room, tending to people who Ioanna supposed had been caught by falling stones. Guilt clenched at her stomach as she realized that had been her own doing. What had come over her that she'd been so thoughtless, so careless, so pointlessly violent?

The realization that she'd been no better than her sister was mortifying. This whole time she'd been so convinced she was better than Netheia, but in the end was she really?

She would never do this again. She would never allow her blessing to overtake her as it had today, no matter what was at stake. She'd never have thought Iolar's magic was capable of being a corrupting influence, but perhaps the god behind the magic was less important than she'd always assumed. She'd have to discuss it with the paladins later.

Vitaliya was among the injured sitting down on a low-cushioned bench dragged in from one of the other rooms. A few healers were gathered around her, but they all backed away when they saw Ioanna coming.

The bruises on Vitaliya's face had faded significantly since the last time they'd seen each other, but it still pained her to look at them. Ioanna knelt so she could embrace her properly.

"You're you again," murmured Vitaliya. "I was so worried you'd be gold forever."

"I'm sorry. I didn't mean to frighten you."

"Actually, it was very impressive." Vitaliya smiled. "I'll have to commission someone to do a painting of it."

Ioanna laughed. "I'm so glad you're safe. I don't know what I'd do without you."

"Let's not ever find out." Vitaliya curled closer. "But..."

"What?"

"I think I'd like to go to my father's wedding."

Of all the infinite things Vitaliya might have said in that moment, Ioanna thought this was the one she'd expected least. "You do?"

"Don't laugh," muttered Vitaliya. "Just, I came so near to dying. I thought I might never see my family again. And after that—after *everything*—Father remarrying hardly seems important at all. It's like being angry about a stone in your shoe when your arm's been cut off. I'm sorry. I just said I wanted to stay with you, and now I'm wanting to leave—"

"No," said Ioanna firmly. "Don't apologize. I'm happy you've forgiven him. Good fathers aren't always easy to come by."

"Maybe he loves her the way I love you," Vitaliya murmured. "And if that's the case, I'd be a hypocrite if I said he shouldn't be with her, wouldn't I? She'll never be my mother, but..."

"I don't think anyone can reasonably expect her to be your mother," Ioanna said. "Especially not at your age."

"I'll come back." Vitaliya's eyes were bright with determination. "The moment the wedding's over—I'll come back. Don't you dare hold a formal coronation without me; I've got to make sure you invite everyone who needs inviting and leave out everyone I'm angry at!"

"I don't think a formal coronation will happen for quite some time," said Ioanna. "Given everything that needs to be done."

"I wish you could come with me," Vitaliya sighed. "You could meet my family. Or are you going to continue the Xytan tradition of never showing up for other people's weddings?"

Ioanna laughed. "No! I'd come in an instant if—" She glanced over at the injured palace residents, then at the cracked and damaged wall. "—if I didn't have so much to do."

"You, and the stonemasons!"

"I don't know what came over me! I know it was foolish and wasteful."

"It was symbolic," asserted Vitaliya. "And given what I've seen of Xytae, I'll bet everyone is more impressed than angry."

Vitaliya was probably right about that. Ioanna supposed she ought to be grateful, but she just felt sad. It would take decades, maybe even longer, before Reygmadra's influence on their culture would fade away.

"I feel bad for her," she murmured.

"Who? Netheia?"

"No. Well. Yes, I feel bad for Netheia. But I was actually thinking of Reygmadra."

Vitaliya made a distasteful face. "Her? Why do you feel bad for her?"

"Because of what she said to Dayluue. She was so hurt—"

"Wait," interrupted Vitaliya. "In the dungeons. Could you understand what they were saying?"

"Yes." Ioanna blinked at her in confusion. "You couldn't?"

"No! It was all in some language I've never heard before!"

"Oh." A side effect of immersing so deeply in her blessing? Of her connection to Iolar? She wasn't sure. "I could tell they loved each other. Maybe they still do. But..."

"Dayluue could have anyone in Asterium—or on Inthya—and she loves Reygmadra?"

They're not so different, thought Ioanna. But she was too tired to explain her thoughts, so instead she just kissed Vitaliya's forehead. "I suppose there's nothing we can do. They'll have to work it out for themselves."

"That's too bad. I love getting involved in other people's problems." Vitaliya sighed, and Ioanna laughed.

"Crown Princess?" At the sound of her title, Ioanna frowned. She was not in the mood to be anyone's crown princess right now. But she tore her eyes away from Vitaliya to look at the paladin who was now addressing her. It was Vel, and her mood lifted at the realization. He'd been with them for so long; he did not deserve her anger. "I apologize for interrupting. But Knight-Commander Livius wishes to speak with you regarding the impending arrival of the rest of your forces, and your grandmother says she wants—"

She didn't just have to be their crown princess, Ioanna realized. She had to be their empress.

"Yes, of course," said Ioanna. "Tell them I will be with them shortly."

"How soon is shortly?" asked Vitaliya as the paladin walked away.

"That's a matter of opinion, I think," said Ioanna, resting her head against Vitaliya's shoulder. "An hour, maybe? Or two?"

Vitaliya giggled and curled closer to her, so close that Ioanna could feel her heartbeat. "A week?" she whispered.

"That might be pushing the boundaries of honesty," Ioanna murmured back, pressing a soft kiss to Vitaliya's lips. "But perhaps I can make an exception."

Her amassed army arrived in the city two days later. There was no fanfare as they made their way through the streets, only quiet confusion. The battle they had spent so many weeks anticipating would never come.

Ioanna was glad for that. The last thing their nation needed was more bloodshed. She was still a bit unnerved by how Iolar's blessing had overtaken her mind and body, but she supposed it had saved lives.

Still, she would never allow it to happen again.

In the meantime, there was so much to do. She could not officially be crowned empress until the mourning period was over, but that did not mean she would sit idly by and wait for the time to pass. Grandmother Irianthe was a great help to her, standing at her shoulder while all the courtiers fell over themselves to be first to swear fealty to Ioanna. Curiously, the oaths were not lies. This did not mean they wouldn't eventually change their minds, but she could rest easy for the time being.

Getting the army and the Temple of Reygmadra under control would be a little more difficult. She'd already issued an edict that all the conscripted were to return home, and the Imperial Fields to be vacated. That still left the career soldiers, but they could be stationed around the border, kept busy and separate enough that they would not decide to consolidate their power and march on the capital.

Ioanna was not looking forward to the return of her father's generals, those men and women who had all spoken so eagerly of Xytae's glorious golden destiny. Her grandmother had already selected new posts for each of them, so they wouldn't be in her way, but Ioanna knew she could expect them to turn up on her doorstep once they realized the war with Masim was truly ended. They would be difficult to reason with even with her grandmother at her side. And if she wasn't careful, they'd free Netheia and try to replace Ioanna with her once again.

Ioanna's heart sank as she thought of Netheia, who was still confined to her rooms. She had not visited her sister yet, though not out of spite or anger. She'd simply been far too busy to find the time. She still had no idea what Netheia's ultimate fate would be. Perhaps it was foolish, but Ioanna still harbored hope that they could be allies one day.

"I saw your mother today."

Ioanna looked up from her writing. Vitaliya sat on the bed in her nightdress, smiling her usual happy smile.

"What?" asked Ioanna, still lost in her own thoughts.

"Your mother. I saw her today." Vitaliya would be leaving soon, and so Ioanna was trying to enjoy the time they had together.

"I've seen her about," commented Ioanna. "But she has not spoken to me."

"Will you summon her?"

Ioanna shrugged. Her mother would probably be a useful ally, for she'd spent so many years as Xytae's administrator. But Ioanna was not certain she wanted her mother's aid. She still did not know how much her mother had known about Netheia's plans or about the way their people had starved.

She supposed she could ask, but then she would have to live with the answer.

"I was just curious," said Vitaliya. "I don't mean to pressure you into talking to her. She's been telling everyone who will listen how capable and clever you are. But perhaps she's just realized which way the wind is blowing. Forget I said anything. What are you working on there?"

"A letter to the Masimi." Though really, she still had hardly any idea what she would say. What *could* she say? There was no apologizing for what had been done. And Xytae could hardly afford to pay reparations. Perhaps the army's withdrawal from their lands would be enough, for now. "I hope they'll allow me to send an ambassador, but that may be too much to ask for right away."

"Maybe you can go yourself," suggested Vitaliya. "Meet with them and show them you're nothing like your family."

"It's probably not a good idea right now, but I'd like to someday. Though I'd not blame them for refusing to host me."

"I'll go ahead of you, then!" said Vitaliya. "And I'll threaten them! I'll tell them if they refuse to see you, I'll—"

"Hold your breath until you faint?"

"Yes!" Vitaliya smiled. "How did you guess?"

Ioanna laughed and stepped away from her desk. The letter could wait. It would be weeks, perhaps even months, before she could really begin to think of reaching out to the Masimi people, and they might never forgive her for her father's crimes.

She went to Vitaliya, who reached out her arms to receive her. Ioanna would miss her terribly, but at least it would only be a temporary separation. And she'd have more than enough work to keep her busy in the meantime. With any luck, the weeks would fly past.

"You've been working too hard," said Vitaliya. "What's the point of being empress if you can't order people to do everything for you?"

"Unfortunately, there are some matters that only I can handle."

"I warned you about this! Didn't I? I said it would be much easier to just run away. We could have been fisherwomen in a driftwood hut, but now you're stuck being empress for the rest of your life, and I'm stuck watching you be empress for the rest of *my* life."

They fell onto the mattress together.

"The rest of your life?" Ioanna murmured. Their faces were only inches apart, and Vitaliya's eyes glimmered in the candlelight. "That's quite a long time."

"Longer than you think! I'm going to live forever!"

"You just decided that, did you?"

"Yes, just now." Vitaliya wriggled closer. Then she calmed a little. "Really though. If you ever want to run away, I'll follow you. No questions."

"I won't run away," said Ioanna.

"I know you won't, but it's nice to have options, even if you never use them." Vitaliya smiled at her and wrapped one of her arms around Ioanna's back. "Think about that when you're sitting in those terrible meetings. Think about all the places we could run away to."

"It might be difficult at first," agreed Ioanna. "But I think things in Xytae are going to get better. Once things get settled, and people realize I'm not going to ruin their lives, I think things should improve."

She was also looking forward to the formal assessment of her blessing. Of course, she had no doubt of her status as a Truthsayer, but it would put the matter to rest, assuring both those who supported her and those who still doubted.

Normally, such assessments would be carried out in the privacy of a temple, but Archpriest Lailus had rather gleefully suggested they assess her in the palace before the entire court. Ioanna could think of no reason to refuse. They were only waiting on the arrival of Justices from the Order of the Sun so the assessment would not have to be done twice.

"I told you they'd love you," said Vitaliya. "Didn't I? And I was right."

"It's still a bit early to say—"

"No, it's not! I've been wandering around the palace all day, and nobody has a single bad thing to say about you. Even when I hide under tables to listen in. They're even talking about attending Sunrise services. So much for Reygmadra!"

"It's as you said. They know which way the wind is blowing." Ioanna sighed. "But I suppose it's a start. Until I can win them over truly."

"You have time," encouraged Vitaliya. "You have years. And I'll be here too. Once the wedding is done, I'll be back before you know it. And then..." Her voice trailed off as though she was uncertain.

"What?" asked Ioanna.

"I expect there will be a prince or two—"

"Stop that!" Ioanna sat up and seized a pillow, striking Vitaliya with it until she shrieked with laughter and feathers filled the air. "There will be no prince! There is only you! Now tell me you understand!"

"All right! All right!" Vitaliya gasped for air through her wild laughter. "I'm sorry! I take it back!"

Ioanna released the pillow and lay back down beside her. "You don't really think I'd accept anyone else trying to court me, do you?"

"No," Vitaliya said. "I don't."

It was not a lie. It was the truth. Ioanna reached her arm out again to pull Vitaliya close once more, determined to savor what little time they had together before her departure. "Maybe they'll come, but I'll send them away. I'll be very clear about it. I'll accept no would-be suitors so long as you're with me."

"You might never have a suitor again, in that case."

"That is my hope," said Ioanna. "That, I think, would be ideal."

Major Gods of Inthya

INTHI: God of Creation and First of the Ten. Inthi is a contemplative and peaceful god who encourages innovation in their followers. Their plane in Asterium is called Ithis, and it is there that Inthi is said to design and build marvelous creations beyond the comprehension of mortals.

MERLA: Goddess of the Sea and Second of the Ten. Like the sea itself, she cannot be reasoned with and appears to lack empathy. However, she is not malevolent and can just as easily be a friend to lost sailors if the mood strikes her. Her plane, Salis, is an endless ocean.

EYVINDR: God of the Harvest and Third of the Ten. Eyvindr is a generous god who appreciates hard work and dedication, and farming communities usually feature his temples at their center. His plane, Cembra, is farmlands surrounded by verdant forests.

IOLAR: God of Law and Fourth of the Ten. He is the patron of regents and lawmakers. He commands people to be orderly, compassionate, and to value the collective over the individual. His plane, Solarium, is a city where those who have upheld the law are allowed to spend eternity.

TALCIA: Goddess of Magic and Fifth of the Ten. She is the patron of hunters, hermits, and magical creatures. She created unicorns, dragons, gryphons, and many species who all call her their mother. Her plane, Dia Asteria, is a mountainous wilderness.

PEMELE: Goddess of Family and Sixth of the Ten. She is the patron of parents, families, and midwives. Her teachings emphasize strength in numbers and the importance of community. Her plane, Vela, appears to viewers as the place where they spent their own childhood.

DAYLUUE: Goddess of Love and Seventh of the Ten. Dayluue is a joyful and carefree goddess, though her anger is a terrible thing to see. Her teachings emphasize the formation of healthy relationships and knowing one's own wants, needs, and limitations, as well as respecting others'. Her plane, Vanya, is an endless summer garden.

REYGMADRA: Goddess of Warfare and Eighth of the Ten. Reygmadra values the pursuit of victory and freedom over all else. Her plane, Vailyon, is a battlefield where history's greatest warriors gather to test their skills against one another.

ERAN: God of Dreams and Ninth of the Ten. Eran is a strange and enigmatic god associated with sleep, the future, and the subconscious. They devised dreams as a way for mortals to explore their own minds and discover new possibilities within themselves. Their plane, Ivoria, exists as a place of light and mist where anything and everything can happen.

ADRANUS: God of Death and Tenth of the Ten. He is the patron of healers and scientists. He encourages his followers to attempt to comprehend the unknown whenever they can. His plane, Iestil, is the final resting place for any mortals who have not been invited into the planes of any other gods.

About the Author

Effie is definitely a human being with all her own skin, and not a robot. She writes science fiction and fantasy novels and lives with her cat in the greater Philadelphia area.

Email: effiecalvin@gmail.com

Twitter: @effiecalvin

Website: www.effiecalvin.com

Other books by this author

The Queen of Ieflaria
Daughter of the Sun
The Queen of Rhodia

Also Available from NineStar Press

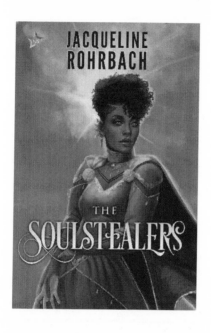

JACQUELINE
ROHRBACH

THE

SOULSTEALERS

Connect with NineStar Press

www.ninestarpress.com

www.facebook.com/ninestarpress

www.facebook.com/groups/NineStarNiche

www.twitter.com/ninestarpress

www.tumblr.com/blog/ninestarpress

Made in the USA
Las Vegas, NV
23 February 2023

67992002R00189